HIS
LOVING
WIFE

BOOKS BY MIRANDA SMITH

HIS LOVING WIFE

MIRANDA SMITH

Bookouture

Published by Bookouture in 2021

An imprint of Storyfire Ltd.
Carmelite House
50 Victoria Embankment
London EC4Y 0DZ

www.bookouture.com

ISBN: 978-1-80019-720-6
eBook ISBN: 978-1-80019-719-0

For Harrison, Lucy and Christopher

CHAPTER 1

12 months ago

Whatever Kate had been dreaming—something magnificent, she believed—retreated mercilessly. She tried to remember, pulling at her thoughts like a fisherman reels in his catch, but it was useless. Her dream was gone, locked away in some forgotten chamber of her mind.

Thud.

A sound. Was that what had woken her? She opened her eyes, but couldn't see anything, the blackout curtains performing exactly as designed. Behind them was nothing more than wisps of moonlight. It was the middle of the night. The alarm clock to her left confirmed it.

Thump.

Another sound.

Kate raised herself onto her elbows, squinting to make sense of her surroundings. She saw the outline of the dresser across from their bed, easing her into familiarity.

Clatter.

A chill started in her gut, clenching her insides, snaking its way up through her chest to her throat.

"Andrew?" she whispered.

Her husband was still wholly asleep, perhaps lost in his own dream. He didn't stir.

Two more noises. They sounded closer, clearer. Or maybe that was just because Kate was now awake, fully cognizant. She gave Andrew a hard shove, the kind that was impossible to ignore.

"Andrew. I think there's someone in the house."

He turned his head in her direction, no better capable of seeing anything. "It's probably Willow." He fell back on the pillow like a toy whose battery had run out.

Willow. Their daughter. Fifteen. Sleeping in her bed. The lavender walls of her room plastered with black and white posters of moody rock bands who reigned supreme well before her time. Kate could imagine it with absolute clarity, but it didn't make sense. If Willow were wandering about the house, she'd do her best to be quiet.

That sound wasn't her.

And it wasn't Noah. Their son was only nine. He slept in the bottom tier of a bunk bed they'd found online a year before. He filled the top mattress with his favorite stuffed animals. Noah was much more comfortable with the idea of remaining a child than Willow was. He was still too cautious to roam through the house on his own in the middle of the night. He was more likely to dart down the hall, climb into their bed when he'd had a nightmare.

That sound wasn't him.

"Andrew, something's happening."

Kate knew it now. The feeling inside her had blossomed from paranoia into fact. Someone was inside their home, someone that didn't belong. And they were making careless sounds, almost like they wanted to cause this type of tension before the big reveal.

She threw the comforter from over her legs and scrambled to the wall. "Andrew," she said, her voice an urgent whisper. He ignored her, until she flicked the light switch, drowning the room in sharp colors and light.

"Damn it, Kate."

She wasn't listening to him. She was crouched in front of the bedroom door, waiting for another sound, waiting for confirmation that the fear inside her body was founded. She couldn't be sure, but it sounded like someone was coming up the stairs.

"Did you hear that?" She turned, gave Andrew a spiteful stare.

Andrew didn't say anything, but the look on his face confirmed he'd heard it, too. He wasn't as alert as Kate, wasn't as on edge, but that last sound had proved he wasn't dreaming.

Footsteps. Right outside their door. Instinctively, she flicked the lock. The one they'd installed a few years ago, when they realized it was their only hope of intimacy away from their two curious kids. The doorknob jangled. Once, twice. Two gentle turns letting them know someone wanted in.

This time, Kate was too afraid to say anything. She turned, staring at Andrew with wide eyes. *Do something*, they said. *Tell me what to do*. But she didn't say it, only her expression did.

"We'll call the police," Andrew said. It came out like a guess. Should we? Is that what people do in these types of situations?

They didn't own a gun. And they didn't have neighbors who could hear their screams. The family next door, the Robertsons, had left for vacation that very day. The world, which only yesterday had seemed so big and colorful and vibrant, shrank to the size of a rice grain in those short, intense moments of panic.

The doorknob moved again. This time the whole door shook. The attempt to enter the room was angry, impatient.

"Get away from the door," Andrew said, fumbling with the chargers beside their bed. He was trying to find his phone—the one he always turned off at night because his colleague said the radiation was slowly killing him over time. Kate tried to calculate how long it would take for him to find the phone, unplug it, hold down the power button for it to turn on, dial the number… Each task seemed to take off another year or so of her life.

"What about the kids?" she asked. Now her mind was filled, again, with those familiar images. With whoever was on the other side of this door walking down the hallway, watching Willow sleep in her bed surrounded by posters. Seeing Noah dozing beneath his balcony of stuffed animals.

"The kids," Andrew stammered, as though in just this moment he'd remembered them. His fingers were pecking at the phone, pressing too many buttons to do anything productive.

She didn't have a choice, she realized. Whoever was standing there, jangling the lock, in the dark, in the middle of the night, was not a figment of her imagination. This was not a dream. Whatever it was, was too big a threat to keep out there even a second longer. What if one of the children had heard the same commotion, had stumbled out of their beds to see…

She slung open the bedroom door.

The man was tall, his shoulders disproportionately wide in comparison to the rest of his narrow frame. It was hard to tell really, as he was wearing all black. His face was covered by a mask, slits at his eyes and mouth. His mouth was open beneath the fabric, she could tell. He seemed shocked she had opened the door so abruptly.

Kate screamed.

CHAPTER 2

Now

We need a break. From the world. From the children. From the dark thoughts rumbling around in our minds.

I look admiringly at how the pink skies swirl above the cerulean waters. I think, *I never want to leave this place.* I close my eyes, inhale deeply. The salt from the sea and the passing wind refreshes me. My hair blows back, off my shoulders, dancing in the air. And it's quiet here. Secluded. Like we're the only ones in the world. It never feels that way back home. It never feels peaceful or complete. Ever since that night, we've been struggling to feel whole again. But not here. This vacation has brought us closer to the family we were before our lives were ripped apart.

I'm afraid once we return, we'll lose everything we've worked so hard to repair.

"Kate?"

I open my eyes and look behind me.

Andrew is cruising the planked walkway leading from our rental house to the beach where I sit. He is wearing khaki pants and a button-down shirt. In his hands are a bottle of tequila and two shot glasses.

"Want a drink?"

"Yes." I turn back to the sea, watching as another wave crashes onto the shore. "But it's the last night. I've not even started packing."

"It's still your vacation. One drink won't hurt," he says, with an almost forced cheeriness.

Out of habit, my eyes scan the beach first. I have to make sure both my children are safe. Noah is standing at the water's edge, his pants rolled up to his knees. He's trying to catch sand crabs before they burrow away into the earth. Willow is sprawled out on her beach towel, where she has spent most of the day. She holds her phone above her body, two white cords snaking down to her ears.

I look back at Andrew. He's smiling, holding out the bottle for me to take.

"Fine. You win," I say, an attempt to keep him happy.

He sits beside me, setting the glasses in the sand before he pours two shots. He hands one over, making his own cursory check of the kids before he speaks.

"To vacation," he says, clinking his glass against mine.

"Vacation."

Andrew sips his drink, but I swallow mine whole. The taste is bitter, and I quickly lick the salt lining the rim to help mellow my palate. I'm still grimacing when I look back at Andrew and laugh.

"Look at us," he says, wiping his mouth with the back of his hand. "It's like we're two college kids all over again."

"Almost," I say, clearing my throat, trying to dislodge the stinging aftertaste. We're at least pretending there aren't any problems between us. "Except we have two children in tow. One of whom is a teenager now."

"Don't say that. It makes me feel old."

"We are old," I say, leaning my head on his shoulder. The sudden burst of tequila has left me dizzy.

Really, we're not. In fact, we're young to have a sixteen-year-old. We were both only twenty-two when she was born, which puts us just shy of forty. But I feel older, and I'm sure Andrew does, too. Parenting generates an ache you can feel in your bones, a tiredness that never seems to cease. This is the closest I've felt to relaxed in… I don't know when.

"Mom?" Noah comes running up to meet us. "What's for dinner?"

"Burgers."

He kicks the sand and rolls his eyes. Suffice to say, it's not his favorite meal.

"It's the last night. We need something fast and easy," I say, sitting upright. "Have you started packing yet?"

Instead of answering, Noah stomps back to the ocean. He passes his sister, who barely stirs on her blanket. The blaring music in her ears means she can't hear us, but I'm sure she'll have her own insult about tonight's menu.

"Maybe we should just order a pizza?" I say to Andrew. "That would give us more time to pack."

"Burgers sound delicious," he says, pouring two more shots.

"I thought you said *one* drink wouldn't hurt?" There's an irritation in my voice that's difficult to hide.

"To vacation," he repeats, pushing the glass into my fingers.

I hold eye contact as I down the second drink. He's rarely been this optimistic in the past year, and I'm reluctant to ruin it.

I close my eyes again, savoring the refreshing feel of the breeze against my warm skin. "I need to start packing."

"Do me a favor," he says, standing, his balance stable. "Let's eat, and then we'll start packing. Okay? I'd like one more family meal before this all comes to an end."

I nod and smile. Andrew is right. This is the most we've been like us since… I'm reluctant to even think it. Since the invasion. It's like our lives have been in marathon mode ever since that night, trying desperately to keep up, not run out of breath. Here, we've been present for the first time in a long while. Hunting for sand crabs. Listening to music. Drinking tequila by the sea.

"I'm going to start the grill." Andrew wipes sand off his shorts. He starts to take the bottle with him.

"Leave it," I say.

He chuckles. "That's what I like to hear."

He walks away, leaving me alone on the shore.

We've been together over seventeen years now, an amount of time that seems to have blinked past. I think back to when we first met. Our senior year of college. We'd somehow managed to live in the same thirty-mile radius, attend the same parties, frequent the same library, and still never cross paths. That first time I saw him, it was an immediate connection. Not love at first sight, exactly. That is too abstract for either of us to ever believe. But there was a definite something, a stillness in the air, a quiet voice within telling me this was right. The two of us were meant to meet. Meant to be.

The attraction was instant. Not that Andrew was particularly good-looking, but something about him dared me to look closer. When he smiled, his eyes crinkled into two thin slants. There was something mysterious behind those eyes. Something quizzical worth exploring. I wanted to know more.

A member of his college fraternity, he was used to having girls around, even if they were after more alpha types in the pack. When Andrew looked at me, I don't think he saw what he'd seen in girls past. I barely spoke at parties in those days, let alone flirted, until I found myself staring at those alluring blue eyes. In a trance.

For months, I remained locked in that stupor. It didn't matter that I was dating someone else at the time. Everything else in my life seemed washed away the moment we met. Andrew and I never discussed exclusivity or labels. Our relationship with one another was understood. We wanted every spare moment to be spent with each other. Exploring different dive bars around campus and local hiking trails. Every minute, every second seemed like it wouldn't be enough. Our need for each other was ravenous, insatiable. Both of us in a fever dream that we didn't want to end.

Like all dreams, of course, it did.

Graduation was on the horizon, but that very adult step was preceded by the revelation I was pregnant. Due six months after we would receive our diplomas. Our relationship, so beautifully undefined, now felt bound within a certain set of parameters. Decisions had to be made. Choices that would affect our careers and education and relationship, not to mention our own wavering identities.

The night we found out, Andrew settled his hand on my lower back, rubbing in soft circles. "We don't have to decide now, you know."

"Decide what?"

"If you…" He waited, gripped his chin with his hand. "I'm saying, I support you no matter what you want to do."

"I don't know what I want to do," I said, defeated. I didn't appreciate the burden being placed on my shoulders. Andrew was trying to alleviate that stress, but I could still feel its weight.

"I'm not used to this," I said.

"Being pregnant? I'd hope not."

"No." I laughed. "Things not going according to plan. I'm used to being in control."

"You are in control. That's what I'm trying to tell you. Whatever you decide, I'll be here for you. I love you."

We'd said it before, usually in the heat of lovemaking or as a joke. This time when he said it, I felt the words' impact. Those three syllables branched out through my body, filling me with warmth and confidence.

"What about our plans?"

"I've already been accepted to the graduate program for the fall. I'll be here another two years at least. I feel confident I can complete my degree and parent at the same time." He waited. "I understand it's different for you."

Briefly, my life seemed to flash before my eyes, the way they say it does when you die. I'd been offered a writing grant by the university. I thought I'd stay on campus another year, use the opportunity to hone my skills. It would be a first step toward what I believed would be an illustrious writing career.

"I've still not accepted the grant. There's no way I'd be able to enter a program pregnant, let alone complete it with a newborn." I bit my lip. "But I love you too and even though there's barely anything inside me, I love it. Him or her."

"We're young. We still have our whole lives to figure it out. And we'll both have our degrees within the month. Some things might have to be put on pause, but we can do this. Together."

He kissed my hands. A single tear trailed down my cheek, and I was smiling. The fear, the love, the indecision… it was overwhelming. But in those moments with Andrew, it all felt right.

"We should get married," he said.

My mouth fell open. "Married?"

"I know, right? Truth is, I can't imagine a future without you. And I hate to break it to you, but a baby is a much bigger commitment than a couple of rings."

"Married," I repeated the word like a hex.

"One thing at a time." He wrapped his arms around me, pulling me closer. "We'll think about it. We don't have to decide our entire future in one conversation."

That's how it started. Not I *want* to marry you. We should. It was a practical decision, even if the hormones in our brains made us believe otherwise. Sometimes I think every decision I've made since then has been the same—practical, logical, methodical. Except for that night in August.

Willow is walking away from the sea, her phone in her hand. The ends of her hair are damp, clumped together in narrow strands. Her skin is ivory. Even after a week, she doesn't have the tan the rest of us do. She looks angelic. So, so beautiful. It's hard to imagine the topic of our conversation all those years ago has developed into this full person before me. At sixteen, she's only six years younger than I was when I made the decision to be her mother.

"What's for dinner?" she asks when she gets closer.

I'm staring at her, smiling, lost in thought. I clear my throat, raise my book as though she interrupted my reading.

"Burgers."

"My gosh. Could you guys get more boring?"

She returns to her towel and plops down, her legs and arms sprawled out like she's about to be outlined in chalk. Her ears are plugged again with the headphones, and she's retreated to a world where I no longer exist.

I stare at her a while longer, my smile dropping ever so slightly.

CHAPTER 3

Now

The meal came together easily, and eventually Willow got over the "basic-ness" of burgers. Andrew's burgers aren't basic at all, really. He has this special marinade he uses on the meat, which makes them taste savory with just a hint of sweet. Of course, they would have been better if we were back home and Andrew was using his familiar grill, but the one at the rental is in good condition, and by the time I take a bite, I can barely tell the difference.

"Good?" Andrew asks, waiting for approval.

"Delicious."

"Mine's great, Dad," Noah says, even though his burger is nothing more than bread, meat and cheese. No toppings or condiments.

"What about you, Willow?" asks Andrew, equal parts joking and testing.

"Not bad," she says, fighting against herself to smile. "You know I always like your burgers, but it's the last night. I guess I was thinking we might do something special for dinner."

"I'm happy you mentioned that," Andrew says. "I actually have a surprise for all of you."

"What is it?" Noah asks.

"Yes, what is it?" I ask, my voice noticeably more serious. Andrew isn't the type to spring surprises, but I did notice something off about his behavior earlier. I settled on the fact he was probably anxious about returning home, as we both are, but I suppose I was wrong.

Andrew smiles. "This isn't actually our last night."

"What do you mean?" Willow asks.

"When I booked this place, there was a two-week minimum. It turned me off at first, but there were already so few places available, considering we booked last minute. I checked over my schedule at work and my vacation days were stacked high. I thought, why not? Let's really go all out this year."

Noah, with his dramatic flair, stands, pushing his seat away from the table. His eyes are glistening. "You're saying we have a whole other week at the beach?"

"Yes, that's what I'm saying." Andrew looks over to me, fidgeting a fry between his fingers. "And that's why I've been trying to stall your mom from packing all day."

"This is awesome," Noah says, jumping before getting back in his seat.

"You've known this since you booked the place?" I ask. I'm smiling, but I fear it looks strained. "Why didn't you tell me?"

"Well, I wanted to surprise all of you. We've never taken a family vacation this long before, and I thought it would catch you off guard."

"It worked," Willow says, beaming. "All day I've been bummed about going back. This is, like, the best surprise ever."

"That's the reaction I was hoping for," Andrew says. He turns to me. "Two-week vacation. Pretty cool, huh?"

He asks the question like it's no big deal, but I know he wants my approval. Off the top of my head, I can't think of any reason why it would interfere with our schedules. I'm still on summer break at the community college. The kids won't start school for another three weeks. The only person who would be impacted is Andrew. Financially, he's the penny-pincher more than I am. If he's okay with paying for another week's rent, I should be celebrating. Who wouldn't want another week of relaxation? And yet, part of me wonders if he's done this intentionally. Because there is one reason why neither of us want to return to Hidden Oaks just yet.

"I think it's a great idea," I say, because I know he needs to hear it more than I actually believe it. "And that means I can have another cocktail. No packing tonight!"

"Atta girl," Andrew says, raising his drink in a mock toast.

"Wait a minute," Willow says, her pitch high and urgent like something awful has just happened. She's staring at her phone, leaning over the table. "No. No. No."

"What is it?" I ask.

"Sonja's birthday is next week," she says, still staring at her screen. "If we're here, that means I'll miss it."

I don't try to hide my annoyance. Willow—all teenagers really—have the ability to make the mundane sound like the biggest crisis on earth. Based on her tone, you would have thought Sonja had been hit by a bus, not invited a bunch of teens over to watch movies and eat pizza in her basement. I know from overhearing conversations that Willow and Sonja's friendship has cooled in recent months. They are more frenemies than anything, and my daughter is probably more worried about what Sonja might say in her absence than actually missing the festivities.

"She'll have other birthdays, sweetie," Andrew says. "Just tell her I sprung this on you, and I'm sure she'll understand."

"Yeah, Dad. Thanks for the heads-up," she says dryly. She stands, stomping toward the kitchen with her plate.

I put a hand on Andrew's shoulder, trying to ease the blow. "Don't worry about it. Sooner or later, she has to find something to complain about."

"Teenagers," Noah says, followed by a sigh. Trying and failing to sound like one of the adults. Once he's gauged our reaction, he stuffs another ketchup-drenched French fry in his mouth.

After dinner, Noah helps me clear the table and load the dishes into the dishwasher. Willow has already strayed back out to the dock. Noah joins her when we finish cleaning. I pour another drink, and wander into our bedroom. I'd like to sit outside with them, curious to see if Willow's mood has improved; it's typically more tumultuous than a storm at sea. I'm searching for a light cardigan to wear against the wind when Andrew walks up behind me. He kisses my cheek, then remains standing, like he's waiting on me to say something.

"Another week," I say, not realizing I've spoken aloud. I force a smile to recover. "Quite the surprise."

"We deserve it, don't we?"

"We do. We really do."

He leans in, hugging me. My body trembles, tears of happiness pooling in the corners of my eyes. I think back to where we were a year ago. I remember the trauma of that night, and now there's another layer of emotion fighting to break free. A pang of guilt.

"Do you think we should tell them? That Paul has been released."

Andrew's features turn stiff. "There's no point in worrying them. They'll feel safer believing he's behind bars."

"But they're not safe. Paul could get them, and they don't even know to keep an eye out for him." My breathing hastens. "It feels like we're lying to them. We think we're protecting them, but what if we're not?"

"Hey, it's okay." Andrew holds me tighter. "He can't get us here."

"He got us *there*," I whisper.

"If we've ever needed more time as a family, it's now. I did this because I thought it would make you happy."

"And it does. I am so happy. I guess I was just preparing myself to getting back and facing everything head-on. Now we—"

"Now we live," he interjects. "We don't let that asshole take anything else from us. I won't let him."

Andrew is trying. This is what I've been wanting.

"I love you," he says, pulling me in for another hug.

"I love you, too."

I say the words. I feel them. I mean them. But there's something else, hidden beneath every conversation, an emotion neither one of us will dare voice.

Fear.

CHAPTER 4

11 Months Ago

Memories from that night ambushed Kate, confronting her at the most random moments. When her SUV was queued at the car wash, rivulets of pink soap splashing across her windshield, she'd suddenly recall the pain in her lower back when the intruder knocked her to the ground. When she opened the freezer door in the grocery aisle, she'd think of the panic she felt when he tightened his hands around her throat. When she was in the middle of lecturing her students about themes and motifs, she'd remember the soul-stopping sound of Willow's scream.

"Kate?"

The voice belonged to Mary Richardson: married, mother of four, her neighbor from two doors down. Kate had been staring out the window, watching as the mailman deposited letters in the mailbox, reminiscing about the cool night air clammy against her skin when she finally rushed out of the house.

She cleared her throat and turned in Mary's direction. "I'm sorry. What did you ask?"

"Would you be willing to make brownies?"

"Brownies," Kate repeated, wondering how long she'd been checked out this time.

"For the back-to-school fundraiser."

Kate looked around the room, at the half-dozen other mothers staring back at her. Most of them were neighbors, all of their children attended Hidden Oaks Middle School. This was the first

Fundraising Committee of the new school year, the first time she'd been around most of these women since the attack. She wondered if they noted this the same way she did.

"Right," she said, giving an assured nod of the head. "Yes, I can make brownies."

"I think that's everything," Mary said, holding her notebook vertically and tapping it on the table. "You'll let us know about using the community pavilion, Sarah?"

Kate was standing and already in the foyer before Sarah answered. She couldn't wait to get out of there. She'd been dreading this meeting for over a week. It was the first in a series of formalities she'd have to endure; she could no longer languish in the lazy fog that had enveloped her since that night. Andrew was back at work. The kids were back in school. Her own classes would resume next week. Their responsibilities continued, there was just a layer of anxiety at the base of it all.

Dana Smith-Peters, Kate's closest friend in the neighborhood, followed her out the door. She tapped Kate's shoulder. "You okay?"

Kate exhaled and shook her head. "Yeah. Sorry. I just zoned out in there."

"No one can blame you for that," she said, walking beside her on the sidewalk. "Mary's meetings are always a bore."

Kate laughed at that. Most of the other parents used the Fundraising Committee as an excuse to at least offer tasty food or potent drinks. Mary was all business. Kate remembered she was scheduled to host the November meeting, and a new wave of angst washed over her. She hated being in her house, knowing what had happened there, and now she had to invite others in; she wondered what her neighbors would think.

"Everything else good with you? Happy to have the kids back in school?"

Kate stuffed her hands in the back pockets of her denim shorts. "We're adjusting."

Dana nodded, tucking a strand of hair behind her ear. She was an expert at letting Kate know she cared without prying, which is probably why she was the only friend she'd stayed in contact with since the attack.

"Maisie is thinking about joining the volleyball team this year. It's got to be better than swim team, right? No ridiculously long practices and meets."

"That's good," Kate said, easing back into normal conversation. "You know, Noah is always—"

She stopped speaking when she turned the corner leading to their row of houses and spotted a police car parked in her driveway. Dana saw it, too. Both women halted, like they'd just been marked in a game of Freeze Tag.

"Is everything—"

"I don't know," Kate said, picking up her pace. "I'll call you later."

Her steps pounded against the cement, mimicking the thudding of her heart. People often had this reaction when the police arrived at their house unexpectedly. But Kate was familiar with cops. They'd been in constant contact since the attack, mainly because the intruder was still at large. For the police to show up unannounced during the day, it had to mean something.

Her stomach dropped further when the front door swung open, and she saw Andrew. Normally, he didn't arrive home until after seven. It was unusual for him to be home in the middle of the day.

"What's happened?" Kate said, her breath exhausted. "Are the kids—"

"The kids are fine." Andrew held out his hand to steady her. "They're at school."

Kate looked at the car in the driveway, then back to their front door.

"Then why are you here? Why are the police—"

Detective Marsh poked her head around the corner. She was a petite woman with dark skin and curly hair tied tight into a low bun. She was wearing a gray suit that looked too long for her small frame.

"Kate, are you okay?"

She took a deep breath. "I just saw the car and thought something might have happened."

"I tried calling you," Marsh said.

"She called me, too," Andrew said. "That's why I left the office at lunch."

Kate pulled her cell phone from her pocket. It was still on silent, revealing she had three missed calls. She exhaled with equal parts relief and embarrassment. So this wasn't an impromptu visit. Nothing bad had happened.

"Sorry, I didn't see you called."

"It's fine," Detective Marsh said. "I called you both because we do have a major development, and I thought it would be best to discuss it with you when the kids aren't around."

Detective Marsh had been with them since the beginning. Local deputies were the first on the scene that night, but Marsh followed soon after. She gave Kate a cup of coffee, wrapped a blanket around her shoulders. From that point forward, she'd been Kate's main contact. She had the ability to make Kate feel like a person, more than a name in a case file.

"Have you made an arrest?" Andrew asked, taking a seat on the sofa.

"No." Marsh, still standing, looked down at the beige carpet beneath her feet. "We don't have a person in custody, but we now know who entered your home and attacked you that night."

"Who?" Already, Kate's pulse was racing again. "If you haven't made an arrest, how could you know?"

"We pulled prints from the doorknobs and windowsills around the house. There was only one set that didn't match someone living here. It's taken us a while to run them through the database, but we got a hit. Turns out the guy has a couple of DUIs so his prints are already in the system."

"What's his name?" asked Andrew.

"Paul Gunter." She paused. "Does that name sound familiar to either one of you?"

The air stalled in Kate's throat. For a second, she felt woozy. She took a step closer to the window, staring out at their front lawn, as if the peaceful scenery could help clear her thoughts.

"Paul Gunter," Andrew repeated. Kate didn't have to see her husband to know what he was doing. His thumb and pointer finger pinching his chin, his brow furrowed, trying to place the name. "I think we do know a Paul Gunter, actually. He went to college with us, right?"

"Yes," Kate said, her voice so low she wasn't sure either of them heard her.

"When is the last time you saw him?" Marsh asked Andrew.

Kate, still facing the front lawn, closed her eyes. She winced as her mind took her back.

Six months ago. She was at Andale's, her favorite post-work restaurant. She made a habit of going there when she wasn't already committed to the kids' activities. She was sitting at the bar, halfway through a margarita, when she felt a tap on her shoulder.

At first, she expected to see a stranger, but after a few seconds, familiarity set in. She recognized the dark hair, still thick after all this time. She remembered his dimples.

"Paul?"

"I thought that was you."

She stood and hugged him. His gait, his smell, the texture of his denim jacket worked in unison to take her back to the last time she had seen him. Senior year of college.

He pulled away, looking her up and down. "Kate Richards?"

"Kate Brooks now." She wiggled her left hand, then immediately regretted it. Paul was who she'd been dating when she met Andrew all those years ago, and even now the comment felt too forward.

Paul seemed unfazed. "Talk about a blast from the past."

It was exactly the kind of corny line she'd expect him to use. "What about you? Married? Kids?"

"No." A subtle sadness fell over his face, then he smiled again. "Am I interrupting you?"

"No. Please. I'm just grabbing a quick dinner."

They rambled through the basic introductions. Kate: college professor, mother of two, amateur writer. Paul: auto mechanic, divorced, no kids. After they'd sifted through the present, their conversation turned to the past. Old keggers and cramming for finals. They'd shared a lot of memories during college, even if the last one—their breakup—wasn't her best moment. The fact Paul was an ex-boyfriend struck Kate as an afterthought. Their conversation, which left her giddy with laughter and nostalgia, was catching up with an old friend. Nothing more.

Kate wished she'd never seen him again after that first meeting.

"What about you, Kate?" It was Detective Marsh.

Kate's mind was still stuck in the memory, on that warm night when Paul came back into her life. "I'm sorry, what?"

"Andrew just said he's not spoken to Paul since college. What about you?"

Kate's eyes darted toward her husband. He was waiting for her response, which should have been an easy one. But Andrew didn't know about the encounter at Andale's, or about any of the events that followed.

Kate clenched her eyes shut. "Yes, I've seen him recently."

"When?" asked Detective Marsh.

"Six months ago."

"You didn't tell me that," Andrew said, now standing.

Detective Marsh looked at Kate with sympathy, like she was a drowning woman in need of a life raft.

"It wasn't a big deal," Kate said. "At least I didn't think it was."

Marsh pulled a notebook out of her blazer pocket. There was a pen hanging from the spiral binding. "I need you to tell me everything."

Kate took a deep breath, preparing to revisit her story, this time aloud. She had a sinking feeling inside that she should have known it was Paul Gunter all along. Maybe part of her did know but was afraid to acknowledge it.

Kate didn't want to admit that all of this had been her fault.

CHAPTER 5

Now

My heart pounds, like I'm running. My palms are sweating, my fingers stretching and recoiling, trying to grasp something that isn't there. What? I don't know. Everything is dark, and yet, in the distance, I can see something.

A shadow.

A person.

It's Paul. He drifts into focus, slowly, like heat waves on a scorching summer day. He floats closer, frighteningly near, still shrouded in darkness.

Darkness? My eyes are closed.

I open them. Above me, the ceiling fan lazily circles around. I turn my head to the left, squinting at how bright the morning sun is as it streams into our bedroom. I hold my breath, taking in the quiet, then hear the gentle roar of a wave as it crashes outside.

We're here. At the beach. At the rental house.

There is no Paul. There is no darkness.

"Bad dreams?" Andrew asks.

I turn quickly, unaware I wasn't alone in the room. Andrew is already dressed, coming out of the bathroom. I get a whiff of his mouthwash as he walks past.

"I'm fine," I say, flattening a palm against my chest.

He nods in understanding but doesn't press further. In an attempt to keep the peace, we avoid talking about that night. I'm not the only one who has flashbacks. Andrew has them too, and the kids. It's hard to say which of us has them the most or whose are the most severe. I know I've not had as many night terrors lately. In fact, this is the first since we've been on vacation. This realization comforts me, allows me to believe I'm slowly headed in the right direction.

"Heading off somewhere?" I ask.

Andrew looks as though he's been awake for a while. Fully dressed, eyes no longer puffy. I must still look a mess.

"Noah's been bugging me about checking out that boat rental place down the road. I told him I'd drive us down there. At least check the prices."

"I'm sure they're astronomical," I say, turning again to look out the window, my eyes just now adjusting to the brightness.

"I already told him. If it's too expensive, we won't do it. But we have another week here now. I don't think I can get away without visiting the place." He pauses. "Are you okay with this?"

No, my mind screams. I'd thought we'd avoided this discussion about the boat. I know how much it means to Noah, but I'm not comfortable with my baby boy being at the ocean's mercy. Andrew watches me, trying to gauge my expression.

"You know it worries me."

"And I understand why." He sits on the bed, placing his hand over my blanketed legs. "You know I'm experienced on the water. I wouldn't suggest going out there if I didn't think I could handle it."

Experience can't prepare you for everything, my conscience interrupts. Suddenly I feel like I'm struggling to breathe, like a swell has already overwhelmed me, is pulling me under. Then I see Andrew's eyes, how desperately he wants to share this experience with our son.

"Check the prices. It's your call," I say. "Where's Willow?"

"By the pool." He stands, seeming pleased with my lack of interference about the boat. "She claims to get better reception out there, although she complained about her phone not working at breakfast."

Breakfast. Usually, I'm the first one up and out of bed, preparing the first meal for the family. Eggs and bacon for everyone but Noah, who prefers waffles. I'm not used to the family carrying on without me.

"What time is it?"

"Almost ten. You deserved to sleep in." He leans over and kisses my forehead.

I'd already slept in later than usual, and yet I was tempted to lie back in bed. Why not? Everything I thought we'd be doing today—loading the car, filling up the tank, googling directions—is no longer relevant. We have an extra week here. It feels like more of a gift than the rest of the vacation up until this point, like when I was growing up in the mountains of North Carolina and we'd get hit with a snow day. No more worrying about studies and sports practices; we'd officially have the day off. A true free day. Kids don't get enough days like that. Adults get even fewer.

I pull my cell phone off the dresser, surprised to see that I have full reception. It's been patchy since we arrived. There were four bars our first day, then zero. There have been short periods of reception since then, but after an hour or so, it's back to nothing. Andrew said the owners had warned about this in their listing. As I'm about to get out of bed, the phone rings.

It's my sister, Aster. I wonder if she's tried calling already, or if the fates would have it that the one time she calls reception is clear as glass. I debate whether to answer, then remind myself I'd regret it if something was happening back home and I ignored her. With the patchy reception, she might not be able to reach me again.

"You on the road yet?" Aster asks when I answer.

"No."

I regret answering the phone. I can tell by the lackadaisical tone of her voice nothing serious is going on. She's just calling for a chat, and I'm not really in the mood.

"Well, why not? It's nearing eleven. You should have left earlier. It's going to be nothing but traffic this late in the day."

I exhale, having had an entire lifetime of hearing that voice with that tone. Aster is two years older but acts as though she's some soul that's on her fifth or sixth go around, and I'm on the first. That's how she talks to me at least, her little sister with the husband and kids and menial teaching position. Aster is married to a man named David, and they have no children. They're both college professors, like me, I would say, but she would be quick to tell you their careers are different. While I teach creative writing at the local community college, they're both on the tenure track at the University of Georgia. David specializes in anthropology, and Aster focuses on psychology. They're both leading experts in their respective fields.

My career ambitions stalled after having kids. Pursuing a career as a writer no longer seemed as important as ensuring a stable income for my family. Aster, on the other hand, has achieved every professional goal and then some. It's never bothered me living in my sister's shadow, I just don't know why she has to be so damn smug about it. And, of course, there's a lot of animosity between us when it comes to our parents. I'm not used to bragging about anything to my sister, so when I realize I have the opportunity to tell her about Andrew's little surprise, my limbs tingle with excitement.

"Actually, we're not leaving the beach house today. Andrew surprised us with booking the place for another week."

I wait for Aster's response, and much to my pleasure, there's a long pause.

"Oh. You're staying two weeks?"

"Yes. Andrew just told us last night. After the year we've had, he says we deserve it."

Aster knows about what happened to us a year ago. Everyone does, it seems, but she's one of the last people I want to talk about it with. I don't need her psycho-analyzing my every move and claiming it comes from a place of professional expertise.

"Of course you do," she says, her only acknowledgement of the incident in months. "That's awful nice of Andrew. I'm impressed."

"I am too."

"Of course, you have all the time in the world for it. David and I are lucky to get a week off, even in the summer."

And there it is. Because their jobs are so much more important. Not only do they sign up to teach summer classes (with student waiting lists a mile long, she'll tell you), but they also sit on department boards.

"We've been on the road since six, but we won't check into the hotel until late afternoon. We decided to split up the drive this time."

I'd forgotten they were using this week for their vacation. They're driving down to their beach house in Florida. A property they own, don't rent.

"I have a fabulous idea," she says, in that tone that makes me think it will be anything but. "We're going to be passing right through your area tomorrow. We should stop by your place for dinner?"

Shit. This is what I get for bragging. In my mind, I'm already listing reasons why it won't be good enough upon Aster's arrival.

"I don't know, I just—"

"Please, Kate. You can't tell me you have plans. You didn't know you were staying another week until last night."

She's got me there. "I'm just thinking about you and David. You've already spent so much time in the car. I'm sure you'd rather start your vacation. Before you know it, you'll be back at work."

"Don't remind me," she says in the fakest voice. "But I'd really love to see my niece and nephew. It's been, what, Thanksgiving since we've seen each other?"

"Yeah, I guess so."

I've dodged every invitation to visit them since then and offered a half dozen excuses why they can't come see us. I'm sure she thinks what everyone else does when I turn them down. *She's been through a lot.* And the people who think that are right, except when it comes to Aster. She's my sister and I love her, but my irritation wins every time.

"It would be nice to see you too, you know," she says, then pauses. "David thinks we'll be passing through about six tomorrow. Want to aim for six thirty?"

"Sure," I say, unable to offer up a good excuse.

"Fabulous. Text me the address. Send the kids my love."

I click off the phone, half tempted to call it a day and roll over in bed. I can't do that now, though. We used up all our groceries thinking our vacation was nearing an end. Now that we have another week here, we'll need to restock on staples. And now that Aster has invited herself over for dinner, I'll have to do more than that. I'll have to entertain, the last thing I want to do.

CHAPTER 6

Now

Already, I'm imagining Aster using phrases like "shabby chic" to describe the décor, whereas I would describe the place as a tropical oasis. Our rental is one level, a floor plan that seems to stretch out into comfortable corners. Each of the three bedrooms has a different color that reminds me of seaside homes in Key West or cascading down hillsides in the Cinque Terre—shades like buttercup, pear and powder pink. The color scheme would be too harsh at home, but it seems perfect for a rental. Perfect for an escape.

After getting dressed and pulling the hair away from my face, I wander into the living room. The ambiance is peaceful with the pale blue walls and white shiplap ceiling. The far wall is fitted with sliding glass doors, allowing for a view of the private swimming pool and beachfront beyond. In some ways, the transparency and seclusion of the place make me feel exposed, and yet, ironically, this is the safest I've felt in a long time.

I walk into the kitchen, which is located in the far-left corner of the open concept design. There aren't any barriers between one place and the next. The space is white and clean with distressed ceramic floors that remind me of a shipwreck. The décor flows seamlessly, although our exposed cabinets are now noticeably bare. We'll definitely need more food now that we're staying another week.

"Lazy much?" Willow says, wandering in through the sliding glass door that leads to the patio.

"Morning," I say, smiling before opening the fridge. "I'm heading out to the store as soon as your dad gets back. Need anything?"

"Where did he go?"

"He took Noah to that boat rental place down the road."

"Are you really going to let him get one?"

"If that's what they want to do." I keep my back to her, pretending the idea of renting a boat for the week isn't as terrifying as I really think it is. "Tell me what you need from the store."

Willow rambles off a list of toiletries and snacks she just *has* to have. Eventually, I have to stop investigating the refrigerator to grab a pen to write everything down. You would think we were going to be here another month.

"Dad said you cooked yourself breakfast this morning?"

"Cereal." She sighs.

"I'll be sure to get up early and cook omelets for everyone tomorrow. Maybe you can even help me."

Willow smiles at this. In her eyes, eating an omelet sounds much more sophisticated than eating scrambled eggs.

"By the way, Aunt Aster and Uncle David are stopping by the house tomorrow."

"Really?"

Willow's tone perks up. She's always had a good relationship with her aunt, the few times a year they actually see one another. When Willow was little, Aster treated her like she was a stain on my life. She did the same with Noah. Babies were yucky and needy and dependent; only people who didn't have anything better to do had them. Aster much preferred children, especially teenagers. Now that she's older, Willow is easily fascinated by stories her aunt tells about traveling to different conferences around the world. Sometimes I wonder if the main reason Aster shows Willow any attention is to get under my skin.

"They're driving down to their vacation home for the week. If we had left today, we would have missed them. Since we're staying a bit longer, they thought they'd join us for dinner."

"Sweet." Willow looks down at her phone and starts walking toward the sliding glass door. Before she opens it, she stops. "Do you want me to go to the grocery store with you?"

I smile at the fact she at least thought to offer. "No. You enjoy the sunshine. I'll be back in time for lunch."

I watch her walk outside, checking my phone to see if there are any messages from Andrew. It's hard to gauge how he'll react to Aster's visit. The two don't necessarily dislike one another. They tolerate each other for civility's sake. Aster thinks Andrew is too simple, and he finds her too domineering. Of course, he's not used to our family dynamic.

My parents divorced when I was ten years old, igniting a contentious relationship that lasted until my father's death two years ago; Andrew's parents have been married almost forty years. My mother worked two or three jobs to support us, while my father pursued a high-flying career in advertising and wrote a check twice a month. Andrew's father is a preacher. His mother is the church organist. I have a complicated relationship with my sister; he is an only child. It's another reason I feel pressure to patch up my relationship with Aster; she's the only aunt my children have, and they'll never have any cousins.

Andrew's upbringing was different from mine on almost every level—financially, relationally. And yet, we reached a comfort with one another that we'd never found anywhere else. Either in our own homes, or in the arms of other lovers before each other. I certainly never had those feelings when I was with Paul.

Paul.

For years, he was someone whose name only popped up in passing. I could hardly remember anything about him, let alone anything we did together. Our relationship was that insignificant. Now, he's always there, hiding in the recesses of my mind, waiting to reappear. I can't even think about the milestones I've had since our breakup—my marriage to Andrew, my children—without fearing he might somehow interfere.

I fear he'll take them away.

I fear he's not only hiding in my psyche, but on the outskirts of my life. Our lives. Waiting to make his next move.

CHAPTER 7

Now

It took Andrew and Noah longer to return from the boat rental place than expected, although they did secure a reservation for later in the week, much to Noah's excitement. I try to focus on his elation and not the impending sense of doom I have at the thought of my beloved children being out on the water. Then, just as I was about to leave, Willow had a meltdown because she couldn't find her phone charger. Her phone was almost out of battery, and she would just *die* if it lost power. By the time I found my spare in the bottom of a suitcase, the shoddy reception was back, so Andrew and I had to listen to her stomp around the rental, huffing and puffing to no avail, like a little wolf confronted by a house of bricks.

Due to the tension and hours wasting away, I didn't want to tell Andrew about Aster's visit. I wasn't sure how he'd take it and was afraid one more meltdown would nix my trip to the grocery store entirely.

When I clapped the car door shut, I might as well have been at the spa. The hot leather at my back could have passed for hot stones, and the scented tree hanging from our rearview mirror might as well have been essential oils. The immediate removal from all the chaos was that transformative. I sat in the driveway for a minute, half expecting someone to come running outside with another item they'd forgotten that I needed to pick up. Alas, when no one did, I put the car in drive and rode to the grocery store in silence.

I've always juggled responsibilities since I've had the children—I don't know a mother who hasn't—but I haven't always felt so frazzled about it. Sometimes I wonder if the trauma we've endured this past year makes it harder to cope, or if these emotions have always been there, beckoning to break free.

At the store, I take my time wandering through the aisles, making sure everything on the list makes it into my cart. By the time I check out, I'm mourning the end of my hour alone. I take my time, lazily peering at the items on display between the register and the front door, when someone passing catches my eye. It's a tall man with dark hair, a baseball cap pulled low over his face. The way he brushed past me—was he trying to get my attention?—makes me think of Paul.

He's found us, I think. My whole body freezes up. I stand, motionless, watching as the man stops in front of a vending machine in the front lobby. I take a step forward, equal parts scared and curious. I dread seeing Paul, and yet, I have to know if it's him. The man bends down, retrieves his drink from the machine dispenser, then takes off for the parking lot.

I follow him, but there are several shoppers with carts in my way, blocking my ability to go after him. Then we're outside, and the tropical heat is suffocating, the bright sun bouncing off passing cars and blinding my eyes.

The man walks down a row of cars. I leave my cart on the sidewalk, jogging across the street to where the man—Paul—is headed. I see him duck into a white sedan. Could it be a rental? I have no idea what car Paul drives. I've still not had the chance to see his face. By the time I reach his vehicle, it's too late. He's pulled into a line of cars and is exiting the parking lot. Between his sunglasses and ball cap, I have no way of knowing if it's him.

It can't be, I tell myself. *I'm being paranoid.*

But every time I try to think logically about Paul, my mind runs off in a different territory. *What if?* Those are the only two words I need to send my confidence in a tailspin.

*

When I return to the rental house, everyone is swimming in the backyard pool, Andrew and Noah playing a game where one person throws a Nerf ball and the other cannonballs into the pool whilst trying to catch it. It makes me laugh, and I shudder at the selfish glee I felt only an hour ago to be away from them.

Andrew notices I'm back, and quickly dries off. He walks outside, looping grocery bags around his forearm as he helps me into the house.

"Was it busy in town?"

"I didn't really notice." I won't tell him I thought I saw Paul. I don't want him to think I'm as paranoid as I feel.

"The guys at the rental place said they're calling for storms later in the week. I was afraid it might be a madhouse." He waits. "You're not upset I rented the boat, are you?"

"No," I say, but my tone is unconvincing. I clear my throat. "When are you getting it?"

"Two days from now. The rental is just a couple of blocks from here. I'll drive down and get it, then I can pull it up to the dock."

Andrew is experienced on the water. I focus on this and not on the fear I have about my family being out at sea. He spent his summers visiting different church camps, usually the ones his father's congregation was sponsoring. I've always thought it sounded like a choppy way to spend your time, never having a stable home for the summer. But of course, I spent my summers back and forth between my mom's house and whatever apartment Dad had that year. All our childhoods are uneven if you examine them for too long. And at least Andrew's experiences taught him a variety of skills: how to garden and play tennis and sail boats.

Since the children are still outside, I figure it's a good time to tell him about Aster.

"I got a call from my sister today," I begin, filling him in on the conversation and the fact she and David will be driving just past our rental tomorrow afternoon. "Anyway, I couldn't really tell her no, so I guess we'll have guests for dinner."

Andrew, still putting away food into the cupboard, doesn't look at me, and I can't help wondering if it's intentional.

"Is that okay?" I ask.

"Why couldn't you tell her no?"

It's a fair question, but I'm insulted he felt the need to ask. "Because she's my sister. I put my foot in my mouth by bragging about this place, so it's only natural she'd like to visit. Plus, she's not seen the kids since Thanksgiving."

"And whose fault is that?"

"Both of ours, if we're honest."

He slams a cabinet shut, then leans against the counter, looking down at his feet. "I just don't want this to turn into some mock therapy session. Like she's trying to get to the bottom of things in our marriage."

"That won't happen," I tell him, but sense he needs more reassurance. "Aster doesn't know we've been seeing a counselor."

"Thing is, she'd probably shut up faster if we just told her we were seeing one, after we divulged every gory detail of our sessions, of course."

I laugh because it's true, but part of me feels a bit stung.

"Look, I don't want this to spoil our time here."

"Are you doing this because I rented the boat?" he asks abruptly. His shoulders clench ever so slightly.

"No, Andrew. Why would you even think that?" It was never my intention to retaliate. "If Aster stopping by bothers you this much, I can think of an excuse to give her."

He pauses, like he's thinking over something. "No. It's only one dinner, right? We can get through it."

"Thank you."

All I can hope is tomorrow night passes quickly.

CHAPTER 8

10 Months Ago

The Hidden Oaks neighborhood was ready for Halloween. Proactive parents had already dressed the sidewalks and light poles with reflective stickers. Each front porch had a menagerie of carved jack-o'-lanterns and hand-painted decorations. Some of the more ambitious residents even draped plastic skeletons from their front doors.

It was all too macabre, in Kate's opinion. Not only because of what they'd experienced that summer, but because a much more gruesome act was currently underway in her home: a showdown between mother and teenage daughter.

Willow stomped around her bedroom wearing a black sports bra and cotton shorts with fishnet stockings underneath. Her heavy eye makeup was already beginning to run from the tears, making her look very ghoulish indeed.

"You shouldn't even have a say in this," she screamed.

Kate stood in the doorway, her arms crossed.

"I'm your mother. Of course, I have a say."

"But it's my outfit! My body!" With each word, Willow slapped one hand against the other, as though her argument needed this physical punctuation to get her point across. "You told me I could go to a costume party."

"And you can still go, if you get your attitude under control." Kate nodded to the wad of fabric on the bed. "I just don't want you wearing that."

It wasn't worthy of being called a costume. It was barely a garment. The Lycra material shrunk up to the size of a hand towel when it wasn't stretched across the skin. When Willow had tried it on, the fabric was practically see-through. Kate had demanded she take it off immediately. There was no way she would allow her teenage daughter to go out in public in something she herself would blush to wear around her own husband.

"It's a costume, Mom. It's the one night of the year you're allowed to be a completely different person."

"And for some reason the fashion industry has twisted that to mean women should dress as scantily as possible."

"Do you realize how judgmental you sound?"

Kate opened her mouth and closed it. She hadn't ever pictured herself being in this scenario, where she'd have to argue about how a woman should or shouldn't dress. She wasn't protesting her daughter's costume choice because of her gender, but her age. The outfit made her look too mature, and Kate feared her daughter wasn't capable of handling the attention that might bring.

"Call me judgmental. Call me an old-timer. I don't care."

"I plan on telling Doctor Arrington about this."

Noah and Willow had both been going to therapy since the home invasion, but Kate suspected her daughter liked the opportunity to vent about her problems, outside what happened that awful night. It gave her a little spotlight, something every teenager craves. Right now, Willow was using her sessions as a threat, a way to pressure Kate into more lenient parenting, but Kate refused to take the bait.

"Feel free to tell Doctor Arrington whatever is on your mind," she said, crossing her arms. "If you want to attend that party, you need to find something else to wear."

Willow let out a ferocious howl. Kate turned on her heels, cradling her head with her hands. A headache was coming. What had once been the family's most celebrated night of the year was turning into a nightmare. And as much as she'd like to blame the events from the summer, she worried something more organic was at work. The fact her daughter was getting older, bolder, wriggling from her grasp so quickly she didn't know how to pull her back.

"What do you think?"

The quiet voice at the other end of the hallway belonged to Noah. He was standing in his doorway wearing black sweats with neon skeleton bones sewn onto the front. Kate couldn't help but smile.

"You look terrifying," she said.

"Do you think ten is too old to dress up for Halloween?"

"I don't think there's an age limit when it comes to fun." She knelt down in front of him. "Besides, it's your favorite holiday."

"Yeah, but it doesn't feel the same."

Kate sighed. She'd been dreading this reaction all month. Ever since they moved into this neighborhood, the Brooks family hosted their own Halloween party. They had a great street for trick or treating. Parents would take turns caravanning the children around the block, then meet back at theirs for snacks and spirits. As much as she wanted to continue the tradition for her children, Kate couldn't do it. These days, she ducked around the corner when she spotted a neighbor or friendly face. She couldn't very well invite those same people to her house and fake being jovial all night.

"There's always a big celebration at the park. Give it a try this year. You might enjoy it."

"There's too many people there. Half the kids in my grade don't dress up anymore, and I don't want them to see me and make fun. I just want to stay here, like we always do."

"No one will make fun of you," she said, hoping it was true. Noah was at that age between child and teen, and she wanted him to stay in the former category for as long as possible. She pinched his nose. "You're too scary for that."

There was the sound of a door opening downstairs.

"I think that's Dad," she said, cupping his chin. "Let's see what his plans are for the night."

When Kate reached the main level, Andrew was standing in the kitchen, still wearing his coat. The refrigerator door was open, and he was looking inside. When he heard Kate behind him, he startled slightly, then looked back at the fridge.

"The traffic once I got off the highway was ridiculous," he said. "Cars are already lined up entering the neighborhood."

"It feels different this year, doesn't it? Because we're not throwing the party."

"I suppose." He closed the door without retrieving anything.

"Noah might enjoy going to the community park. Maybe we could take him."

"Crowds aren't really my thing." Above them, there was a rhythmic thudding. The unmistakable sound of Willow's stomping. "What's that about?"

"I don't approve of Willow's costume. She's not very happy about it."

"What's she supposed to be? A witch or something?"

"I'd describe her costume as Victoria's Secret model meets Bratz doll."

Andrew arched his eyebrows and made a whistling sound. If Kate felt unprepared to handle their daughter's teenage fits, Andrew was even less so. He didn't know much about women in general, but Kate had made it easy on him. Willow was testing his limits altogether.

She took a step closer to her husband, putting a hand on his forearm. "Maybe after we get back from the park the two of us can watch a movie together. Pour some wine. Munch on popcorn."

Andrew pulled his hand away. "I told you, I'm not very keen on going to the park."

But she felt what he meant to say was that he wasn't keen on spending a romantic evening with her. There'd been a gap between them ever since the attack really, but the divide had deepened after she fessed up about her encounters with Paul.

"This is usually such a fun night for us. As a family."

Upstairs, they heard a door slamming. Both their heads jerked in the direction of the sound.

"Well, things are changing," he said.

Kate bit her bottom lip and shifted her weight. She wasn't one for drama, but she'd rather have a confrontation and lay it all out. Andrew was more inclined to pout, and it had been almost an entire month of detachment. She'd been foolish in thinking tonight, a holiday, might change things.

"You have to stop this. I swear I didn't do anything wrong. How was I supposed to know that Paul would—"

She stopped talking when she realized Noah had joined them in the kitchen. He stood with his treat sack in front of him, his skeletal makeup perfected.

"Look at you," Andrew said, walking toward him. His smile was wide, and his voice was chipper. He turned into Dad mode at the turn of a dime, something Kate admired, but she wondered if his eagerness had more to do with their conversation being on pause.

"Do you think I'm too old to go trick or treating?"

Andrew looked at Kate, then back at their son. "Not if it's something you'd like to do. Mom mentioned something about going to the park—"

"I don't want to go there. We always go trick or treating around the neighborhood, then we come back here for the party."

Andrew rustled his son's hair. "Things are a little different this year. That's all." None of them needed him to elaborate as to why. "Would you like me to walk you around the neighborhood?"

Even beneath the globs of black and white makeup, Kate could see her son's enthusiasm.

"Would you?"

"I'm already wearing my coat. Let's get going before the spooks come out."

"Andrew, I think we should finish our conversation."

"Another time," Andrew said gently, putting his hand on Noah's shoulder. "We'll be back later. Pour yourself a glass of wine. Relax."

Even with his gentle tone, the words sounded like an order. Worse, they sounded like the only response she'd gotten for the past month: he wasn't ready to talk about what had happened. Or what she'd done.

She followed them to the door. As she watched them descend the porch steps, Dana was walking up. She was wearing an orange and black Lululemon ensemble and carrying one of those recyclable shopping bags from TJ Maxx.

"You two have fun," she said, as she passed them. She stood in front of Kate, holding out the bag. "I've brought alcohol. Tell me that's enough to get me in."

Kate nodded for Dana to follow her. "Don't have plans with the girls tonight?"

"Their dad has them this year. I get them for Christmas. Besides, my Halloween plans have always been to come here. Even if you've canceled the party, I don't see why that should change."

As they were walking into the living room, Willow came storming past. She was wearing the same fishnets but had a black tunic top on that draped just above her knees.

"Heading out?" Kate asked.

Willow didn't say anything. She stood at the kitchen counter, grabbing her wallet and phone.

"What are you supposed to be?" Dana asked.

"A non-slutty witch."

Willow strode to the front door. Kate managed to holler out, "Curfew is eleven," before the door slammed shut.

Dana whistled. "Is that what I have to look forward to in four years?"

"Pity me now. You'll have *two* teenage daughters to deal with."

"Do you think we were ever that bad?"

"I'm sure we were. But I don't remember my mother being this exhausted."

"It's been a hell of a year." Dana poured two glasses of wine and shoved one in Kate's direction. "I figured neither one of us needed to be alone tonight."

Dana and her husband had finalized their divorce a few months back, even though it had been in the works much longer. She knew her friend was happy to put an end to her marriage but regretted the time she now spent away from her daughters.

"Normally, we take all year getting ready for tonight. It's something we can look forward to together. Now, it's like we're all off doing our own thing. Willow's trying to be an adult. Noah's trying to stay a child. Andrew is ignoring me altogether."

"Why is he ignoring you?"

"He's been mad at me ever since the police found out my ex invaded our home. Andrew won't say it, but I know he blames me."

"Didn't you say you all went to college together?"

"Yeah, but he's mad because I ran into him six months ago and never told him about it."

Kate went into the story of her chance encounter with Paul at Andale's. She explained how she walked away from dinner that night with pleasant thoughts about their impromptu reunion; she wasn't expecting to run into him again a week later, at the very same restaurant.

"Are you becoming a regular?" she asked, having spotted him walk in across the room. They had made eye contact, and he scampered over to her, as though being pulled by some invisible force.

"I think this is the best salsa I've ever had." He winked. "And I've been pleased with the company, too."

He ended up pulling up another chair. Again, the two found themselves lost in conversation, talking about the good 'ole days, their younger selves. For a few moments, Kate was transported back to that person she'd once been, the young woman who dreamed about being a writer, carving out her own path in the world, before she became responsible for the paths of so many others. It felt nice to be taken back to that person. Although she'd met Andrew in college, they were bound to the same responsibilities now—kids, bills, jobs. With Paul she could fully immerse herself in the splendor of yesteryear.

Kate flicked her finger in the direction of the waiter and asked for her check. They'd already devoured two bowls of chips and salsa, and Kate wasn't keen on ordering another margarita. Three would be too much for her to drive.

"It feels good catching up with you like this," Paul said. "It seems like I never run into anyone from the old crew."

"This has been nice," Kate said, honestly.

For the first time that night, Paul's gaze lingered a millisecond too long. "Being a wife and mother suits you."

Kate looked down, chuckled nervously. "You think?"

"From the outside looking in." Paul hunched over the table, holding his hands together. He lowered his voice, like he was whispering a secret. "Are you happy?"

"Peachy." Kate didn't know how else to answer the question other than sarcasm. The entire tone of the evening had been light, playful. It suddenly felt like Paul was moving into intimate territory.

"No, really. Are you?"

"Yes." Kate didn't attempt to hide her cool tone. She'd answered his question already and didn't appreciate being pushed.

Paul pursed his lips together. He looked across the way, at the front door, before looking back at Kate. "I need to tell you something. I didn't run into you tonight by mistake. Or last week."

Kate felt a tingle of something at the base of her spine. "Excuse me?"

"You get dinner here every Thursday," Paul said, nonchalantly. "After your afternoon class ends. On all the other nights, you have activities. Willow's math tutor. Noah's guitar lessons. But if you don't have somewhere you have to be, you're not rushing home to spend more time with them. You spend it here. Alone."

Kate paused, replaying back everything Paul had just told her. The details. The names. The silent accusation. And what little she'd told him. Their conversations had centered around the past, not the present; she couldn't even recall telling him the kids' names. "Paul, how do you know all this?"

"I've been watching you." He waited, perhaps for a response, but Kate remained silent. "You see, I think we have a lot of unfinished business, and, sooner or later, we're going to have to discuss it."

Kate's skin flushed and her thoughts whirred. What was Paul saying? Why was he saying it? He couldn't possibly think—after nearly twenty years—she owed him anything. Could he?

Kate told Dana about their contentious discussion at Andale's, how their friendly catch-up turned into something more sinister.

"It was so bizarre. I just wanted to forget about the whole thing," she said, fingers splayed as she moved her hands with the rhythm of her words, not unlike her daughter during her fit of rage earlier.

"But you couldn't?"

"I did. At first. Then Paul started trying to contact me in other ways." Kate took another sip of her drink. These were the details she had kept hidden from her husband, the ones she was compelled to reveal after their conversation with Detective Marsh. "At first it was emails. I guess he was able to get my contact information from the university website. I responded once, telling him I felt uncomfortable with his tone and would like him to stop contacting me. That's when he started calling my cell phone." She took another drink. "I still don't know how he got that number."

"What would he say?"

Kate couldn't tell her the full story. Not that she didn't trust her, rather, it felt like saying Paul's accusations aloud was like speaking his thoughts into existence. What he said during those phone calls was impossible. But she never thought he was dangerous.

"Just threatening stuff. Telling me we needed to meet. Saying we needed to talk. I think he was fixated on the idea of the two of getting back together."

"How did Andrew react to all of this?" Dana asked.

Kate opened her mouth to speak, then pursed her lips. She inhaled and exhaled through her nose, slowly.

"At the time, I didn't tell him about it."

"Oh." Dana shifted in her seat. "I guess that's why—"

"That's why he's so pissed now. I know I messed up, but at the time, I didn't see the sense in worrying him."

More honestly, she had already predicted her husband's reaction if she told him her ex-boyfriend had started stalking her. At first, he would have played it off, pretended it was nothing. Then, he would have become fixated. It was what he did when there was a problem he couldn't figure out. Kate had believed she could handle Paul on her own—her first mistake—but she also feared bringing Andrew into the mix would lead to more suspicion. She dreaded the idea of Andrew turning on her, and she knew that was why she'd kept quiet more than anything else.

"I had no way of knowing Paul would break into our home."

"How could you? No one would ever think this guy would go so far as to attack your family."

"I know. But sometimes I think I should have known better. Andrew thinks I should have known better. He won't say it, but he thinks what happened this summer was my fault."

"You know that's not true, right? Some psycho ex-boyfriend started creeping around again. For most people, that would be an annoyance, not a reason to tighten security."

"If I'd known then what I know now—"

"You didn't." Dana moved in front of Kate, forcing eye contact. She wanted what she said to sink in. "This isn't your fault."

Kate tried not to blame herself, to accept the fact Paul was responsible for his own actions. Still, when she re-examined Paul's anger, Andrew's resentment and the true motive behind the invasion that night, there was only one common denominator.

Her.

CHAPTER 9

Now

The next morning, Andrew wakes up early and heads to the living room for a meeting with his Second Chances group.

Our therapist, Dr. Sutton, is the one who suggested we each try to find our own way of dealing with our trauma, outside our own therapy sessions and conversations with each other. For me, self-defense classes helped me release the tension I felt building throughout the day.

When Andrew first found the Second Chances support group, I thought the entire thing sounded atypical for him. He's always been an introvert. Sometimes I forget we met each other at a frat party; it's so unlike the man I've known for the past seventeen years. It's no easier to imagine him sitting around sharing his feelings with a group of strangers now than it was watching him stand around the beer pong table with his housemates back then. Neither of them fit the true Andrew.

Still, he was taking our therapist's advice to heart, which I appreciated. When he told me what the group was for—men looking for a second chance at self-acceptance—I thought it sounded a bit odd. These men gathering around their computers to talk about their emotions. It's a sexist thought, I admit. How many groups are there out there for women? It's completely acceptable for women to lean on each other, share their deepest fears for the sake of finding common ground. Why can't men?

He relies on Second Chances most, it seems, when he's overwhelmed. In the past year, we've had our ups and downs, both individually and as a couple. It's obvious Second Chances has helped bring Andrew out of his shell. My husband from six months ago wouldn't have suggested any vacations, let alone tack on another week. Six months ago, it seemed he'd rather bury himself in work or drown himself in happy hour cocktails than confront his emotions. I'm happy we've moved beyond that, and I can't deny the group's influence in helping him.

I pull the covers over my head and doze for another half hour before hopping in the shower. After I'm dressed, I wander into the living room. Andrew is seated on the sofa, his laptop resting on the coffee table in front of him. He's plugged into his computer, video chatting. I can see the familiar *Brady Bunch*-style windows on the screen, filled with blurry faces.

I touch his shoulder, and he turns, immediately closing the computer.

"What?" His voice is harsh, and I wonder if Aster's visit is bothering him more than he's willing to admit. Maybe that's why he started chatting with the group so early this morning.

"Are you going to stay inside all day?" I ask, my voice intentionally airy.

"No. I'll head out soon enough." He starts putting away his laptop, and I sense he's embarrassed he reacted like he did.

"Who were you chatting with?"

"Some of the guys from Second Chances."

"Still?" I wait. "You've been in here almost two hours."

"The internet is as patchy as the cell phone service, it seems. I had a strong connection for the first time in a couple of days, so I was using the time to catch up with some of the guys."

"How is everyone?"

I only know a few names, the ones he talks to the most often. He's careful about telling me what their specific issues are, but I wonder. There must be something pulling these men toward one another, driving them to find solace with other likeminded people online. And yet, they can't all be victims of violent crime, like Andrew. Sometimes I find it hard to believe he can find comfort comparing his own issues to those that are bickering with their wives or behind on bills.

"Everyone's good. Just catching up." He looks at me, then continues talking like he expects me to ask more. "Raj is going through some things. Thought I'd offer him my ear."

Raj is a name I've heard him mention several times, mainly because they both work in finance, and it seems Raj has a mean sense of humor. Another one is Vincent. The way Andrew talks, I'd say his sole job is chatting with these men online. I don't see how he'd have time for anything else.

"Are you sure everything is okay?" I ask. There's something about the tight lines around his eyes, the flushed hue of his skin.

"Fine. Why?"

"If this dinner with Aster—"

"I already told you. It's not a problem."

And the way he says it this time, I actually believe him. My thoughts from earlier, that he'd logged online to vent with his friends, are all but confirmed, but at least they've made him feel better.

There aren't many people along our stretch of beach, another advantage to renting a house. We're used to staying with the resort crowd, waking up early to stake out our square of sand for the day. Here, we're able to take the vacation at our own pace.

I'm trying to soak up as much of the glorious weather before Aster arrives. I flip through a few pages of my magazine, but the sun is at full attention, making it hard to read anything without squinting. I toss my magazine and look out at the ocean.

Andrew and Noah have wandered onto the dock. Tomorrow is supposed to be the big fishing expedition on the rental boat—yet another reason for me to feel uneasy—and they're preparing by practicing casting techniques. Willow has wandered down the beach. Her phone is propped up in the sand, and she's videoing herself run through a dance routine.

Alone in my chair, I laugh. Don't teenagers ever think of how ridiculous they look? Of course, each generation has their own trends and fads. When I was younger, nineties pop and chunky sweaters with high-waisted jeans were all the rage. Thankfully, documenting every moment of the day wasn't yet a thing, so there's very little proof of it. I wonder, sometimes, if Willow will grow up regretting the amounts of selfies and TikToks and tweets she's shared with the world, or will it be a normal part of GenZ culture? Maybe everyone will have their own unique time capsule encrypted on hard drives.

Sometimes I can't ignore how much Willow is turning into the person I once was. She's rebellious, always pushing the limits. She even has a flair for the creative, like me. I've found half-written poems and short stories in her room, although she wouldn't dare say she wants to be a writer. Right now, wanting to follow in my footsteps at all is a buzzkill, but then again, she's the product of a wannabe novelist, not a real one.

This certainly isn't the life I predicted for myself. Mother of two. Community college professor. No, when I was Willow's age, I envisioned a life where I'd be traveling the world. Maybe working for a travel magazine, writing opinion pieces about the best places to eat tapas and go skinny-dipping. Eventually, I'd funnel all those experiences into writing the next great American novel. That was the dream, anyway.

It's not that I'm unhappy with where I've ended up. I may not be writing my own articles and books, but my vocation still has plenty of room for creative outlets. I'm able to explore various genres with my students—romance, fantasy, crime. I've even seen some former students make it in the industry. Just last year, one of them published his first book in a new crime series about a former mafioso entering the police academy. I spent hours helping him put together his book proposal. It's a good feeling knowing I've contributed to someone else's dreams coming true, even if I've not quite fulfilled mine.

At least I have my family. I certainly can't imagine a life without Willow and Noah, and the events of last August made that abundantly clear. If I lost them… my mind won't even go there. Still, I sometimes think of that other life, the one I would have chosen for myself had my real life not gotten in the way.

There's shrieking from the dock. Noah is standing with both his hands out in front of his body. Andrew is behind him, helping him guide the line from the water to the shore. A gray fish the size of my forearm flounces out of the water before sinking back in. Together, Andrew and Noah hoist the fish out of the sea, until it's flopping on the dock.

Noah, his cheeks pink with excitement, suddenly looks frightened; he's never caught a fish this big before, and it's clear he doesn't know how to handle it.

"Hold it steady," Andrew says, turning around to rummage through his tackle box.

I'm closer to the dock now, feeling the instinctive need to help my son, even though I know little about fishing. But I know when he needs backup, and his wide eyes tell me he's afraid of messing this up.

"That's a big one," I say, watching as the fish fights with noticeably less abandon.

"Thanks," he says, smiling. He's back to feeling proud, as he holds one hand on the fish's slimy belly, begging it to keep still. "I thought we were going to lose it."

"Good thing you had your dad here to help." Over my shoulder, I can still hear Andrew searching for something.

"Maybe we can get a picture—"

Noah's words are cut off by the chop of a knife cutting into the thick flesh of the fish, the blade slicing right through the head, so that the tip thuds against the dock. Noah pulls back his hand, his gaze fixated on the motionless fish.

My mouth agape, I look from the fish to Andrew. He's standing beside us, holding the knife.

"Andrew!" I shout. "What the hell are you doing?"

The smile leaves his face at a slug's pace. "We're fishing. Surely you don't expect us to throw it back in. This can be our dinner."

My heart is pinging in my chest. I'm not sure why, but the suddenness of the moment has left me unnerved. Noah looks shaken, too.

I motion toward our son. "Noah's hand was right there."

"I told him to hold still. I had to do something before it flopped back in the water." He wraps an arm around Noah. "You're okay, aren't you, bud?"

He nods and smiles, but shakily, like a deer learning to walk on wobbly legs. "Yeah, I'm fine."

"Proud of you," Andrew says, raking his hand through Noah's hair. "Now help me clean up this mess. It won't be long before Aunt Aster arrives."

Noah and Andrew tend to their decapitated catch. I watch as the blood runs down the dock, dripping into the sea.

CHAPTER 10

9 Months Ago

Kate started cooking their Thanksgiving meal the night before. She had to prepare the casseroles, mix the desserts. Normally, it would be Andrew's job to cook the turkey, but she didn't feel like asking him. Not this year. He always seemed so preoccupied, and she didn't want to owe him anything. It was much easier to send Willow to the restaurant down the street to pick one up.

Willow walked in carrying a tin tray with both hands, her car keys hanging from her knuckles. "Where do you want this?"

"Sit it on the counter. I'll move it over to a tray and pop it in the oven, so it stays warm." She looked up to see Willow smirking at her. "You're not going to mention this to Aunt Aster, right?"

"Secret's safe with me." Willow made the motion of drawing a line across her lips with her finger. It wasn't like Willow had much loyalty to her mother anymore, but having this tiny secret shifted the power dynamics into her favor, however marginalized.

Kate would rather die than tell her sister they'd ordered a turkey. It's not like Aster was an expert chef or anything. Rather, Aster was an expert at finding problems and narrowing in on them. Whether that be Kate's weight, Andrew's attitude or Noah's table manners.

In fact, once Aster and David arrived, all three had been mentioned by the time they sat down for dinner.

"I'm just saying, you look a bit frail," Aster said, circling back around to her first dig of the day.

"It's been a hectic school year."

"Beginning junior year, Willow? You'll be applying for colleges before you know it."

"She's already made a short list of where she'd like to send applications," Andrew said. He usually let Aster's digs fly by without addressing them, but it was harder for him to remain silent when she targeted the kids. "Our girl will probably have to fight them off."

"I'm not that great, Dad," Willow said under her breath, but her face morphed into a smile. She still liked to pretend her parents were a nuisance, but there was the rare moment when she actually seemed pleased by what they had to say.

"That's all nice to hear," Aster said, taking another spoonful of sweet potato casserole. After swallowing, she angled her body to better face Andrew. "How about you? How have you been holding up?"

Kate's eyes boomeranged between her sister and her husband. If anything, Andrew's spirits had plummeted further in recent weeks. He often came home late and would almost sprint to the refrigerator to grab a beer. He wouldn't stop drinking until it was time for bed. He was never around on the weekends either. He claimed to be golfing or meeting up with work colleagues, but more than once Kate had wondered if he'd been doing little more than driving around the neighborhood in an attempt to ignore her.

He'd been better today, though. He didn't cook their turkey, but she noticed he hadn't drunk as many beers during the football game either. And he'd at least tried to hold a conversation with Aster and David. It spoke of his loyalty to his wife; it was no secret Kate was on edge whenever her sister was around. Now, she was sitting as still as stone, waiting for her husband to answer.

"Like Kate said, it's been a hectic year. Work is always busy right before the holidays it seems."

Kate breathed a sigh of relief. She was thankful for Andrew's neutral answer. The last thing she needed was for Aster to pick up on the fact they might have problems in their marriage. It was her nature to pick at a loose string until the entire tapestry unraveled.

Aster stared at Andrew a second too long, like she was trying to unpack the meaning behind what he'd actually said. Then she took another bite.

"The turkey is delicious," she said.

Across the table, Kate and Willow locked eyes and smiled.

After dinner, Willow ran upstairs to her bedroom while the boys wandered into the den. Andrew returned to watching football, Noah was plugged into his Nintendo Switch and David was settling in for his second nap of the afternoon. Kate would have been satisfied doing the dishes on her own, but Aster insisted on "helping," which meant drinking a glass of wine while leaning against the counter.

"Do you like your students this semester?" Aster asked.

"As usual, half the students are there to earn a required credit. There's a handful of students who have real potential, if they keep developing their skills."

"I guess that's one of the differences in teaching at a community college. Most of my students are already committed to their field of study. They eat up everything I say." Aster laughed and waited for Kate to chime in. When Kate didn't, she continued. "What about your writing? How's that going?"

"I'm trying to write more in the afternoons," she said, stretching the truth. Aster had never been a fan of Kate's passion. Even the way she said *writing* made it sound like it was nothing more than a hobby, which at this point, it was. Kate hadn't had time to write since the kids were little, and the events of the past year had further quenched her creativity.

"So, tell me," Aster said. "Is everything really okay with you?"

"It's fine. Why wouldn't it be?"

Kate immediately regretted her defensive quip. All she'd done was invite her sister to bring up the one topic she'd tried so desperately to avoid.

"Your family has been through a trauma, Kate," she said in her most professional voice, and Kate wondered if Aster had ever been properly slapped while on the job. "It's natural for there to be some type of adjustment period."

"There is no adjustment period. We're fine. I just wish you'd stop going on about it."

Most people would have backed off at that comment, stayed in their lane. Aster stepped closer and Kate could smell the wine on her breath. "I'm your sister. I can tell when something is bothering you."

Kate pushed her tongue into the side of her cheek and exhaled. "I've been preparing this meal since yesterday afternoon. I'm tired." She slung the dishtowel on the counter, worried that wouldn't be enough. "And honestly, I'm missing Mom."

"Oh, please. She's not had to lift a finger all day and probably had a delicious meal served. Where was she going again? Karen's or Sasha's?"

"It's not the same. She's spending Thanksgiving without her family."

"Which was her choice. You're completely overreacting. She's spent half of our Thanksgivings without us, if you remember."

Kate furrowed her brow but didn't say anything.

"If you're going to miss someone, miss Dad," Aster said. "If he were still alive, he'd be doing everything he could to be here with us."

"He missed half our Thanksgivings, too. If you remember."

"Of course, he did. But he missed them *because* of her."

Kate looked at the floor. She could feel an argument brewing. She had a lot of differences with her sister, but she couldn't help but wonder if this was the root of every disagreement they'd ever had. When their parents had divorced, they unintentionally took sides. Kate supported her mother. Aster supported their father. And it was an argument that all these years later, even after their father's death, didn't seem likely to end.

"After all these years, do you still have to be so critical of her?"

"I'm not criticizing. You're the one who is too forgiving. If she hadn't tried so hard to change Dad, maybe he never would have left."

Kate was about to go in for a response when she felt her phone vibrate. It was an email from Detective Marsh. She opened it, reading the introductory sentences, unaware Aster was still talking.

"Do you hear me?"

Kate looked up, putting the phone in her pocket. "Sorry, I need to read this."

"Every time we get onto this topic, you shut down. I really think it would be much better for both of us, and our relationship in the long run, if you'd quit running away from this conversation."

What was the conversation again? Oh, yes. Their parents. Kate's mind was already focusing on Detective Marsh's email.

"I'm sorry, Aster. I really need to get to the bottom of this."

She untied her apron and left it on the kitchen island. She caught a glimpse of Aster grimacing, but she didn't care. She walked through the noisy downstairs living room and entered the family study.

She logged into the desktop and pulled up the email again. Now she was able to read in relative quiet, and really take in what Detective Marsh had written:

Kate,

Sorry to bother you over the holiday, but I figured you'd want to know straight away. We've made an arrest. Turns out Paul Gunter returned to Hidden Oaks for the week. I can officially tell you he is behind bars. Hopefully, this will give you a little something to be thankful for. I'll reach out Monday with more information.

Take care,
Anne Marsh

Kate read the words over and over again. She felt a wave of euphoria wash over her. It didn't eliminate the fear she'd been holding onto since that night, but she did feel somewhat safer. Like wrongs could be righted.

After a few seconds, she switched over to the search engine and typed in the name Paul Gunter. After clicking through a few local newspapers, she found a recent mugshot. And there he was. A grimace on his face. Disheveled hair. His image trapped within the camera's frame, just as he was presently trapped behind bars. He couldn't get to them. Not anymore.

"Who's that?"

Kate looked over her shoulder. Willow was standing in the doorway, her face fixed on the computer screen.

"What are you doing down here?" Kate's voice cracked when she spoke.

Willow ignored her mother's question. "Is that him?"

For the past few months, Kate had been trying to shield them from updates, protect them from the truth. But Willow especially was old enough to deserve answers. It would make her feel safer to know the person responsible for breaking into their home was caught.

"Yes. Detective Marsh just told me they've made an arrest."

Willow walked inside the study and leaned over, taking in the face. Kate hoped this would help her daughter. Let her see this was no monster—just a man. A man who could no longer hurt them.

After a few seconds, Willow spoke: "I've seen him before."

"Yes, he was here that night—"

"No, I don't recognize him from then. He was wearing a mask the entire time, remember? I saw him before that."

"Saw him? Saw him where?"

"Outside my school. He talked to me."

"Talked to you?" Her voice sounded strangled, felt the way it did when Paul's hands wrapped around her throat the night of the invasion. "What did he say?"

"Not much. Just made conversation about the weather, things like that."

Kate wasn't listening anymore. Her mind was traveling back to when Paul had first made his ridiculous accusation.

After their tense exchange at Andale's, Paul had tried contacting her in other ways. As she told Dana, he'd reached out to her via email. Called her office. Called her cell phone. She blocked his cell from her phone, and refused to answer unknown numbers, in case he tried to contact her again.

Then one day, as she was leaving work, she spotted him. He was leaning against her car, waiting for her.

"You need to get away from me," she warned him, stopping in her tracks. "If you don't stop contacting me, I'll get the police involved."

"And what will you tell them?" The words came out like a challenge. "That your old friend only wants to have a conversation."

"I'll tell them that you've been harassing me, following me, watching my every move." All of which was true.

"Tell me more about Willow." His words dropped with the intensity of a heavy weight. "She's, what, fifteen? You must have gotten pregnant during our senior year. Does that sound about right?"

The air seemed to stall in Kate's throat. "Paul, I don't know what you're insinuating—"

Paul lowered his head, never once breaking eye contact. She stared directly at him.

"She's my daughter, Kate. Did you really think I wouldn't figure it out?"

Kate scrunched her face, could feel her cheeks reddening. "That's not true. You can't possibly think that."

"I know it. You've kept her to yourself all this time. But not anymore."

Kate should have known then how far Paul would be willing to go to wreck her life. He threatened her that day, not with violence, but with an accusation. She wanted to believe that's all it was—an accusation from a scorned, desperate man.

Looking back, Kate realized she should have been more vigilant. That was the moment when she should have taken action. She should have told Andrew that same day, maybe even alerted the police. She should have told Detective Marsh about Paul Gunter the very night of the invasion, but she didn't want to admit how far she'd let events spiral beyond her control.

Kate couldn't admit that she had never actually been his target. All along, he'd been after Willow.

CHAPTER 11

Now

My eyes ricochet between the oven and the digital clock above the microwave. Aster and David are due to arrive any moment. Andrew still hasn't returned with the fish. He insisted we cook Noah's catch and took it to a local fish market to debone the fillet.

I was hoping he'd be back a half hour ago. The vegetables are roasting in the oven and the noodles are being kept warm on the stove, but we'll have to wait for Andrew to cook the fish when he arrives.

There's a noise outside. I walk to the front door but hear nothing. From behind, the sound returns, coming from the patio. Willow pulls back the sliding glass door and walks inside. She's wearing a bikini top and unbuttoned denim shorts.

"What are you doing?"

"Just came in from the pool."

"I thought you were already getting ready."

"Chill, Mom. It's just Aunt Aster."

Looking at Willow, I don't see anything wrong with the way she's dressed, but I'm familiar with Aster's standards. And anything unsatisfactory she sees in Willow won't be aimed at her, but at me.

"Will you just wash up and put on something nice? Dinner should be ready soon."

"Where are Dad and Noah?"

"Still getting the fish."

"But *I'm* the one that better hurry," she says, skulking down the hallway.

Before I can answer, there's a knock at the front door. Aster is here, and the meal isn't even close to being ready. I look back at Willow, no longer trying to disguise the frustration on my face.

"Please, just get dressed and help me set the table."

"Fine," she says bitterly.

I take a deep breath to compose myself and iron out my apron with my palms. I walk to the front door and open it.

"Katelyn!" Aster says, her arms already spread wide to give me a hug. She's wearing a turquoise blazer and white linen pants. Behind her stands David, dressed in khaki shorts and a navy windbreaker. He makes a hmm sound and nods his head.

"Welcome," I say, waving them in like this is my home, when we both know it's not.

Aster charges forward, her head tilting upward to get a better look of the shiplap ceiling and massive fan.

"It's nice. Not quite what I was expecting based on our conversation, but cute."

I knew I was too brazen on the phone, although this is a dream rental by my standards. Aster is impossible to please.

"Two weeks here feels like a little slice of heaven," I say.

"I'm sure. I've been teasing David the whole way over. What's the point of owning a place if we only visit it a few days at a time?"

"Because the rental fee we charge covers the mortgage and then some," David says. His voice has always reminded me of a dried-up slug, if I even knew what one of those sounded like.

"I guess that's what we get for working nonstop," Aster says. "It's difficult to pull ourselves away."

Unlike our jobs, where it's so easy to drop what we're doing, I think. Not important. I have to stop reading into everything she says, reacting as though it's a dig. I should think better of her, but it's hard. After all, I know my sister.

The front door swings open. Noah skips inside, stopping in front of Aster and David. He initiates a hug. Andrew walks in behind him carrying a Styrofoam cooler.

"Sorry we're late," Andrew says.

"We've just now arrived." Aster nods at his hands. "What's that?"

"This is our dinner for tonight."

"Dinner?"

"I caught it," Noah confesses, happily. "The man at the market said it's a grouper. Dad's going to cook it on the grill."

"That's very impressive," Aster says, squeezing Noah's shoulder. Behind her, she nudges David. "I told you we should have picked up a snack along the way. I'm practically starved."

"Sorry," I say. "It was really important to Noah that we eat his fish."

"I understand, I understand." She holds up both hands, graciously letting us know she forgives our faux pas.

Andrew already has the fish out of the cooler and on a platter. The stench is fetid and sickly. He grabs some olive oil and seasonings from the top cabinet, balances them on the tray.

"It's only fish, Aster." He walks toward the backyard grill, pausing to stare down at Aster with the platter in his hands. "It won't take but a few minutes to cook."

Aster seems caught off guard, or maybe she's bothered by the stench. Maybe she realizes how rude she sounds, after inviting herself over for dinner, complaining that it's not yet ready, but that's a stretch.

Andrew walks outside, the glass door clacking shut behind him.

"He's right. It won't take long."

Willow joins us in the living room, her grin growing when she catches sight of Aster.

"There she is," Aster shouts, holding out her hands for an embrace. "My goodness, you get more beautiful each time I see you."

Willow blushes. "It's been a long time since we saw each other."

"Thanksgiving, if I remember correctly."

"Well, we should probably set the table," I say. "Willow, care to help?"

It doesn't take any pressing at all. Willow scoops the noodles out of the bowl and into a serving dish. I take the vegetables out of the oven and do the same. Aster holds out a bottle of wine.

"We did stop by the liquor store to get this."

"That was nice of you." I stop momentarily to fetch a corkscrew out of the drawer. "Care to pour me a glass?"

"I would be delighted."

"So, how far away is your summer house from here?" Noah asks.

We've never been, nor have we been invited. Our schedules never seem to line up. While we're dependent on the school calendar, Aster and David only seem capable of getting away on long weekends.

"It's a little over two hours away from here," she answers.

"And you're driving the rest tonight?" I ask.

Aster looks to David.

"We were wanting to talk to you about that," he starts, a noticeable tremble in his throat. I pity his present students.

"We've been on the road so long as it is," Aster says. "And David always feels so lethargic after dinner. I was wondering if maybe we could stay here for the night?"

"Here?" The word comes out more irritated than I meant.

"We could always get a hotel if it's too much trouble," she says, then looks around. "Or if there's not enough space."

"There's plenty of space," I say.

"It shouldn't be a problem," Willow cuts in. "Right, Mom?"

She looks at me, and it's hard to tell whether she's pressuring me or trying to help.

"One night won't be a problem. I hate for you to get back on the road too late," I say.

"Splendid." Aster claps her hands together. "We'll bring in our luggage after dinner. Like I said, I'm starved."

I nod to the bottle in her hands, a reminder. "How about that wine?"

CHAPTER 12

Now

By the time everyone has gotten their drinks and taken their seats, Andrew returns with the fish. This time the smell is much more pleasant, and I can feel my mouth salivating.

"That was fast," I say, taking a drink.

"The guy at the fish place gave me this easy recipe. It's a little spicy. Hope everyone can handle it," Andrew says, placing the platter in the middle of the table. The meat is flaky and bronze on the outside and white and juicy on the inside when I take a bite. Even if it had been a slab of lard, I would have eaten it, just to make Noah happy. In his seat at the other end of the table, he is beaming.

"Good job, fishing buddy," Andrew says to him.

"Tomorrow will be even better. I can't wait to fish off the boat."

"You're renting a boat?" Aster asks, her tone a hair alarmed.

"Just for the rest of the week," Andrew says. "Noah's been hounding me about deep sea fishing."

No one says anything for a few minutes, but it's easy to guess what people are thinking. They're well aware I'm not looking forward to a day out at sea.

"Well, the kids could be mighty fishermen. It runs in the family," Aster says, breaking the silence. She nods to Noah and Willow. "Your grandfather lived to be on the water."

He died there, too, I think to myself. I gulp my wine, refusing to make eye contact with anyone at the table.

*

As dinner winds down, Willow looks at me. "Mom, I told Sonja I'd call her."

"You're finished eating. Go ahead before the reception cuts out," I say. Noah looks at me expectantly. "You can leave, too."

We smile as the children scamper off to their respective bedrooms, then a thick silence hangs about the room.

"I must say, I'm proud that you're even considering going on the boat tomorrow," Aster says to me. "That shows growth."

"You didn't have to mention Dad. I don't want the kids thinking of him every time they are on the water."

"You seem to be the only person who has that problem." She looks at David, making a tut sound. "Are we supposed to stop talking about him? It's not like they don't know what happened."

"We've toyed with whether or not to buy our own boat," David says, perhaps trying to change the subject. "Not sure if it's worth the investment."

"But it would be fabulous to have," Aster chimes in. "Some of my happiest moments were made on the water."

I take a big gulp from my wine glass. "Considering how much you two work, you may not get to enjoy it much."

Beside me, I see Andrew smirk.

"It's only a thought," Aster says.

"How is work, by the way?" I ask.

"Busy as ever. David is working with graduate students now, which means all sorts of activities."

"Lots of travel," he says.

"And I'm not sure if I told you, but I've been working on this project focusing on young offenders. Really gripping stuff. I practically had to go to the beach house just to wipe my mind from it all."

"Sounds dark," I say.

Aster's eyes light up. She looks from David to me.

"I do have some news, though. I've been waiting for the right time to share it."

"Oh?"

"As I said, I've been working on this research for a while. One of my colleagues put me in touch with a literary agent. They think the material has some commercial potential. We've worked together over the past few months, and a publisher finally signed me up. I got a book deal!"

I'd been chewing my food until she made it to the last part. The food stalls in my throat and I cough, half choking.

"Are you all right?" asks Andrew.

"I'm fine." I wipe my mouth with my napkin, then look at Aster. "You're writing a book?"

"Yes! Isn't it fabulous?"

I can feel the heat climbing through my chest, to my neck, to my cheeks, and I'm not convinced it's just because I nearly choked.

"Since when have you wanted to write a book?" I ask dryly. "For years you've said that's nonsense. What sellouts do. You've said your work is strictly academic."

"Well, it is, but my agent says people are fascinated by true crime, especially adolescent offenders. It's basically like I'm bringing my lectures from the classroom and putting it all in a book."

This sounds like a sales pitch coming straight from her agent.

"And you're actually writing it?"

"Well, I have a ghostwriter helping me. You know how busy I am. Don't have the time to write an entire book, but it will be my words, so to speak. And it will be my name in big fat letters on the cover."

I get up, carrying my plate into the kitchen. I stand in front of the sink, steadying myself and trying to take deep breaths.

"We're very proud of her," David says. "The university wants to host a little launch party closer to the release date. The two of you should try to make it."

My back still to the table, I let out a dry laugh. There's a pause, and then Andrew speaks.

"We'll have to check our schedules."

"Kate, I hope you're okay with this. I mean, I know you used to talk about writing a book one day. Ages ago, it seems."

"I don't talk about it. It's something I still want to do. I still write, when I can."

She should know this, but then again, she spent so long telling me what I was doing was a waste of time, a childish dream, I eventually quit telling her about it. After all those digs, now she's releasing her own book. Rather, having someone write it for her. And she's just now telling me?

"I know it's an incredibly hard industry to crack," she says. "That's why I thought you'd be the happiest for me."

I turn quickly, just in time to see that thin smile on her face. The one I memorized as a child, the one I still see every time she makes a quip about Mom. Leading with my anger, I start marching toward the table. I stop when I see Andrew is standing.

"What's your aim here, Aster?"

"Excuse me?" she says.

"You don't know your sister any better than this? You didn't think this news might have upset her?"

"I don't know what you're talking about. I thought she'd be happy for me. She's the one who knows how hard it is to get a project like this off the ground."

"You're not even writing the book!" Andrew shouts. "And yet you couldn't wait to rub it in her face."

"That's not what I'm doing."

"Oh, forget it. You've probably been pissing yourself the whole way here just thinking about telling her."

I cover my mouth and momentarily forget to breathe. I've never heard Andrew talk to Aster like this. I've never heard *anyone* talk to Aster like this.

"There's no need to be rude," David says, standing.

"Oh, hush. Aster's been asking for this. She practically came here begging for a reaction."

I put a hand on his shoulder to calm him. "Andrew, pl—"

But he's not done. He leans over the table, pointing at Aster and David. "You invite yourselves over, intrude upon our vacation, even have the gall to complain about the food not being ready. Now you're trying to upset my wife?"

"That's not what I'm trying to do," she says.

There were a million other times she could have told me. Aster used to listen to me whine over rejection letters. She's seen me squirm in discomfort when someone asks how the writing is going and I have nothing to say. And she's somehow mastered the fine line of putting down my writing career and academic success at the same time. As emotionally intelligent as my sister is, she must have known this news might upset me, but she was begging to share it anyway.

"Well." Aster pulls the napkin from her lap and places it over her plate. "I certainly didn't expect my news to put a damper on the evening."

"Like hell you didn't," Andrew says. "I hope you aren't feeling too *lethargic*, David, because the two of you won't be staying here tonight either."

"You must be joking," David says.

"You're seriously going to kick us out? Make us get a hotel room this late?"

"Take it out of the boat fund," Andrew says. With that he grabs his plate and walks into the kitchen.

David gathers his things and quickly walks outside, leaving me alone with Aster.

"That was just…" She starts but doesn't know how to finish. "I can't believe you'd allow him to speak to me that way."

"I think we both know tonight's outburst wasn't just about the book. This is how you treat us. Like we're sitting in the audience of the great show that is your life. You treat Mom that way, too."

"Don't start in on the Mom stuff. She blames Dad—"

"Newsflash, Aster. Dad isn't around anymore. Mom and I are the only family you have left. If you don't start treating us better, you're going to be awfully lonely."

Her cheeks are flushed. She clears her throat.

"Thank you for dinner," she says curtly, and walks away.

I watch her leave, then I join Andrew in the kitchen.

"I'm sorry," he says, his back turned to me as he loads dishes into the sink. "I'm just sick of her bullshit. I wasn't going to let her act like she doesn't know what she's doing. She always knows."

He faces me, and I can see the apprehension on his face. He's worried he's crossed a line, overstepped the boundary between a partner and in-laws.

"Kate, say something," he says.

I step closer, pulling him in for a hug, resting my cheek on his chest. "Thank you."

He pulls back, aiming for a look at my face. I'm at a cross between laughter and sadness, wishing tonight hadn't gone sour while also grateful Aster got her comeuppance. Andrew often skirts confrontation; it's that reluctance to get involved that has pushed us away from each other in the past year. Tonight, he sensed I was struggling and came to my defense. I feel a connection to him that I feared may have forever been broken. The man I first loved, the man who would do anything to protect my happiness, still exists, and I've just had a glimpse of him.

He kisses me. I'm surprised by how right it feels, my body pressed against his. We continue kissing, careless about the exposed windows across the way or the children nearby in their bedrooms. A ripple of desire swells like I haven't felt in years, like we're somehow being transported to those young, spontaneous kids we were when we met, before life and all its accompaniments became so daunting.

I grab his hand and lead him toward our bedroom. We lock the door behind us, as though retreating from the obstacles of life is that easy.

CHAPTER 13

8 Months Ago

There's something strange about being on school grounds after hours. Kate always felt that way, ever since she had her first lock-in at her elementary gymnasium. Now an educator, she still felt that eerie sensation whenever a midterm or final exam kept her on campus later than usual. And she felt it now, sitting in the narrow hallway of Hidden Oaks Elementary, waiting to meet with Noah's teacher.

Across from her, the classroom door opened. Ms. Peterson entered the hallway, waiting as the couple before her left. Everyone was smiling and nodding, offering well wishes for the upcoming Christmas holiday. After the couple was a few feet down the hallway, Ms. Peterson turned and held out her hand to Kate.

"Mrs. Brooks?"

"Yes." Kate struggled to jerk her hand from beneath her winter coat and briefcase in order to shake Ms. Peterson's. "Thanks for agreeing to meet me late."

"Not a problem," she said, nodding for Kate to follow her inside the classroom. "You're also an educator, correct?"

"I teach creative writing at the local community college."

"Exciting," she said, sitting behind a desk. "I always say I'm going to write the next great American novel one of these days."

Kate smiled tightly.

"And will Mr. Brooks be joining us?"

Kate cleared her throat. "He's busy running errands with the kids."

"That time of year, isn't it?"

"We're a bit like ships passing in the night these days." She added a chuckle, so it came across as a joke, even though there was more truth in the statement than she preferred to admit.

"Let's talk about Noah." Ms. Peterson cupped her hands together. "Very bright student."

"He is. Noah is our easy one. His sister is just as smart, but we always have to push her to complete her work."

Kate pinched herself. There she was again, comparing Willow to Noah. She didn't mean to. Maybe it was a repercussion of having two children. Especially two children so distinct.

"I was surprised you wanted to meet," Kate continued. "His grades are high. Like I said, he doesn't give us much trouble."

Being a professor, Kate rarely dealt with her students' parents. When she did have consultations, it was always with students who were in danger of failing. She'd been asked to meet with Willow's teachers over the years, but it never had to do with grades. It was usually about punctuality or back talking or skipping class.

Ms. Peterson smiled. "Noah's certainly not trouble. But I do have concerns." Her smile deflated. She placed her hands on the table. "Has Noah talked to you about anything that's been going on at school?"

Kate wiggled in her seat. "No. I mean, he tells me about his classes."

"Does he tell you about his classmates?"

"Noah is very much an introvert. He pretty much pals around with the same group of kids he's been with since kindergarten."

"He does seem to have one or two close friends. However, he's had a few issues with some of his other classmates. They've been giving him a hard time."

"A hard time?"

"Saying things to him during class, in between class change. There have been a few incidents during recess. One day a male teacher found Noah crying in the bathroom."

The image of her bright, beautiful son balled up in a bathroom stall was enough to make Kate want to cry or lash out at someone. She wished Andrew were here with her. Firstly, because she didn't want to be alone. Secondly, because she didn't want to share this information later.

"He's not said a word to me about any of this. Are you saying Noah is being bullied?"

"He's at the right age for it. Thankfully, the politics surrounding bullying have gotten better over the years. People no longer look at it as child's play."

"But why? What are they giving him a hard time about?"

Kate was biased, sure. But when the image of Noah, her son, came into her mind, all she could see was his sweet face. She thought of his wit and playful sense of humor. The idea someone was targeting him—making him cry!—pained her in a way that was difficult to explain.

"Noah is an exemplary student. He's kind, generous. All those things put him on the right track for being a decent human being. Unfortunately, he's also a bit passive. It makes him a target for more aggressive types."

"I can't believe he's not told me about this." The words left Kate's lips in a whisper. She wondered at first if she'd even said them out loud.

"I can assure you we've addressed every incident we're aware of, but I'm afraid there might be more happening that he's not admitting."

Even though Ms. Peterson had been as kind as possible, Kate felt a flash of rage. There was no one else around for her to blame, other than herself—and she already blamed herself for so much.

"I have to ask. Why is this the first I'm hearing of this? He's never had an issue with bullies before. If it's a recurring issue, you should have contacted me sooner."

Ms. Peterson stiffened in her seat. "We did try calling your office."

Kate could feel herself blush. She was never good about returning messages, but she felt certain she would have flagged one that came from Noah's school. Of course, this entire semester had whirred by like a vicious storm. She hated to admit she'd let that cloudiness impact her ability as a parent.

"I'm sorry. I wasn't aware you had reached out."

"I also had a conversation about this with your husband. That's why I was hoping he would join us tonight."

Kate furrowed her brow. "You told Andrew that Noah was being bullied? When?"

"Back in the fall. After the second incident."

Ms. Peterson continued talking, but Kate struggled to absorb her words. She was lost in her own thoughts now. This was the first she'd heard about Noah being bullied, but Andrew knew. And he'd never told her. He'd been nothing but bitter toward her since that visit from Detective Marsh. She'd hoped Paul's arrest would improve their relationship, but it didn't. Kate couldn't believe he'd let his resentment toward her outweigh their responsibility to protect their son.

These thoughts tumbled over one another for the rest of the meeting, fought harder once Kate was alone in her car. By the time she had arrived home, her anger had peaked. Her skin was flushed, and she was using every ounce of control she had left not to burst into tears.

She stomped into the living room, not even bothering to take off her coat. Their living room was already decorated for Christmas—Noah had insisted—and she found Andrew sitting alone by the tree.

"Where are the children?" Kate's voice was uncertain. The silence of the house made her fear something awful had happened.

"They're over at Dana's," he slurred. "I'd thought you'd be home sooner."

"I had a conference with Noah's teacher." The memory of the conversation returned, bringing with it the anger she'd carried with her the whole ride home. "Why didn't you tell me you'd spoken to Ms. Peterson?"

Andrew shook his head, like he was trying to recall the memory. "It was a long time ago. She called my office sometime last month."

"Did she tell you that Noah was being bullied?"

"She mentioned something about it."

"*Mentioned something about it.* You didn't think that was something I needed to hear?"

"Did she tell you about it?"

"Yes. It's the whole reason she called me in tonight."

"Now you know." He stood shakily. That's when she noticed the glass beside the sofa.

"Are you drunk?"

"Does it matter?"

Kate wrestled with her coat, taking it off and throwing it over the sofa.

"I'm sick of this, Andrew. I can't live this way. Ever since Detective Marsh told us Paul Gunter was the one who broke into our home, you've been giving me the cold shoulder. You might not want to talk about what happened that night or anything that happened afterward, but you can't let your issues with me interfere with this family. You can't allow it to neglect our own children."

Andrew laughed.

"Is something funny?"

"The irony of what you've just said. You're upset I didn't *tell you* what was going on with Noah, that you had to hear about it from a practical stranger. How do you think I felt to hear from Detective Marsh that the person who broke into our house was your ex-boyfriend?"

"Don't you think if I knew he was capable of something so demented I would have offered up his name from the very beginning?"

"That's exactly what you should have done!" he yelled. "Or you should have at least involved me!"

"I didn't believe we were in danger." Her voice was flat, her eyes averted. She wanted it to be true. She wanted to believe Paul wasn't capable of violence, but she was wrong, and now Andrew wouldn't let her forget it. "I wish I had acted sooner. I wish I had said something before this got out of hand, but I didn't think Paul would go this far. Even after that night, I still thought it was more likely some random burglar than my ex-boyfriend!"

"Maybe you had reasons to stay quiet."

There was a pregnant pause.

"What does that mean?"

"It means maybe I'm not concerned about what happened that night or after. I've been wondering what happened *before*."

"I told you what happened before. We ran into each other at a restaurant. He got all weird. Then he started trying to reach out to me, but I ignored him every time."

"You didn't tell me about any of this until after he had broken into our home."

"I didn't want to worry you. You can get so judgmental at times."

"Judgmental?"

"Like the way you're acting right now! Like I've done something wrong."

"Have you done something wrong? I'd much rather hear about an affair now than have it dragged out at Paul's trial."

"You're drunk," she said, hoping to end the argument. She'd rather have this conversation when they both had clear heads.

"It doesn't matter whether I'm drunk or sober. I think about the two of you all the time. I think you know more than you're letting on. I think you've always known." He plopped back down onto the sofa and crossed his arms. "Maybe I needed some liquid courage to finally ask you about it."

"I was not having an affair with Paul Gunter. I've always been faithful to you."

"Then I need you to explain to me why, Kate." He hunched forward, resting his elbows on his knees. "Why did this man that you've not seen in almost twenty years pop back into our lives in such a sinister way? You know what the officers told me they found after he was arrested? Tape and zip ties and blindfolds. It's like he planned on taking you away with him. Why would he do that for some girl he dated back in college if there wasn't more to it?"

Kate blinked hard. She'd tried to forget what Detective Marsh told them about what they found in the car. And after she learned Paul was the person in their house that night, she'd tried to pretend she didn't know what it all really meant.

"You're my wife, Kate. I can tell when you're holding back from me."

Kate revisited everything that had happened in her mind. From her meeting with Paul to the first phone call to the moment she found out it was him who had invaded their home. She thought of the fear that creeped up her spine when she realized he'd made contact with Willow, that he'd concocted this fantasy in his mind, and he was deluded enough to act on it. In that moment, she realized maybe she'd done Andrew a disservice in trying to keep this to herself. Maybe she needed him to know the ugly truth about Paul and his allegations.

"Paul didn't plan on taking me that night," Kate said, crossing her arms across her body. "He planned on taking Willow."

"Willow?" For the first time during their conversation, Andrew appeared genuinely shocked.

Kate took a deep breath, preparing to say the words she'd hoped she never would have to say. Preparing to witness the pain she had hoped she would never cause.

"Paul has this crazy idea that Willow is his daughter."

"What?"

"It doesn't make sense. That's why I completely shook him off. I mean, the timelines don't even add up."

For several seconds, he remained silent. She hoped, even in his drunken haze, he was finally piecing things together. She hoped he was finally realizing how delusional Paul Gunter was. Maybe he'd start forgiving her.

"How long had we been together when you found out you were pregnant with Willow?"

"Don't you remember?" She waited a beat before answering. "It was months."

"And you left him for me?"

"Like I said, the timing doesn't make any sense."

"And you weren't ever with him again? After we started dating?"

The question might as well have been a slap. "How could you even ask me that?"

In some ways, this accusation was more hurtful than the one from earlier. An affair was one form of betrayal… but this? He was accusing her of building their entire lives together on a lie.

"I'm just trying to understand. Paul must have some reason to think she's his daughter. He wouldn't break into our home intending to kidnap her otherwise."

"He's crazy, Andrew! None of it makes sense. He came up with this bizarre theory and targeted our family. Maybe he's still bitter about how everything ended between us years ago. I don't know! But I shouldn't have to defend my actions against a madman."

The front door opened and they both jerked their heads. Dana walked in carrying a Tupperware container. Willow and Noah were behind her.

"We have cookies!" Dana raised the container. Her smile fell when she picked up on the tension in the room. "Everything okay?"

"Fine." Kate touched her cheek, turning so the children wouldn't see. Thankfully, they were both plugged into their devices. Ignoring their parents, as usual.

"We need to finish talking about this," she said, lowering her voice.

Andrew drained the rest of his glass and stood. He marched past her, nudging her shoulder as he did. She couldn't tell if the shove was intentional.

CHAPTER 14

Now

Last night, Andrew and I made love in a way we hadn't in years. Over time, sex becomes a series of familiar motions, greatest hits you've played again and again. It's hard to be present with your partner for the thousandth time when you have everyone else's worries bouncing through your head. And in the past year, especially, there's been a distance between us that's been hard to ignore.

Last night, none of that mattered.

When I wake, I smell coffee before I even open my eyes. I smile, bracing for the bright sunlight pouring into our room. Andrew is seated at the foot of the bed with a cup in his hand.

"Coffee?"

I lean up and reach for the mug. "That was nice of you."

"I made breakfast, too. Nothing special, bacon and eggs. It's in the kitchen."

"You didn't have to do that."

"You've been running around this entire vacation taking care of us. You deserve to be spoiled every now and then." He looks down. "Last night was pretty great, huh?"

"It was." I place my coffee on the bedside table and stretch, falling back on the downy mattress. "We shouldn't have waited so long to have a night like that."

Andrew laughs. "Time just gets away from us, I guess." His expression changes. "About Aster—"

"Don't even worry about it. It's about time someone put her in her place."

"But she's your sister. I could have held back, but when I heard her going on and on about her book deal… I don't know. Something just came over me."

"You only said everything I was already thinking. Really, I'm the one who should have put her in her place years ago. You're right. I give her too many passes."

"It's easy for an outsider to judge your relationship. I don't know what it's like, growing up alongside someone, watching your family be torn apart. That's why I care so much about you guys. You're the only family I have."

I lean up, reaching for his hand and squeezing it. "Promise me this. Can we not think about Aster for the rest of the trip?"

"It's a plan."

He leans forward and kisses me. I lean into him, then pull him on top of me, the white comforter between us. I'm on the brink of pulling him underneath the covers and reigniting the passion from last night when I'm interrupted by the sound of bickering in the other room.

"Should I lock the door?" Andrew asks.

"No," I say, playfully pushing him away from me. The kids sound wide awake.

"Yeah, I need to get moving anyway. I have to be at the boat rental place in less than an hour."

"No wonder the kids are full of energy. Today we're going sailing."

Andrew stands, adjusting his clothes and begins to walk to the door. "Are you coming with us?"

"I think I might try. And Andrew?" He waits inside the door-frame and looks back. "Thank you for everything."

He smiles. "Let's just make today the perfect day, okay?"

"Deal."

CHAPTER 15

Now

I used to love the water. As kids, it seemed to be the only activity Aster and I both enjoyed. We didn't like the same games or toys or television shows, but we both loved going to the lake in the summer.

After my parents' divorce, Mom stayed in the home where we had grown up. Dad bounced around from city to city, until he eventually retired and bought a small cabin by the lake. After the kids were born, we began visiting him in the summer, and it seemed my love for the water outweighed the bitterness I had toward him.

"Are you ready?" Andrew asks, interrupting my thoughts. He's standing on the dock, having just brought the boat back to the vacation house.

It's a standard fishing boat with a covered center console and a motor on the back. It's over twenty feet in length, mostly white, with a thick black trim around the sides and chrome railing along the edges. There are padded seats on either end of the boat. The idea of stepping onboard makes my knees buckle.

"Awesome," Noah shouts, running up behind me. "I've already got our fishing gear ready to go."

"I have a few more things I need to check," Andrew says. "It wouldn't be a bad idea to take some sandwiches for the trip."

"I'll make some," I say, almost too eagerly, turning back toward the house.

Andrew grabs my arm. "You're okay with this, right?"

"I'm fine," I say, but my words sound like they are choking. "It'll be fun."

On my walk back into the house, I pass Willow. Her eyes are wide, fixated on the boat.

"Cool," she says. "Noah, take my picture."

I go back inside, standing by the counter. I exhale and close my eyes, try to shoo away the worries in my mind.

Dad lived at the lake house up until his death. We'd continue to visit him there; his social calendar was far too busy for him to see us. I did it out of duty and the fact I thought my children deserved a grandfather more than I deserved the right to hold a grudge. We made many great memories there, not quite powerful enough to wipe away the bad ones from my childhood, but enough to let me know I made the right decision in allowing him to remain in our lives.

Two years ago, my dad went out fishing in the afternoon, as he always did. Everything had been typical, except for the fact he never returned. Another fisherman spotted his boat the next day. It was floating in the middle of the lake, empty except for a lunchbox and some fishing gear. Dad was nowhere to be found.

The initial worry didn't settle in until much later. My father was stubborn and selfish, but undeniably self-reliant. A series of assumptions crossed my mind about what might have happened. Maybe he returned as usual, his boat had become untethered and drifted away, and Dad was out and about somewhere, unaware there was currently an active search taking place. Or maybe he'd run into trouble, but found a way out of it, again unaware how the situation might present itself to onlookers. Wherever he was, he was safe, the same old son-of-a-bitch he'd always been.

Four days later, we received the call that divers had found a body in the lake. We still don't know exactly what happened. Dad followed safety regulations to a tee; I can't imagine he would enter the water in an unsafe area, let alone leave his lifejacket on the boat. Whatever happened, the end result was my father had died, his body already bloated and swollen. At least that's the image Aster conveyed after she made the identification.

Selfishly, I was happy she'd been called to identify his body and not me. Although I'm too stubborn to admit it, Aster is in some ways the stronger of the two of us. The most like Dad. She was always his girl, and I was always Mom's. Whether they'd intended for that to happen after their divorce or not, our allegiances were divided, a separation that impacts my relationship with my sister to this day.

I had a complicated relationship with my father, but that didn't ease my mourning. I missed him intensely, in a way I might not have predicted before his death. I'd lived a vast majority of my life without him—that part wasn't new. I suppose I thought when the time came, I'd have some type of warning. With Dad, that wasn't the case. He was there, then he was gone. The last time I'd seen him—three months before he died—there was no indication it would be the last time.

Aster and I had planned a weekend to sort through his belongings at the lake house—we were the only two left. Dad was an only child, and the only family he had left other than us was a long line of bitter ex-wives, our mother included. We spent the days going through each drawer and closet, mostly trashing what was left behind. In the afternoons, we'd unwind on the dock, looking over the water that had taken our father's life so suddenly. A peaceful looking beast, it was.

By the end of our trip, Andrew had decided to drive up with the kids. Aster had talked us into taking the boat out, and that's when the panic first set in. Out there on the water, the land and trees a pinprick on the horizon, I felt like I was suffocating. Like the same dangers that had claimed my father's life were rising, ready to swallow me whole.

A few months later, when I returned to the local community center for my weekly swims, I was grasped by that same terror. The water, a living breathing organism, had plans to destroy me. I've not been swimming since.

It wasn't a reaction I was expecting to have after his death. It seemed like I could almost imagine the currents overpowering him, pulling him under, squeezing the last breath from his lungs. Perhaps I wouldn't have such a reaction if there were more answers about his death. But answers, I don't have.

"Mom, are you coming?" Willow walks inside, sliding the glass door closed behind her.

"Just finishing up." I turn around and grab a Tupperware off the counter. My hands begin to shake, and I drop it, the plastic plopping against the floor.

"Are you okay?" Suddenly, Willow sounds mature beyond her years. Kinder.

"I'm fine." I smile, tucking a stray hair behind my ear. "Didn't get much sleep last night."

Willow nods, unconvinced. They know I've had a complicated relationship with water after Dad's death. I still appreciate it from a distance—much like my relationship with him my entire life. In the past year or so, I forced myself to get over this mental block, if not for my own well-being then for my children. They didn't have the same fears I did. They didn't sense the impending doom I felt when the water surrounded me. And I didn't want to inflict my own fears on them. So, I took them to pool parties and swim meets and even days at the lake. I'd watch them more closely than before, but I'd let them enjoy the moment because it was theirs to have. I pushed my fears to the side.

Maybe that's something I owe to Paul Gunter, too. Our latest trauma has replaced my previous one.

CHAPTER 16

Now

The motor's whirring helps drown out my thoughts. Andrew cuts the engine, and the boat rocks from side to side, balancing on the waves of the Atlantic. I'm sitting toward the back, crouched down in an irrational attempt not to fall over the edge. There's a small chance of that happening, but my anxieties make it feel like it's inevitable. *If it could happen to my father…*

I focus, instead, on Willow and Noah's gleeful expressions. This is the happiest they've been the entire vacation. Noah stays at the wheel with his father, his head whistling from left to right, taking in every view. Willow's hair blows away from her face. Her eyes are closed, as though she is pocketing this sensation.

I remind myself Andrew is an expert boatsman, having spent years maneuvering lake currents with my father, and even before then, during his own childhood. We've not taken a boat on the ocean in several years, but he looks as comfortable as ever.

Until he doesn't. Now that we've stopped in the middle of the sea, land so far away you have to squint to catch a glimpse, his demeanor has changed. It's a subtle shift. Not even the children pick up on it. It's something you only notice after several years with a person. It's the way he fumbles with equipment, the way he looks over his shoulder, as though he's expecting someone else to be here in the middle of nowhere. That's the impact Paul has left on us. We question our abilities in a way we didn't before, doubt our safety, all too aware of the dangers beyond our control.

"Dad, can we lower the line?" Noah asks.

"Sure, sure," Andrew says, both hands on his hips. He cocks his head toward Willow. "You want to fish?"

"I'm fine," she says, her phone raised above her head. "I'm just going to relax and take some pictures."

It's all she's done since the boat stalled. She's snapped dozens of selfies and expertly poised shots. Her ankle and manicured toes by an anchor in one, her hand reaching over the side of the boat to feel the water in another.

"Dad, the stuff?"

"Right." Andrew shuffles to the back of the boat, where I am, and starts rummaging through bags.

"You okay?" I ask, my voice low.

"Great. It's a beautiful day." An artificial smile covers his face. "How about you?"

"I'm okay," I say, my tone conveying he needn't worry. After he walks back toward Noah, I take a sip from my water bottle and stand. I make my way to the side of the boat, my balance shifting at first, and look at the surrounding water.

My fears aside, the view is beautiful. The sun's rays beam across the water, creating the impression of dazzling diamonds across the surface. The sky is a clean, calming shade of blue, only a few bulbous clouds in sight. I even value the scent of salt and sweat. I try to focus on these sensations, and not on the image of my father's last moments in a similar setting.

"Mom, where are those sandwiches?" Willow asks.

"In the basket by the cooler." I take a seat across from her, my back against the side of the boat. "Sure you don't want to fish with the boys?"

"Maybe later," she says, snatching a triangular sandwich and taking a bite.

"I'll hold you to that," Andrew shouts from the other end of the boat. "I'd like to see you both give it a try."

Andrew knows I'm not one for fishing. We're fortunate I've made it this far on this little excursion. Noah casts his line into the ocean. Andrew monitors him from behind, but every so often he'll glance back at me and Willow, like he's trying to keep tabs on us, too. I know he's trying to look after me, be the protector he feels he has to be. Sometimes I wish his attempts weren't so obvious. If he doesn't think I'm worrying about Paul Gunter, he believes I'm paranoid about the water. It makes me feel fragile.

I lean back on the boat, pulling my hat over my eyes. It's easier to concentrate in this position. I can hear everything around me without having to see it. Willow's chewing. Noah's excitement. Andrew's praise. Water splashes against the hull and, every so often, I hear the squawking of birds overhead. I feel the gentle rocking of the boat, and it almost puts me asleep. I can feel my lids getting heavier, my reaction to everything around me dwindling.

"Dad!"

Noah's voice wakes me before I'm fully asleep. I sit up, watching as he wrestles with his fishing pole.

"I think I got something!"

"Impressive," Andrew says, taking a step back.

Noah pulls harder on the line but doesn't gain any distance. "Whatever it is, it's big. I don't think I can get it."

"Keep trying." Andrew's voice is low, his eyes on the side of the boat.

Noah tries to yank the pole toward him, but it's useless, his feet shuffle closer to the side.

"I can't get it, Dad. I need help."

There's a moment where Andrew does nothing, just continues to watch. Then he wraps both arms around Noah, trying to steady his grip so Noah can reel it in.

"Put a little muscle in it," Willow says.

"I'm trying," Noah shouts, and his voice sounds so small. Willow lets out a wicked laugh, whereas I feel torn.

Andrew lets go. His eyes never leave our son, but he's no longer there to provide the strength he needs to reel the fish in.

"Dad, I'm losing my grip. I need your help."

Andrew wraps his arms around Noah again. I stand, making my way toward them.

"Just give up," Willow says, turning away from the excitement.

"It's too heavy," Noah says, and it sounds like there's fear in his voice.

"Hold on." Andrew lets go again, moving to retrieve something else from the other end of the boat.

Just then, Noah loses his grip on the pole. It goes into the water as though there is some type of magnetic pull underneath. As it goes over the edge, Noah reaches after it, slamming his body against the side of the boat. He loses his balance, and in one swift but excruciating moment, his body topples over the side, landing in the water.

At the sound of the splash, we all rush to the point where Noah just stood. Within a few seconds, it seemed, he was gone. The panic rises from my stomach to my chest, clenching my heart with icy knuckles. I grasp the side of the boat, staring at the ocean in hopes Noah's head will break the surface.

A second later, it does. He takes a gulp of air, then plummets beneath the water again.

I scream. A thick, terrifying sound, more visceral even than the one I released on the night of the invasion. That night I'd felt I didn't have a chance to react; in this moment, my greatest fears are coming to fruition, and my child is at the center.

"Andrew, do something," I shout, but my words are followed only with silence. Noah's head pops up again, only to be overwhelmed by another current, and he goes under once more.

I turn around. Andrew is sitting, his eyes fixed on the scene in front of us. His mouth is partially open, as though amazed, and his left knee is rapidly shaking. But he's still. He looks afraid, horrified, but does nothing.

"Andrew!" I shout.

For a brief moment, we make eye contact, but his expression is blank, paralyzed by fear. It's written all over him—the worry, the defeat. But he doesn't act.

"Noah!" Willow yells, and I can now hear the fear in her voice, too. "There he is."

I follow the direction of her finger, and catch sight of his head in the water, his body being pulled further away by the current.

I take another deep breath, but it feels as though no air has entered my lungs, and in one jump, I'm in the water.

The sudden coolness stuns me and awakens my senses all at once. Water seeps into my mouth and rises up my nose, a fishy, salty taste. I spread out my arms and pop my head through the surface. From this angle, the waves appear larger than they do from the comfort of the boat. I look back, and can see Andrew is standing again, Willow at his side.

"Kate!"

I turn away from his voice, back to the open sea, and shout. "Noah!"

I spot his pale skin bobbing against the waves, and I start swimming in that direction. Long, deliberate strokes, like I used to do during my weekly swim sessions at the community center. After a few strokes, it feels like I'm getting nowhere. I dive beneath the water, thinking I might gain more distance that way.

When I rise for air, I hear Willow again.

"Mom, he's right there."

I swim rapidly toward him, until I feel my body crash into his. He grasps for me, but his life vest isn't fitting properly, hindering his ability to swim. He's panicking.

"I'm here, Noah," I yell. "Try to stay calm."

Hearing my voice, feeling my body beside his in the cold water, soothes him. His breathing becomes less haggard and his movements less frantic.

When I turn, I see we've already drifted at least ten feet from the boat. I'm trying to get closer, but it's challenging when I'm swimming for both of us. Noah's grip loosens, and I feel his arms gliding through the water beside me.

Up ahead, to my left, there's the sound of something hitting the water. I see Willow has thrown over a life preserver, the other end still tied to the boat by a rope.

"Come on," I encourage Noah, reaching out with all my strength to grab it.

After a few more seconds, my fingers finally reach it. I hold it for balance, using my other arm to bring Noah closer. I pull him in front of me, making sure he has a tight grasp on the preserver.

"We got it," I shout.

Willow starts hauling, but it's not enough. "Dad, pull them in while I lower the ladder."

At last, Andrew moves. He pulls the rope closer to the boat, but he still has that stupefied expression on his face. By now, we're within reach of the boat. Willow lowers the ladder. I allow Noah to climb up first, then me. He falls on his knees and coughs. A gulp of sea water splatters onto the deck.

"Are you okay?" Andrew asks. He kneels in front of our son. Whatever daze he was in is gone, and he looks genuinely worried.

"I'm fine," he says, trying too hard to act as though what just happened wasn't as scary as it was. His embarrassment acts as a sign that he's okay.

"Mom?" Willow looks at me.

I'm drenched, shivering from a combination of adrenaline and panic. My breaths come in short, rushed bursts. My eyes focus on Andrew, and my anger renews.

"Let's head back," I pant between breaths.

Willow wraps a towel around my shoulders. She does the same to Noah. Andrew, at the wheel, starts up the engine. I watch him, trying to understand his reaction, why he did so little to help our son. I can't imagine displaying that amount of passivity. It's not in my nature, and yet seems to define his.

I close my eyes. I no longer wonder about the fear my father must have felt in his final moments, I realize.

I've just lived it.

CHAPTER 17

7 Months Ago

Kate's favorite season had always been winter. Most people enjoy the freedom of summer, the colorful landscape of fall, the bright freshness of spring. Something about a new year brought Kate peace, always had. Outside, the skies were gray, cloudless. When she squinted, she could see snow flurries drifting to the ground, disappearing almost as soon as they hit the concrete. It wasn't cold enough. Yet. By the end of the week, the temperatures would drop and the snow would build, each flake bonding to the other, until the roads were so thick with it they'd have to call off school. Kate liked having the children home with her. She enjoyed sending her students a message that said, *Sleep in! Classes will resume next week.* Days like that felt like a gift.

Kate was bundled in layers, a thick red scarf wrapped around her neck. The specks of snow that fell on her hair stayed there, wetting her strands. She moved quickly, both hands in her pockets, with Noah at her side. They were the only two people on the sidewalk as they walked from the car. That was another element of winter she enjoyed. Usually only the brave ventured out, and she was one of them. For a few, cold weeks, it was like she had the world all to herself.

"Let's just go back home," Noah said.

"Come on. I thought we agreed we'd do this together?"

"You *told me* we'd do this together."

"Hey." Kate stood in front of her son and bent down, forcing him to look at her. "This will be good for both of us."

"Are you doing this because of what my teacher told you? She's really making a big deal out of nothing. I'm not having problems at school, and if I was, I can just talk to Doctor Arrington about it. I don't have to take some stupid class."

Except Noah wasn't talking to Dr. Arrington about the bullies. Kate had already asked him. At this point, she was more concerned with his self-esteem; she believed taking this class would improve his confidence.

"This will be good for both of us, all right? Just give it a chance."

He responded with an eye roll, pushing past her to enter Hidden Oaks Fitness Center.

There was a small waiting room at the front, heat pumping through the vents. By the time she approached the counter, Kate could already feel a thin layer of sweat at the back of her neck.

"Kate and Noah Brooks," she said. "I pre-registered us online."

The man behind the counter was short, but his shoulders were broad, his biceps practically bursting from beneath his short sleeves.

"I've got Noah in the beginners karate class, is that right?"

"Yep." She tried to ignore her son's loud sigh.

"Did you want to sign up for a certain class, or are you here for the open gym?" the man asked Kate.

"I'll take a look around. Maybe sign up for one of the classes later."

"If you're trying to find something during his karate class, we offer Self-Defense in Studio B and Zumba in Studio D."

"Good to know," she said, although neither were up her alley. Kate couldn't stomach the idea of dancing around a room of strangers; if it weren't for her phobia of water, she'd hit the pool. Now she wasn't sure what to do, but it was important to her that Noah found an activity that would keep him busy and improve his confidence. She thought it might help him at school.

The man behind the desk looked to Noah. "Your class is in Studio C. There are lockers in there for your bags. Follow me."

Before he walked off, Kate grabbed Noah's arm. "Give it a chance, okay?"

He nodded, a small smile beginning to peek through.

She followed them into a narrow hallway that led to the main gym area. To her left, was a wide arena of bare space, a line of mirrors on the far wall. She stared at her reflection as she passed. To her right was the more crowded area of the gym. Machines and dumbbells and more mirrors. Kate tried to remember the last time she'd been to a gym. She used to frequent the gym on campus, before the children's activities filled her week. She'd abandoned her former discipline, but now she was making time for herself again. This was her resolution.

Another aspect of the new year Kate enjoyed: she was good at making a plan and sticking to it. Lose ten pounds. Stop buying coffee. Read a new book a month. She carved out these changes as best she could. This year, her goal was to find her physical strength. She needed to start a new adventure, even if all she could manage as a wife and mother was joining a gym down the road. At least it would be an hour to herself a couple days a week. Maybe she'd quit by the end of the month, as most new year hopefuls did, but Kate doubted she'd be like that. She was committed.

After she undressed in the locker room, she locked up her belongings and walked out into the open arena. A jolt of insecurity cemented her where she stood. She looked around, unsure what she should do first, where she should go. Should she try the treadmill? The machines were too intimidating, already saved by meatheads that seemed to know what they were doing. She didn't want to make a fool out of herself.

She peered into one of the studios, watching as people prepared for the next class. She was surprised to see the room was made up mostly of women. About half were her age, the others about a decade younger. None of them had the aura of insecurity she had; they all seemed at ease.

At the front of the room, she saw a familiar face. Detective Marsh. Their eyes locked at the same time, and Marsh offered a wave. She looked different in her neon-colored active wear. She wandered across the room.

"Kate, I didn't know you were a member at this gym."

"I just signed up. Noah's taking karate classes, and I thought I might as well break a sweat while he's doing that." She looked around the room again. "Do you take this class?"

"I'm the instructor. It's a self-defense class." She took a sip from her water. "Thinking about staying around?"

Now, Kate felt awkward. Detective Marsh was the one person who understood exactly why Kate should take this class, and she suddenly felt on display.

"Let's get started," Marsh said, looking around the room. Her eyes seemed to connect with Kate's, but maybe it was just her self-awareness acting up again. "Line up."

They did an initial warm up, running and hopping in place. Kate immediately began to feel herself sweat, but she no longer felt as self-conscious. At the exact point when she thought she might collapse, they had their first break. She and the other members stood around the mat, watching as Marsh demonstrated a series of moves with another participant, someone who actually knew what she was doing. They broke off into pairs, and tried to mimic what they'd just seen.

Kate would have sworn no more than five minutes had passed. She was laser focused on each hit, each duck, each sprint. It was the first time in a long time—who knew how long—her mind wasn't focused on some errand, some responsibility, traveling away from her, back to where they were that night in August. Now, her mind was only focused on this room, the people in it, and her next move.

"Is that it?" Kate asked when the class ended, her breath shaky.

"Flies by, doesn't it? That was an hour." Detective Marsh wandered over, grabbed the towel that had been draped over her shoulder earlier and wiped her forehead. "Will I see you next week?"

"Yeah. I think you will."

"Glad to hear it."

Marsh seemed happy. Kate didn't have to go into her reasons for joining the class, but it was clear Marsh thought it was a good decision. Kate felt good about it too. Doing something for herself. Something that made her better, both inside and out. Already, she knew she wanted to experience the sensation again.

This is what it was about. Fresh beginnings. Hope. She prayed that was what this new year would bring.

Noah's class finished around the same time. He skipped out the door, high-fiving some of his peers on the way out. She was happy his class had improved his demeanor.

She welcomed the cold air filling her lungs when she stepped outside. The drive home felt like its own little luxury. She sang along with the radio, bobbing her head and waving her hands like she did when she first started driving as a teenager.

As usual, she stopped at the mailbox before pulling into the driveway. She was still humming a melody as she flipped through the envelopes. Bills. Flyers. And something else. A letter addressed to her.

She opened it, her eyes scanning the first few sentences. And the fear came flooding back, as though it had never left.

CHAPTER 18

Now

We don't speak much after we return home. I think our minds are still at sea, reliving that horrific scene out on the water.

"Anyone hungry?" Andrew asks, making his way to the kitchen. It's the first sentence he's spoken since we started our trek back to shore.

"I think I might take a nap," Willow says, walking lazily toward her room. I know what happened this afternoon scared her, and I'm sure she feels guilty for taunting her brother only moments before she risked losing him.

"I could eat," Noah says. Always eager to please and also trying to pretend he wasn't the focus of this afternoon's scare. "Although, I am pretty tired."

"Rest up. That would be good for you," Andrew says. "I'll order us some pizza in an hour or so. Something easy."

Noah toddles down the hallway and closes the bathroom door behind him. It hurts, even having him out of my sight for a few seconds. We were so scarily close to losing him this afternoon. I turn and look at Andrew.

"Are you hungry now?" he asks, intentionally avoiding my gaze. "I could make you something."

"You didn't do anything," I say. My voice sounds like it's coming undone, an undercurrent of rage beneath.

"Kate, everything happened so quickly—"

"And you just stood there." My body shakes. That's how hard I'm trying to stifle my rage. "Our son was drowning in the ocean, and you took a fucking seat!"

"He wasn't drowning." He stops, reconsidering his response. "He was struggling, and I was shocked. I didn't know what to do."

"You do what I did," I say, pointing my finger at him. "You do what you have to do to protect them. Jump in, throw a raft. You don't sit there like some moron as we watch our son drown."

He pauses, still refusing to meet my gaze. He's silent. Then, "I was scared."

"I was scared, too. I'm terrified of the water, and you know that, but I still jumped in because Noah needed me. You... you didn't do anything."

"I'm sorry—"

"No!" I'm yelling now, then lower my voice so as not to attract the attention of the children. "How am I supposed to go through life with someone who I can't depend on?"

"That's a low blow." He waits, no doubt thinking about that night, how our fear has followed us both since then, tainting our actions. "It's like Doctor Sutton said, our bodies have three reactions to trauma: fight, flight or freeze. Clearly, you're the fighter between the two of us."

"I'm tired of fighting. I'm tired of feeling like I'm the only person this family can depend on." I break into sobs, as though I can physically feel the weight of all these worries atop me. "I thought we were making progress, Andrew. I thought *you* were making progress."

"I am." Finally, he looks at me, only for a moment. He's ashamed to look any longer than that. "I messed up today. Thankfully, you were there to do what I couldn't."

"Why did you let go of the fishing pole?"

"What?"

"When Noah was struggling with the fish, why did you let go? One minute you had your arms around him, and the next you'd taken a step back."

"I was going to get a harness to help him reel in the catch, and the next thing I knew he was overboard. It all happened so fast."

And yet, there was another moment where that wasn't the case. He let go twice. Why, I don't know, and I'm not even sure if he knows the answer.

"I can't keep doing this—"

"Can't keep doing what, Kate?" He slaps his hands against the counter, and I jump.

How can I tell him I've lost my respect for him, my trust? And his reaction, whether he's wounded or not, doesn't make it any easier.

I don't answer. I back away, wandering into the bedroom, away from the sight of him.

You'd think after a trauma, we'd pull together. I imagine that's what most families do. Mine doesn't. We go our separate ways, trying to work it out for ourselves before reconvening with the group. I learned that after the home invasion, and tonight we're no different, each escaping to different corners of the rental property, hiding beneath excuses.

When the pizza arrives, we gather at the table, each doing our part to pretend this afternoon didn't happen. For several minutes we eat in silence.

"We should come back to this place next year," Noah says, in between bites of food.

"You think?" Andrew looks quizzical.

"I love it here," he says. "There's not all that touristy crap around like in other places we've been."

"Language," I prompt, lowering my eyes in Noah's direction.

"It has been nice. I like having our own pool," Willow adds, her eyes drifting to the sliding glass doors. It's so dark outside, we only see our own reflection. The four of us sitting around the table.

I admire them for trying to ease the awkward tension. This has been the crux of this trip. We're trying to be the people we were before, the people we should have been all along. Before Paul re-entered our lives. Today's accident doesn't change the desire to return to normal.

Andrew's thoughts must be falling in the same rhythm. He says, "It means so much to know you've been happy here."

I reach my hand across the table, laying it over his. I squeeze. I was too harsh with him earlier, even if I was being honest. I don't want what happened on the boat to color our remaining days here.

"We've come so far in the past year," Andrew continues, lifting his head to watch the faces of our children. "We're really lucky we've made it through. Most families don't bounce back after such a tragedy."

I wonder, at first, who he's thinking about. What other stories he might have heard from Second Chances or elsewhere. I wonder what outcomes those families had. Then, I look at our children. I wonder what their reactions to this conversation will be. We rarely speak about what happened that night, and when we do, it's never so openly. *Making it through. Tragedy.* These are words we've chosen to avoid. The kids stare ahead, their eyes on Andrew, but the flush in their cheeks is gone and their jaws are noticeably slacker.

"We've made it a long way," I say, hoping to change the topic to something else. Our nerves are still tender from what happened on the boat; we don't need to revisit the home invasion. "I'm looking forward to the fall."

"I mean just think about it," Andrew continues, as though he hasn't heard me. "Where we were a year ago. What we were going through. I can remember the fear, knowing there was this intruder in our house. Not knowing what he wanted but knowing it couldn't be good. And I knew the people I cared about most in this world were being threatened. I knew then I'd lived my entire life without really being afraid. Without feeling a need to protect. And all at once, those emotions overwhelmed me."

The way Andrew looks right now, the way his head is tilted to the side and his eyes are almost closed, you'd think he was lost in some happy memory. Listening to a song. It's such a strange, open confession, I think none of us want to break him from his trance, and yet I know this needs to end.

"Maybe we shouldn't—"

"Maybe we *should* talk about that night," Andrew interrupts, his eyes piercing through me as though I've just let out a slur. "I'd like to hear what they have to say. About that night."

My mouth is open, and yet no words come out. My eyes dart to the children, Noah, then Willow.

"I… I was scared," Noah says, an obvious attempt to appease his father.

"Yes, we were all scared. But what scared you the most? What were you really feeling in that moment, son?"

"I was afraid something would happen to one of you." His voice is quiet, a small peep that reminds me of a mouse. "I was afraid I might not see you again."

"That would have been terrible, wouldn't it?" Andrew says. "To not see your family again."

I'm enraged, listening to him speak to Noah like this. Almost taunting him. "Andrew—"

"And what about you, Willow?" he continues, cutting me off. "What did you feel?"

Her eyes dart toward me, as though asking for permission. "I was also afraid."

"We've established that. We all were." He stares at her to continue.

"And I was angry. That someone could get that close to us."

"It's infuriating, isn't it? Someone was in our home. Under our roof. Invading our family."

"Andrew, this is enough."

He turns to me. "What about you, Kate? What did you feel?"

"I don't think this conversation is appropriate. We're on vacation. We shouldn't be—"

"Then when should we talk about this? We can't just keep hiding this conversation between the two of us, addressing it when only in the presence of our therapist. It happened to our entire family. We're all impacted by it. And what happened on the boat reignited those feelings in all of us. I think the least we can do is revisit it openly and admit how it might have shaped us."

I feel my eyes prickling with tears, but I clench my jaw, trying to keep them in. I don't want the children to see me cry. They are staring at me, their food untouched, their cheeks pale. I wonder what they're thinking. To hell with that night, I want to know what they're thinking right now. And Andrew's eyes are still on me, casting accusations.

"Were you like Willow?" he asks. "Were you angry someone was able to get so close to us?"

"Yes." All I can manage is that one word.

"And what else?"

Shame, I think. *I was ashamed.*

My eyes bounce between Andrew and the children. "I was heartbroken."

"But we're better now, aren't we? Just look at us."

Andrew is smiling now, like he's impressed with what tonight's conversation uncovered. I'm still not sure why he initiated this discussion. He acts as though it was necessary. I wouldn't describe Andrew as vindictive, but the way he is powering through with this conversation—blocking me when I try to intervene—seems intentional.

"I feel better getting this off my chest," he says, leaning back.

Willow nods. Noah stares straight ahead. I'm still trying to fight back the tears threatening to break.

CHAPTER 19

Now

Andrew's conversation looped through my mind during the night. He didn't say more than a few words after dinner, then spent several hours chatting on his computer. When he did climb into bed beside me, he slept peacefully, like nothing happened. I suppose, in his mind, nothing did. He was simply having a conversation. One he deemed necessary.

I still can't gauge the children's true reactions. They played along, answering his questions and nodding when appropriate. On the outside, they didn't seem bothered by the conversation, which is perhaps what disturbs me so much. I can't decide if I'm being too sensitive, thus supporting Andrew's theory that we should talk openly about that night, or if the children were frightened, but desperately trying to appease their father. Between the two reactions, I'm not sure which one I prefer.

I have a nagging feeling that Andrew did this as revenge. For the way I lashed out at him after the boat, perhaps? He has avoided me since then, choosing to forgo talking to me in favor of venting to his online friends. In a paranoid quadrant of my brain, I wonder if last night's conversation was meant to get back at me. Punish me. Teach me a lesson.

Beside me, Andrew rolls on his side, facing me. I wonder what dreams and nightmares and thoughts are swirling around his brain this very minute. When he does open his eyes, I'm staring down at him. He smiles.

"Good morning."

"Morning." I'm hunched over with my forearms leaned over my knees. "Did you sleep well?"

"Like a baby. What about you?"

I make a face, turning my mouth into a thin, straight line. We're not supposed to keep lying to each other, even for the sake of our feelings. It's better to be upfront about how last night affected me.

"I'm upset about the conversation we had at dinner."

"Upset?" He sits up in the bed. "I didn't bring up what happened last year to bother you."

"I know." I look away, thumbing the seam of the comforter. "But it felt like you sprung the conversation on all of us. We were already on edge about what happened on the boat, then all of a sudden we're back to talking about that night."

"I wasn't trying to ruin the dinner. I'm just trying to deal with our issues head-on, like we've talked about in therapy."

"I think our relationship has improved in recent months." I reach for his hand. "I do. But I think there needs to be a certain amount of discretion when it comes to the kids."

"I think the kids could benefit from talking about what happened as much as we can."

"You don't even want to tell them Paul has been released!" My voice is louder than I intend. I take a deep breath and start again. "If we want the kids to be aware of the situation, they should at least know to be on the look out for Paul."

"I don't want to tell them about Paul because I don't want them to be afraid. Paul won't be able to get to them. I'll make sure of it. Last night was about processing their feelings about what's already happened."

"All I'm asking for is a little heads-up. Maybe you're right, and we should talk more openly with the kids about their feelings. I just don't want to deal with something so heavy while we're still on vacation, okay? What happened yesterday on the boat was hard enough."

He stares at me, then leaves the room.

I get dressed and check on the children. They're antsy to get out of the house, but understandably, none of us are keen about being on the water. The rental boat floats by the dock, a reminder of both the joys and dangers one can experience while at sea.

I find Andrew in the living room. He's ferociously typing on his keyboard.

"Have you eaten breakfast?" I ask.

"Not yet." The entire time he speaks, his eyes stay on the computer screen.

"The kids and I are going to take a walk down the beach. We might grab lunch at the pier. Feel like joining us?"

At last, he raises his head from the computer screen and looks at me. He appears irritated.

"Not now. I'm busy."

"Work stuff?"

"No." He stops and checks his tone, maneuvering his hand over his jaw. "I mean, I have some stuff to look into. Right now, I'm trying to talk with Vincent."

One of his friends from Second Chances. He always turns to the group when he's feeling overwhelmed, it seems. I'm happy he's found an outlet; we all need one. Sometimes I wish he could be as open with me as he is with these strangers online.

"Want us to bring you anything back?"

"No."

He returns to typing, and I exit the room, gently closing the door behind me.

Noah and Willow walk a few paces ahead of me on the sand. The weather is cooler than it has been. Even the sun seems to be ducking behind the clouds. After almost two weeks in the blazing heat, I'm happy for the change. My favorite part of the beach is the breeze, the way the wind steals away the humidity that would suffocate you in a landlocked setting.

There aren't many homes along the shoreline. In fact, we've not seen any neighbors in the time we've been here. About four houses down from our rental, we pass a yellow house with green shutters. There's a family sitting around the picnic table out back. I spot a mother and father, and three young children. As expected, they're all on their devices while the parents are trying to work the grill. Other than each person being preoccupied, they seem happy. I wonder, is this what people see when they look at our family? Are they able to see the cracks?

My phone starts buzzing in my pocket. We must be far enough away from the rental to have service. It's Aster. I'm tempted not to answer, but my curiosity always wins out.

"How are things?" she says, and it's hard to tell from her voice where this conversation might go.

"We're leaving in the next couple of days. It's time to start heading back to the real world," I say. "How are things with you?"

"Honestly?" She pauses. "Pretty shitty. I've not been able to stop thinking about how everything unfolded the other night."

That's a surprising admission coming from my sister.

"Yeah, I don't think that was the best moment for any of us."

"I've been thinking about it, and I feel really awful that you think I'd wave the book news over your head as though I were deliberately trying to hurt you. You don't really think that, do you?"

I grind my teeth. "I don't know if you do it on purpose or not. I'd like to think you don't. But you're smart, Aster. It shouldn't be that hard for you to figure out your news might have bothered me."

"I wasn't trying to make a statement about you—"

"I know. But think about it. I've talked about writing for, how long? And in the past when I brought it up, you laughed it off. Like it's finger painting or something. Then, all of a sudden, you're talking about getting a book deal like it's nothing. You'd think it might cross your mind that maybe my feelings would be hurt."

"It did cross my mind. Yes."

"And yet you just went on and on anyway. Of course, I'm happy for you. I want to be happy for you, but you make that really hard when it feels like you're gloating."

"I'm sorry, Kate." She exhales slowly. "I didn't stop to think how it would affect you. I don't mean to come off so bitchy."

I laugh. "Did you actually just refer to yourself as a bitch?"

"If it walks like a duck and talks like a duck," she quips, then her voice turns sincere. "Sometimes I get carried away talking about whatever is going on in my life, especially if it involves my career, because I feel like that's all I have. You have Andrew and the kids. Your life seems fuller than mine, with or without a book deal."

"Come on, now. You have David."

"David is great, but outside of him, the accomplishments in my career are all I have, and I want to be proud of them."

"You should be. I'm proud of you, too. Especially now that you're willing to admit you didn't handle telling me in the best way. Besides, nonfiction is a totally different genre. The true crime stuff is all the rage right now. I bet your sales will go through the roof."

"Does that mean you forgive me?"

"Yes, it does."

"I've been thinking about what you said concerning Mom, too."

"And?"

"Maybe it wouldn't hurt for me to give her a few more chances. If you can do it for me, it's the least I can do for her."

"I think that would be really good, Aster." I check the time on my watch. "Give me a call when you and David get settled back home. Maybe we could plan a meet up with Mom before we're all back in school."

"I'd like that," she says.

We get off the phone. Ahead, I watch as Willow and Noah take turns kicking at the water as it reaches the sand. Their relationship with one another, even when they are bickering, is much closer than the one I have with my sister.

Our parents' divorce shaped us, and it's meaningless to try and assign blame. Mom made our family a priority, and Dad focused on his career. I know he loved us, he just did so in his own way. And it's easier for Aster to be disappointed in our mother than admit she doesn't fully understand her choices. At the end of the day, Aster and I have followed in their respective paths.

It's another reason why I'm determined to repair my relationship with Andrew; I know how devastating it can be when a family breaks apart.

CHAPTER 20

6 Months Ago

Kate continued going to the gym four days a week. It had only been a month, but she could tell a difference. Her breath was less shaky when she made the march across campus. She fell asleep faster and woke up more refreshed. On more than one occasion, she'd noticed a thin layer of muscle appearing on the back of her arms, the sides of her thighs.

She felt better about herself. Until a flashback to that night came, and her whole body would shudder.

Today, she was afraid memories of that night might take over, as she sat at a coffee shop, waiting to meet the person who had sent her that letter back in January. She watched the other patrons as they lazily wandered in and bought coffee. A college student—had to be, because his shirt was wrinkled, his pants were stained, but his computer seemed brand new. An older couple wearing matching beige cardigans and black slacks. She doubted they planned it that way; they'd probably been together so long they rubbed off on each other without realizing. A heavily pregnant woman in a floral dress. Her face bare, but her hair curled and pulled back with a barrette.

Kate thought back to when she was pregnant with the kids. In both instances, she cherished the little kicks, but she also kept close count of the days until delivery. She couldn't wait for that stage to be over, to move onto the next. Sometimes she wondered if she should have treasured the moment a little more. The pregnant woman in front of her looked so much more at ease than she remembered feeling.

The woman made eye contact and started walking toward her. Reflexively, Kate looked down, blowing on her coffee. The woman stopped right in front of her table.

"Kate?" The woman waited, but Kate didn't respond. "I'm Angie."

Kate stood. For some reason, the image she'd had of Angie in her head didn't quite fit. She'd thought she might be grungier, rougher. An entitled thought, she realized. The woman pulled out the chair and collapsed into the seat.

"I'm happy you finally responded to my letter," she said, relaxing. "Another month, you might have missed me." She patted her stomach.

"You're pregnant." Kate stated the obvious.

The woman gave a weird smile. "I am."

"Is it your first?" Kate tried to stop comparing the woman who had written the letter to the woman sitting in front of her. She tried to speak with her like she would any other acquaintance she had bumped into.

"Yes. A little girl. We're thinking of calling her Emma."

"Beautiful name." Kate smiled, her eyes falling again on the woman's stomach. "Is the father—"

"Paul? Gosh, no. I'm remarried now."

Kate looked at the woman's ring finger. The sparkler looked brand new. "Congratulations."

"Paul and I divorced ages ago, not that that stopped him from reaching out. In the years that followed the divorce, he basically stalked me. Then out of nowhere, he stopped. Dropped off the face of the earth it seemed. Part of me wondered what happened to him, but at that point, I didn't really care. Then I heard about his arrest. I heard about what he did to your family. It all made sense."

"What do you mean?"

All these months later, Paul latching on to her still didn't make sense to Kate. How could it make sense to this woman she'd only spoken to for a few minutes?

"He found a new target. You. I reached out because I thought you might need someone to talk to. Not many people have been on the receiving end of Paul's paranoia. I know from experience it's not an easy place to be."

"You say he stopped harassing you because he started following me. I still don't understand why. Paul and I hadn't had contact in years. Why develop an obsession with me now? It doesn't make sense."

"You were the one that got away." Angie laughed. "You know, back in the early days, you're the last person I could have pictured myself having coffee with. If anything, I envied you. Everyone has that one person they don't end up with who they still think about. You were that person for Paul. He'd casually drop your name, tell stories from college. I'd imagine what you looked like. What you did for a living. If he would have rather ended up with you than me. I know that's silly, but I was younger, you know? And Paul wasn't always so crazy."

"He'd really talk about me like that?"

"I mean, not all the time. I wouldn't have married him otherwise. I felt secure that I was the new *one* in his life. But he mentioned you enough that when I found out he'd circled back round to you… well, it didn't shock me."

"I'm really baffled. Our relationship wasn't even that serious. We dated six, maybe seven months."

"I don't think it was the relationship itself he couldn't get over. I think it had more to do with the way it ended."

"Oh." My cheeks blushed. "So, he told you about that?"

"He said you left him for one of his frat buddies."

"Yeah, I did. But come on, we were kids. And Andrew… our relationship was light years away from where I was with Paul. Or anyone else I ever dated. We married each other in under a year."

"You don't have to defend yourself to me. I really do get it."

"I just can't believe he was so hung up about it."

"I don't think much of anything bothered Paul, until it did. It's like these issues would lay dormant inside him for years, and then they'd rise to the surface and he couldn't let them go. At least that's how it was with us."

"Do you mind me asking, why did the two of you divorce?"

"Paul was my first love. We were so happy together those first few years. More importantly, Paul seemed happy with himself. Nothing like the suspicious person he turned into at the end." She smiled, then her face slowly fell. "He started acting off once we started trying to get pregnant."

"He didn't want a baby?"

"No, he did. We both did. But things weren't working. We went to a fertility clinic and found out the reason we couldn't get pregnant was because of him. Incredibly low sperm count. It's like he refused to hear any of it."

I know fertility issues can weigh heavy on a couple. It's practically what tore apart Dana and her husband. They spent years trying to get pregnant. Eventually, she did, but their marriage was close to over by the time the girls arrived. It's like they lost sense of what they really wanted along the way.

"I didn't leave him because of that, though," Angie continued. "I want to be clear about that. I was willing to explore other options. I would have been fine not having children if that's what he wanted. But it's like that one setback started leading to everything else."

"In what way?"

"He became obsessed with little things. What people at work were up to. What our neighbors were doing. Then he turned that obsession on me. He was never violent, but he was self-destructive.

He'd threaten to hurt himself all the time. I tried getting him help. He found a counselor and got on medication, but then he'd stop taking his pills. That was worse than before he even started. I reached a point I just couldn't take it anymore. His condition was taking a toll on me too. The person I fell in love with, the person I kept fighting for, just didn't exist anymore."

"I'm guessing he didn't handle the divorce well."

"Let's just say his behavior escalated once he moved out. Got worse when I started dating. He almost turned me off the idea of relationships altogether, but then I met Gavin." She twirled the wedding band on her finger. "He was willing to start a life with me, even if it meant putting up with my crazy ex."

"I'm happy you found someone who understands." Kate's eyes fell on Angie's stomach again. "You know, some of what you've said *has* made sense of things. At least, it might explain why he renewed his obsession with me."

Angie sat there waiting. It was Kate's turn to talk.

"When I first saw Paul again, he brought up my daughter. Willow. He had this crazy idea that... maybe she was his."

Angie's eyes widened. "He never mentioned that to me. But again, by the time he moved on to you, I was old news."

"It's ridiculous. We broke up months before I conceived. But now that I know what he'd gone through with you... it seems connected, doesn't it?"

"It's hard to make sense of what Paul's thinking. I almost drove myself crazy trying." She took a sip of her coffee, pointing at Kate. "Almost."

As Kate drove home, she felt better. She couldn't understand Paul, but she could at least understand his motives. That seemed useful.

When she arrived home, Andrew's car was parked outside. Kate guessed he wasn't working, or if he was, at least he was doing it remotely. She hoped he wasn't drinking. On more than one occasion, she'd found empty vodka bottles in the trash can, crunched beer cans in the trunk of his car. Each discovery left her feeling helpless, aware there was little she could do to stop her husband from destroying himself.

Kate walked upstairs. She marched into the bedroom, caught off guard to find Andrew there waiting. He was sitting on the bed.

"I'm heading to the gym," she said, barely looking at him. She was irritated because he was sitting on her stack of clothes, already slowing down her process. "Can you move?"

She looked up then as he stood, got a good look at his face. He'd been crying.

"Andrew? What's wrong?"

"We need to talk."

The one thing they needed to do but he had created every barrier possible from doing. "Talk about what? The kids—"

"The kids are fine."

"Then what is it?"

"I want to talk about us. All of it."

Was it wrong that Kate was irritated? After months of begging her husband to be open with her, he'd finally done it, and it annoyed her. It disrupted the life she was used to living without him by her side. But then again, it wasn't like Andrew to wait on her. It wasn't like him to cry. Maybe after months of holding back his emotions, the dam had finally broken.

"Okay. Let's talk."

"Ever since I found out the person who broke into our house was Paul Gunter… I don't know. I just lost it. In some ways, it seemed easier when it was some stranger, a random criminal. To know he was someone we knew, that he was someone you… had been with. It bothered me."

"It bothered me, too. You can't imagine the guilt I've carried. I did nothing to bring on this attention, but I can't help blaming myself."

"And then you told me you had seen him recently. That he'd been trying to contact you, but you kept it a secret."

Kate wanted to interject, but Andrew wasn't listening to anything she said. He was busy spewing everything he was feeling, getting it out of him before he lost the courage to do so.

"It made me wonder what else you were keeping secret from me," he admitted.

"Nothing. I wasn't trying to keep Paul a secret—"

"I know. I know that's what you said. But it's not what I felt. In one night, I'd come close to losing my family, which I care about more than anything in this world. Since then, we've been doing nothing but crumbling. And I don't know how to put us back together. Not when I'm bottling up these feelings. When you told me Paul believed he might be Willow's father, it put everything else I believed about us to the test.

"Thing is, I'd rather ignore you or drink myself to death than face our problems. I know we can't live that way, but I couldn't move on with our lives without knowing the truth."

"I've told you the truth. I messed up in not telling you about Paul sooner, but since then, I've been nothing but honest."

"I know." He took out a piece of paper from his back pocket, and unfolded it, an act that added more dramatic flair than anything. "But I had to know for myself, too."

"What is that?" Kate asked. She felt something heavy in her chest.

"I ran a paternity test on Willow."

Kate could feel the blood racing beneath her skin, feel her eyes filling with tears.

"I had to do it. I couldn't take not knowing anymore. And I thought maybe seeing it on paper would finally give me confidence."

"I gave you the answers you needed," Kate said, her voice so filled with anger it quivered. "I told you there was no way—"

"I know. The test confirms I'm her father," Andrew cut her off. He took a step closer. "And now I believe you."

"You should have believed me then!" Kate yelled. "I made a mistake by not telling you about Paul in the beginning, but I've never lied to you. I've never cheated on you. But for the past six months, you've treated me like I've done both. You've acted as though I'm not hurting about what happened. Everything you're feeling, I've felt, too. And instead of leaning on you, I've had to suffer through all this. Alone."

"I know. That's why I'm telling you this now. So we can start over with a clean slate."

"A clean slate? You tested our daughter's paternity behind my back. You actually believed it might be a possibility. You believed this mentally ill man over me. Your wife of more than seventeen years—"

"I'm sorry. I had to do this."

"Sorry isn't enough. You're the one refusing to talk to me. You're the one who'd rather get drunk than fix what's happening between us. You're treating me like a villain when I've done nothing wrong. You say you submitted this test to protect our family, to keep us together. You've abandoned me!"

"I don't want to abandon you. That's why I'm telling you this now. I'm sorry I didn't believe you before, but now that I know the truth, we can start moving on."

Kate stood there, her blood still boiling, her temper still fuming. She felt bare. Embarrassed. That her own husband would treat her this way, as though she deserved to be questioned. For the first time in their marriage, Kate wasn't sure she wanted to fix their relationship. She didn't have the tools to do it on her own.

"We're going to counseling."

"Oh, come on, Kate. We don't need counseling. We can work this out, just the two of us."

"No, we can't! It's beyond that now. Standing here, looking at you, after what you just told me… it feels like I'm talking to a stranger. I don't know how to move forward without help, and if you really want to keep this family together, you have to commit to that."

Andrew hunched over, holding his forehead with his hands. He was silent for several minutes.

"Okay. We'll do it. I'll talk to a counselor. I'll do whatever it takes to get my family back."

Kate didn't say anything. She simply nodded. Andrew walked over to her, putting his arms around her. She flinched.

"I'm sorry, Kate. I really am. I'm sorry I didn't believe you."

Kate clenched her eyes shut, a tear trailing down her cheek. She could still feel all of it. The sting of Andrew's betrayal. The slap of rejection. And a renewed anger at Paul Gunter, for what his lies had done to her family.

CHAPTER 21

Now

There's a small arcade in the waiting area of the restaurant; I allow the kids to explore while we wait on our food. Noah is playing a race-car game, the plastic covering his body so all I can see of him is the top of his curly head. Willow has found a group of girls her age and is leaning against the wall talking to them.

"Are they yours?"

There is a woman sitting beside me, and a man beside her. She has short blonde hair and tan skin. Her husband has silver hair. They appear friendly, but I pause before answering, in a way I probably wouldn't have before Paul Gunter re-entered my life.

"Yes," I answer at last.

"It looks like your daughter is cozying up to our girls."

I turn and look. There are two other blonde teenagers on either side of Willow. They have almost the exact same shade of hair as their mother.

"On vacation?" I ask, trying to return the jovial tone.

"Locals. I haven't seen you around before. I guess you're traveling?"

"Yes. We've got a house on Emerald Shore Road."

"Hey, that's right where we are." She reaches out her hand to shake mine. "I'm Jan."

"You must be renting the Billings' place," says the man. "White house with red shutters?"

"That's the one," I say, then immediately regret it.

"First time here?" asks Jan.

"Yes, actually. We thought we'd try some place closer to home this year."

"And where's home?"

I tell them, and we go back and forth talking about superficial stuff. I learn Jan's husband's name is Dan, and by all appearances, they live a charmed life. They're both in the medical field. They have teenage daughters around Willow's age and an older son in college. Our conversation reminds me most people are only seeking connection, they're not trying to deceive you. Then I think back to Paul, how our conversation at a restaurant, not dissimilar to this one, opened a door for chaos to ensue.

"Our girls are probably thrilled to have someone down the road. I'm sure you noticed there aren't many houses our way, which is why we bought the place. When we do have renters in the area, they usually have little kids."

I look over my shoulder at Willow. "Yeah, it's probably good for her, too. I think she's missing her friends back home. We get the worst reception at our house."

"Same problem for us," Dan says. "It's unpredictable, but I guess that's the price you pay for a little more seclusion."

"It's usually worse right before a storm settles in," Jan adds. "Sometimes if you flick the power, it'll reset the system and you'll get better reception."

"Thanks for the tip," I say. "I'll give it a try."

As I sit alone, waiting for our food to arrive, I wonder what Andrew is doing back at the house. It saddens me that he finds more comfort with his friends online than he does with me. It didn't always seem to be that way. I glance over at Dan and Jan, watching the subtle ways they interact with one another. The way his hand cups hers on the bar top, the way she throws back her head and laughs with no inhibitions.

Andrew and I used to be like that. I miss it. In recent months, I thought we were getting back to that place, but after what happened on the boat, it's clear we're not.

When the food arrives, I motion for the kids to join me. Noah talks a mile a minute about the game he was playing, while Willow pouts and fiddles with her phone.

"What's wrong with you?"

"Nothing."

"It looked like you were making friends over there."

"Yeah, they're cool. We exchanged numbers." She looks over at the sisters sitting with Jan and Dan. "I'm just bummed because Sonja's party is tonight, and I'm going to miss it."

Ah, that's why her mood dropped so suddenly.

"You have plenty of parties in your future. Don't let this one get you down."

I place my hand over hers. I look out at the water, then back at the busying restaurant. That's when I see him. Paul.

Or at least someone else that looks like him. It's the same combination of hat and sunglasses, not uncommon at the beach, but it's his visible features that make me think it's Paul. I stand, hurriedly walking away from the table.

"Mom, what's wrong?" Noah asks, but I ignore him.

I push past the people crowding the restaurant entrance and follow the man onto the dock. Except, once I get out there, I no longer see him. There's too many people walking up and down the pier and he's disappeared among them, like a phantom.

I look back over my shoulder, to see Noah and Willow watching me in confused wonderment. I realize they have no idea what I'm dealing with, because I've shielded them from it. They have no reason to know why I'm so scared.

*

On the walk home, the sun comes out. I tell the kids to run ahead and get changed if they want to spend a few hours by the pool. I watch them, never letting them leave my sight. Occasionally, I look over my shoulder to see if Paul—or anyone else—might be following us.

As I approach the rental, I see Andrew. My stomach immediately drops at the idea of telling him I thought I saw Paul. I never mentioned seeing him at the store earlier in the week, but this is twice. Sure, I could still be paranoid, but I could also be right. As I get closer, my determination plummets when I see there's a bottle of liquor beside him.

"I thought you had work to do," I say, and it's all I can do to keep my voice civil.

Already buzzed, he doesn't seem to notice. "Done for the day."

"And Vincent? I thought you were talking with him."

"I was. And now I'm having a drink. On my vacation." There's a bitter defiance laced between his words. He's challenging me to challenge him about the drinking. If only he knew that wasn't my biggest concern at the moment.

"I was hoping we could talk—"

"I don't want to talk about yesterday." He cuts me off and slams his glass on the table. "I messed up, okay? I was scared. *Thank goodness* you were there to save the day."

"Andrew!" I'm shocked at the way he's acting. It's only midday. His words are soaked with sarcasm and booze.

"I just don't know what else you want me to say. I messed up. I'm a failure. I'll say whatever I have to for you to walk into the house and stop bringing it up."

I open my mouth, then stop. It's impossible to reason with Andrew when he's like this. I'd hoped a conversation with the Second Chances group would make him better, but it seems he preferred to turn to his second vice instead. I know trying to communicate with a drunken Andrew will produce more problems than solutions; I'll have to wait to tell him I saw Paul.

Another time. Another day. I'm beginning to fear we don't have many days left.

CHAPTER 22

Now

I'm running down the hallway. I feel the carpet beneath my feet, providing extra buoyancy but doing little in terms of speed. I reach Willow's room, but the door is locked. I pound against it, jiggling the handle.

Nothing.

From the other side, I hear a scream. My daughter's scream, and then Noah's, too. They're in there together. They're calling for me, begging me to find them, but there's nothing I can do.

When I wake, I'm covered in sweat. It's the most vivid nightmare I've had in a while, and I believe all the buried tension is to blame. Above, the ceiling fan is still. The room is dark, random slivers of moonlight peeking in through the blinds. Andrew is beside me in bed, snoring. I remember where we are. We're months away from that horrible night. This beach house is miles away from Paul. *I hope.* I can't shake the possibility that Paul has followed us here, that he's determined to finish what he started that night.

My throat is scratchy. I creep out of bed and wander into the kitchen, pouring a glass of water. I drink the entire thing in only a few gulps, and my senses return to normal. It was just a nightmare. *No one can get us here*, I tell myself. I want to believe it's true.

Before returning to our bedroom, I peek into Noah's room. He's beneath his covers, his arms clinging to his pillow just like they did when he was a toddler. I kiss his forehead and crack his door on my way out.

Willow's door is shut. I creep it open, trying not to wake her. After the nightmare I had, all I want is to see her face. I need to know that she's here with me, that Paul won't ever have the chance to take her again.

When I reach her bed, it's empty, only her gray covers are rumpled together in a mound. It feels like my heart has leaped into my throat. I pat the mattress, thinking surely I must be wrong, but there's nothing there.

I march to the bathroom. The door is open, and there is no one inside. I go to the kitchen. Maybe she heard me walking through the house and she went in there. We could have passed each other in the dark when I ducked in to check on Noah. Maybe she's outside, going for a nighttime swim. I go through every ridiculous scenario possible, turning on the lights and calling her name.

"Willow!"

Only silence. Cruel, sickening silence.

At the restaurant, I thought I caught a glimpse of Paul, just as I thought I'd seen him at the grocery store. I told myself my fear was playing tricks with my mind. Just like last year, I should have taken Paul's refusal to back down more seriously. I should have considered his escalating behavior. Our response to his release was to come here, but that only fooled us into letting our guards down.

I should have accepted that if Paul wants to find us, he will.

He has.

Then, a sound from the hallway. My heart fills with hope, but it's only Noah. He pokes his head out of his bedroom, the skin beneath his eyes swollen.

"Mom, what's going on?"

"Have you seen Willow?" I don't make any attempt to hide my panic.

"She went to bed before me."

"She's not in there. She's not in her room!"

I do another panicked loop around the house, but she is nowhere in sight. There's no signal on my phone, so all the calls I make to her phone fail to go through. I rush into our bedroom and begin shaking Andrew on the bed.

"She's gone. You have to wake up," I shout, pulling at his arms.

He sits up, still unbalanced and dazed. "Who's gone? What's happening?"

"Willow. She's gone." Now the tears come, so fast and strong it's hard to breathe. "Paul took her."

CHAPTER 23

5 Months Ago

Kate and Andrew sat on the same sofa, but they weren't touching. Kate's feet were planted firmly on the floor, her arms wrapped across her body. Andrew leaned over, his elbows on his knees. His foot hadn't stopped tapping since they'd been ushered into the room.

Dr. Sutton looked to be their age, which threw Kate off. She couldn't help wondering what was going on in the woman's life, if she had children, if she argued with her own husband, if she took pity on the couples she saw on a daily basis. In that moment, Kate wished they'd found an older therapist. She believed she'd feel less judged that way. However, Dr. Sutton was the only person who had returned her calls, and Kate didn't want to wait any longer for an opening. She'd barely looked at Andrew since he told her about the DNA test, let alone touched him.

"I understand your home was broken into last year," Dr. Sutton said, her eyes landing on Kate. "That's what you said in your email."

"Yes. It happened in August."

"And the children. Were they there the night of the intruder?"

"Yes," Kate said. "They have a counselor they see once a month."

"I'm curious." Dr. Sutton sat up, twiddling a pen near her mouth. "You clearly thought the children needed counseling to process what happened. Why are you just now seeking help for yourselves?"

"That's my fault, I guess," Andrew said. "I suppose I thought we could handle what happened in our own ways. We thought maybe it was time to try a different approach."

Kate thought it was past time, actually, but she remained silent.

"Clearly you both view this incident as the catalyst for the problems you currently face." They both nodded, but neither spoke. "Then I'll need you to take me back to that night. Tell me everything that happened."

They heard the footsteps coming up the stairs. They saw the shadow blocking the sliver of light beneath the door. Andrew had fumbled with the phone, unable to turn it on. And Kate had suffered through a mental horror show of possibilities in a matter of seconds, envisioned the danger her children could be in if she didn't act fast. That's what prompted her to open the door.

The man—the one they'd later identify as Paul—stood there, a mask covering his face. It turned out Kate's decision to open the door was the first in a series of smart ones. It threw the intruder off guard. He'd expected to be the instigator, but instead, Kate stood in front of him, screaming out a warning for everyone to hear.

The intruder lunged forward, covering Kate's mouth with his hand. His other hand reached for her neck, a way to stabilize his grip, but in Kate's mind, it was another attack. Andrew remained on the bed, watching everything that took place in wide-eyed, open-mouthed horror.

"Shut up," the intruder ordered. "Stop screaming."

But it was too late. Kate's screams had alerted the children. Willow suddenly stood in the doorway to her parents' bedroom. At first groggy, her senses awakened once she caught sight of the man hovering over her mother, grabbing at her face and neck.

Willow screamed.

The intruder turned. Having caught sight of Willow in the doorway, he immediately let go of Kate and started in Willow's direction.

Kate lunged after him, grabbing at his ankles, causing him to stumble and fall to the ground. Willow shuffled back a few steps, her shock preventing her from doing little else but stare.

Andrew remained on the bed.

"Willow, run!" Kate shouted.

Within seconds, Willow was gone. She disappeared into the hallway. The masked intruder struggled to follow her, but Kate refused to let up. It was like her body was made of lead, weighing them both down. Although the intruder was heavier, in that moment, Kate's rage and desperation seemed to compensate for the difference. Like those stories of mothers ripping open car doors to save their young, Kate had an almost unexplainable strength, keeping the intruder in place.

There was movement in the hallway. Kate saw Willow run past, Noah in front of her. She was getting him out of the house. Kate only caught a glimpse of Noah's frightened face, and felt another surge of adrenaline, helping her keep the intruder contained.

As quickly as they appeared, they were gone, and Kate thought—although it was hard to focus—she heard the front door open. They were out of the house. Away from that man. In some ways, it mattered little to her what happened next. At least her children were safe.

The intruder wriggled away from her grasp. He stood, hovering over her. He reared back and smacked her hard across the face. Kate tasted a salty burst of blood in her mouth. When she turned back to face her intruder, he was gone. She chased after him, catching a glimpse of his hooded figure as he exited the house and disappeared around the back.

Part of her wanted to follow him, hurt him—kill him? A rage pulsated in Kate she'd never felt before. Had never believed to exist. The type of rage that could only be exorcised in the defense of one's children, and for that same reason, she chose not to go after him. The only thing more important than making sure that man was punished was making sure her children were safe. She changed direction, jogging the short distance toward Dana's house.

They'd created an emergency plan for the family long ago. If there was ever a fire, Dana's house would be the designated meeting place; the Brooks house was the same spot for Dana's family.

Willow took Noah there, Kate told herself as she made the short, laborious jog across the street. They got out in time. She remembered to take him there. She's smart.

Kate was delighted to find the downstairs lights on, despite the late hour. She banged on the front door, which was locked. Dana's face appeared between the blinds. The door opened, and Kate's heart leaped at the sight of her children. She ran to them, scooping them in her arms. Her tears and her breath and her love poured out of her all at once.

"Willow said there was a man in your house. The police are on the way," Dana said, her face flushed. "Kate, you're bleeding."

Kate didn't care. All that mattered was her children were safe.

"What about Dad?" Noah asked.

Relief exited her body as quickly as it came. She'd watched the man disappear into the night, but she had no idea what happened to her husband. She stood and ran back toward the house.

"Kate, wait!" Dana called after her. "You can't go back over there."

But Kate didn't care. Already, more gruesome scenarios entered her mind. What if the masked man had rounded back and re-entered the house? What if Andrew had gone after him, and he needed Kate's help?

She darted up the steps and found Andrew was in the exact same spot where she'd left him. He was crying, still fiddling with his damn phone. When he saw Kate, he threw it down.

"The kids?" His voice was desperate, full of fear and… shame.

"They're at Dana's. They're safe."

She went to him, wrapping him in her arms. She cradled him as he sobbed.

"What happened? Who was—"

"I don't know," Kate said before he could finish. It was true. She didn't think of Paul. The only certainty was that someone had entered their home with the intention of hurting her family, and she'd refused to let it happen.

"I'm sorry," Andrew whispered, his voice being overtaken by more sobs.

She remained there, holding him, her attention turning to the sound of approaching sirens in the distance.

Questions whizzed through her mind, gratitude pulsated within her heart. They were safe—from what, was unclear. All that mattered was that the people she loved most on this earth were okay.

And yet, in this moment, her arms wrapped around her trembling husband, she felt alone. She'd acted alone, hadn't she? She'd fought back against the attacker, rushed to ensure her children were safe, even returned to check on Andrew, who had barely moved an inch since that first sound woke her in the night. A seed of anger had been planted, would be nurtured by her loneliness in the months to come, until it blossomed into resentment.

CHAPTER 24

Now

I'm trying hard to keep my panic at bay so I can focus. I need to find Willow.

I've told Noah to go back to his bedroom. Andrew is up now, doing his own search of the house. I know it's useless. I've already searched everywhere.

"I can't get reception!" I yell. "We need to call the police."

"Let's stay calm," Andrew says. "We don't need to involve the police just yet."

"What the hell are you talking about? Paul has kidnapped our daughter. The sooner we get people out there searching for her…" I can't finish the sentence. I don't want to think of the alternatives if we don't find her in time.

"There's no way Paul could have taken her," Andrew says, his voice surprisingly calm. "I'm sure there's another explanation."

"The whole reason we're here is to avoid him! Now he's followed us here, and he has taken her."

"That can't be it." He scans the room, his eyes falling on the sliding glass doors. "Let me take a look outside."

Andrew is still searching for an alternate explanation, but it's because I've not told him I thought I saw Paul at the grocery store and the restaurant. I didn't want to worry him, but now I'm convinced he's followed us here. I can feel it in my bones. Part of me feared it would always come to this.

I return to the sofa, trying again to find a signal.

I remember talking with the locals that live down the street, Dan and Jan. They suggested sometimes restarting the breaker box can help with reception. I pull open the front drawer of the coffee table. Inside is the notebook the homeowners left us with all the information we might need. There are cleaning requirements, a sheet of rules, restaurant recommendations and a list of instructions. Halfway down the list, I see the fuse box is in the attached garage—the one place I haven't yet looked for Willow.

I open the door to the left of the kitchen, which leads to the garage. Inside, there are a few random boxes and an array of beach accessories scruffy with saltwater residue, but no sign of Willow. Across the way, I catch sight of the second exterior door. I don't think I remembered it was here until this very moment. I twist the handle, and the door opens with ease. Has it been unlocked this entire time? Is this how Paul found his way inside the house?

I make my way over to the switchbox, trying to figure out how to reset the connection. There's a small table right below the box. It's covered with loose tools and scraps of plastic, then something catches my eye. There's a tied grocery bag with a green and orange logo. It belongs to our Hidden Oaks grocery store. It strikes me as odd, since none of us have been in here, or so I thought. As I untangle the handles, I see that there's a square box inside. It's gray and heavy, but something is clearly on. There's a green light.

I stare at it, momentarily forgetting about Willow, wondering what it could be. It manages to look both familiar and completely foreign at the same time, and yet I feel like I should know what this is. Like I've seen it before but know it's not mine.

Then it hits me.

It's a jammer. A device used to cut off reception within a particular radius. I can remember researching different surveillance items police, and sometimes criminals, use while working on a manuscript with a former student, the one who landed the book deal. That student's story included a jammer; I was unfamiliar with the term and ended up googling it. The image that popped up then looks similar to the item I'm currently holding.

My first thought is, why would the homeowners keep this in their rental? Then I remember the grocery bag. Whoever brought the jammer here is local to Hidden Oaks. Andrew has been stealing random hours to work remotely; a weak internet connection only makes his life more difficult. It certainly wouldn't be one of my tech-obsessed children.

It has to be Paul. He's found us, and this confirms it. None of us would want to cut off contact with the outside world. He's taken Willow and planted the jammer to stall us from getting help.

I flick the button below the green light, and the device turns off. I leave the box where I found it, and rush back to my phone in the living room.

I pick it up to see that I have full service.

"Nothing outside," Andrew says, as he opens the door. "Are you sure we've looked everywhere?"

"I have a signal," I say, ignoring him. I don't have time to explain to him about the jammer. Right now, the only thing that matters is getting help for Willow. Even though we've been here over a week, we know little about the area. I don't know where Paul might have taken her, where the police might begin searching.

"Mom, I have two bars," Noah says, running into the living room with his phone.

"I do too," I tell him. I stare at Andrew. "I'm calling the police."

"Just wait." He raises his hands to me, but he's looking toward the front door. The glare of headlights comes through the entryway windows. "Someone's here."

I push past him, opening the door and running outside. In a matter of seconds, I live through the horrible scenario that the police have already found her. What if Paul hurt her? I have no idea how long she's been gone. They're here now to share devastating news.

It's dark, and the headlights are blinding. I take a step closer and can see that the car in our driveway isn't a police vehicle. I don't know if I should feel relieved or worried. The backseat opens, and Willow stumbles out. I rush to her, holding her up. Her balance is off, and her clothes and breath reek of liquor.

Someone exits the driver's side door. It's Jan, the woman I met earlier at the restaurant. She puts her hands up in a gesture that reads both friendly and defensive.

"Kate?"

"Yes," I say, that desperate tone still in my voice.

"I thought we had the right place." She walks over to our side of the car. "Sorry to disturb you this late."

"We were already awake. I couldn't find Willow and—"

"She's been at our house. Apparently our girls thought it would be a good idea to host a little party in our basement. We had no idea, of course, being heavy sleepers and all. We broke it up about a half hour ago. Looks like the girls got into our liquor cabinet."

I look at Willow. "You snuck out to go to a party?"

"I thought this was a vacation," she slurs, trying hard to sound tough even in her weakened state.

"What's going on?" Andrew is outside now, walking toward us with bare feet.

"This is Jan," I explain. "She lives a few houses down. Willow has been out drinking with her daughters."

"I'm sorry about this," Jan says. "My girls are usually really good, but you know teenagers. Sometimes it feels like you don't want to let them out of your sight."

Andrew opens his mouth to say something, then stops. He's agitated, and like me, embarrassed. "Thank you for bringing her back."

"Not a problem. The least I can do is make sure she gets home safely. Rest assured, Dan is tearing into our two misfits right now."

"Thank you," I say to Jan. "Thank you so much."

Willow will never know the extent of the crisis we just avoided. She doesn't know Paul has been released and could easily snatch her, and I'm hoping Noah didn't overhear us arguing about it earlier. In my mind, I was reckoning with the worst: that I might never see my daughter again.

"Let's get her inside," Andrew says, grabbing Willow's shoulder.

She walks with us, but stumbles every few steps, leaning on us for support. Once inside, Andrew shuts the front door and locks it. Willow staggers to the living room and collapses on the couch.

"Is she okay?" asks Noah. He's sitting at a chair in the dining room. His voice sounds so small.

"She's fine," I tell him. "Go back to bed."

Noah doesn't listen. He's staring at his sister, and I don't feel like arguing with him. All my frustration is reserved for Willow.

"What the hell were you thinking?" I ask her.

She laughs. "I was thinking vacations are supposed to be about fun."

"Well, I'm sorry this vacation isn't living up to your standards, but that doesn't give you the right to sneak out. Do you have any idea how frightened I was when I woke up and you weren't in your room?"

She flinches, a more mature and sober realization sinking in, then her expression morphs into repulsion. "I'm sick of being stuck inside this house with all of you. All I wanted was to have a little fun with people my own age!"

"You don't even know those girls! What if you'd found yourself in a bad situation? After what our family has been through in the past year, I can't believe you would act so carelessly."

Another laugh. "Yeah, you're one to talk. You should know all about letting the wrong types of people into your life."

Even though she's drunk and angry, her comment stings. I'm about to respond, when Andrew pushes past me, positioning himself in front of Willow.

"I've had enough of this shit." His voice is deep, an angry tone I've rarely heard used in all our years together. "You have no right to talk to your mother that way."

The sudden shift is jarring for all of us, especially Willow, who seems to sober up in seconds. I'm usually the target of her disdain. I'm usually the one fighting with her. She's Daddy's Little Girl, and none of us are used to seeing him turn on her.

"Dad, I didn't mean—"

"Shut up, Willow. I don't want to hear your excuses. You worried your mother. You worried me. Even Noah was scrambling around the house trying to find a way to contact you. For someone who tries so hard to act like an adult, you came off very immature tonight."

"I'm sorry. I wasn't trying to—"

"You have embarrassed our family. Do you have any idea how ashamed I am?" He's right in front of her face now. Her cheeks are red and stained with tears. "I've had friends tell me about their daughters acting like trash, but I always thought you were better than that!"

"Andrew!" Even if his anger is justified, his words are cruel. I understand his disappointment, and even admire his initiative, but his reaction seems merciless.

"She needs to hear this, Kate." He glares at me. "She needs to hear how her actions impact those around her."

"I'm sorry." Willow begins to cry.

"Go to your room."

She wanders down the hallway and slams the door. Moments later, Noah follows her trail, scampering to his own room.

"Don't you think that was a little harsh?" I ask Andrew.

"She needed to hear it. This vacation is about creating happy memories together." He stomps toward our bedroom, but I still hear him mutter, "She has no right to ruin it."

Andrew is ignoring the fact he's nursing his own hangover, incurred earlier in the day in response to his own failures on the boat. He's trying to be a disciplinarian, but our biggest concern right now isn't Willow.

It's Paul.

He might not have taken her tonight, but it doesn't mean he hasn't followed us here. I've thought I saw him twice in the past week, and after finding the jammer, I'm convinced he's found us. He's watching our every mistake, waiting for his next opportunity.

Andrew and I are going to have to work together to make sure he never gets it.

CHAPTER 25

Now

I only managed a few hours' sleep.

Knowing Willow was home and safe made me grateful, but the aftershock of those other emotions continued to pulsate: my adrenaline as I raced through the house to find her, my anger when she returned smelling like sour booze, my disbelief that Andrew was so obstructive during the entire ordeal. Most acutely, my fear remained. I thought Paul had finally found a way to take my little girl away from me.

Beside me, Andrew rolls around in the bed, wrestling with his own hangover. At home, his drinking has improved. He's only drunk sporadically on vacation, but yesterday he imbibed too much, reminding me of his behavior from a few months ago. I'd confront him about it, but I already know what he'll say. *He's bothered by what happened on the boat*, as though the unfortunate events in life give him a free pass to behave however he wants.

Thinking back to that afternoon, I shudder. In the past few days, I feared I'd lose Noah to the ocean and Willow to Paul.

Andrew rolls over, facing me with squinted eyes. "I'm sorry."

It's not the first phrase I was expecting to hear. "For what?"

"For how I acted yesterday. I ignored you and the kids and had too much to drink." He leans up on his forearms, turning to block out the sun beaming in through the window. "And I was too harsh on Willow last night."

I'm still bothered by yesterday, but his apology causes a blooming feeling in my chest. "Believe me, I'm angry with Willow, too.

I just think we have to make sure our conversations with her are productive, and if you're yelling and shaming her, she's not going to register anything positive we have to say."

"You're right." He leans up further. "I'll apologize to her for how I reacted, then we'll have a serious conversation."

"Good." I cross my arms. "And about the other stuff, what happened on the boat was hard on all of us. I understand you're coping, I just wish you didn't feel the need to pull away from us when you're upset. I wish you could talk to me."

"That's what I'm trying to do right now." He puts his hand over mine. "I'm so, so sorry Kate. I don't mean for you to feel like you're having to do everything on your own all the time. Believe me, I want nothing more than for our family to thrive together. Not apart."

The blossoming in my chest continues, and I realize it's reassurance. He's continuing to try. He might have his setbacks—like we all do—but he's committed to making this family better.

"There's something else I wanted to tell you about," I look down at the comforter, afraid to see his reaction when I say it. "Yesterday at the restaurant, I thought I saw Paul."

He doesn't look as panicked as I thought he'd be, but he is concerned. "You saw him at the restaurant? Are you sure?"

"Not totally," I answer, honestly. "I lost sight of him on the pier before I knew for sure, but I also thought I saw him at the grocery store last weekend. I've tried telling myself I'm being paranoid, but what if I'm not? What if he's really followed us here?"

"That's why you were so scared last night," Andrew says, like it's all making sense. "You don't think Paul would really do that, do you?"

"He broke into our home, Andrew. At this point, it's hard to say what he won't do." A shiver crawls down my back. "I think we need to be extra careful the rest of the time we're here. We could reconsider telling the kids about Paul's release. It might worry them, but at least they'd know that the risk is out there."

"I don't know. I just think if Paul wanted to confront us he wouldn't be so subtle about it."

"I think I might have proof this time," I say, leaning over and pulling out the jammer from my nightstand. I hold it up. "I found this in the garage last night when we were looking for Willow."

"What is it?"

As expected, Andrew doesn't even know what it is. I wouldn't, if it weren't for that manuscript a few years back.

"It's a jammer. It's something that can block phone and internet connections. It might explain why we've fought to get any signal the entire time we're here."

"Wait." He rubs his temples with his fingers. "You're saying you think Paul planted this here?"

"It was in a grocery bag from a Hidden Oaks store. It has to belong to someone from back home, and clearly none of us brought it along. I know Willow's disappearance last night was easily explained, but it doesn't rule out that Paul is actually here. He could still be trying to mess with us."

"It's definitely odd," Andrew says, inspecting the jammer with his hands. "But there has to be another explanation. If Paul followed us all the way here, surely he'd plan on doing more than cutting off our cell phone signal."

"I don't know what he's capable of doing, but if he's tracked us down here, it can't be good."

He drops the jammer on the comforter and looks away. "If you really believe Paul is here, why is this the first I'm hearing about it?"

I pause, unable to ignore his cool tone. "I'm telling you about it now—"

"You said you saw him last weekend. You said you saw him yesterday."

"I *thought* I did—"

"Then you should have told me right away! You saw what happened last time when you kept things to yourself."

"I didn't want to worry you. I… I thought I might be wrong—"

"Mom!" I hear Noah shout from down the hallway. "It's Willow. She's sick."

I pull my hands away from Andrew, rubbing two fingers against each temple. "We're not done talking about this," I say, turning.

Andrew is fast on my heels as I go down the hallway. Noah is standing outside the kids' shared bathroom, his hands behind his back and his eyes wide. On the other side of the door, I can hear the unmistakable sound of retching. I push on the door.

"Willow, are you okay?"

She's slumped over the toilet, still wearing an oversized sleep shirt, her bare legs sprawled across the floor like a wounded animal. Her hair falls in front of her sweaty face. "Can you get me some water?"

"Sure, honey," I say. Considering my anger last night, I thought I'd feel a little vindicated at watching her nurse a hangover, but instead, all I see is my little girl. Smaller now that she realizes she isn't quite so big.

Andrew comes walking up behind me. I turn to him. "Will you get her some water?"

He nods and leaves.

"How long have you been throwing up?"

"I just started." She speaks, but her eyes remain closed. "My head feels like it's about to burst."

I pull a washrag out of the cabinet and wet it with cold water. I place it on the back of her neck as she leans over the commode, waiting for the next round of sickness.

"You really scared me last night. You should know better than to sneak off like that, especially after last year—"

"I know, Mom. Okay?" Her voice breaks and she covers her eyes with a hand. "I messed up. Especially after seeing how worried you were about Noah. I didn't plan on drinking this much, I swear. I just got carried away."

"What you did was so dangerous. You don't even know those people. I know you think you do, but what if you'd found yourself in a position you couldn't handle? You're not familiar with this town. You might not have been able to find your way back to us."

"I know. I messed up. I—" She freezes, her posture upright, then she leans over, vomiting into the toilet. I pat her back.

"Here's some water," Andrew says, handing over a plastic bottle. "We'll talk more about this when you feel better."

I stand, ushering Andrew out of the bathroom and into the hallway. "Maybe this is a good thing," I say to him. "She'll remember this the next time she decides to take off and start drinking."

"Yeah." Andrew's gaze shifts from me to Noah, who I didn't realize was still standing in the hallway.

"Is she okay?" Noah asks.

"She will be," I say, resting a hand on his mop of hair. "I think we're out of Tylenol. And she could probably use something to settle her stomach. I'll run out to the store and grab some medicine."

"Good idea," Andrew says, still looking at Noah. "Say, you want to help me cook breakfast? Some food will probably make your sister feel better. How about a batch of waffles?"

"Sure," Noah says, taking off toward the kitchen.

"I'll keep an eye on her," Andrew says to me.

"I want to finish our conversation," I tell him. "Later."

We don't have the luxury of discussing our own problems, not when our children need us.

CHAPTER 26

4 Months Ago

Andrew and Kate continued their weekly sessions with Dr. Sutton. During that time, they'd gone over almost every detail of their lives leading up to the attack. They explained who Paul Gunter was, about his obsession with their family. That he believed Willow was his daughter. And then they told her what Andrew had done with the DNA test. After several sessions of stalling, the time had come to investigate the root of their marital problems.

"Kate, can you explain to Andrew why you were so hurt by his decision to take a paternity test behind your back?" Dr. Sutton asked.

"She's already told me. I understand what I did was wrong," Andrew said, before Kate had the chance to answer.

Dr. Sutton cleared her throat, her eyes falling to the notepad in her lap. "Andrew, I believe the words you used earlier when explaining your reasoning for getting the test were *clean slate*. I understand Kate has already told you how she felt, but several weeks have passed since then. If we're going to get to the root of your marital issues, I think that clean slate needs to start here. In a neutral place." Her body shifted, and she looked at Kate. "Can you tell Andrew why his getting a paternity test behind your back hurt you so much?"

Until this point, Kate hadn't talked much. When she did, she was simply providing background about their family and what they'd been through that night. She'd yet to express her feelings.

"It bothered me because it implied I'd done something wrong. That I'd lied to him, so he had to go behind my back and prove me wrong."

Dr. Sutton turned to Andrew. "Is that why you did it?"

"I wasn't trying to prove her wrong." His voice was defensive. He shook his head and started over with a different tone. "I was obviously hoping the results would support her account. I just needed to see them for myself. I had to know, beyond a shadow of a doubt."

"Would you describe Kate as an honest person?"

"Yes."

"You've never had issues with lying in the past."

Andrew looked at Kate. "No. We've always been honest with each other."

"Why do you think this situation was different? She's been truthful with you your entire relationship. When she told you there was no way Paul could be Willow's father, why didn't you simply believe her?"

Andrew thought about his answer. Kate sat there, waiting, hoping whatever he said would make sense to her.

"What we went through that night felt so extreme. This man broke into our house. He was obsessed with our family. For all I know, he intended on taking Willow away from us. I guess a part of me found it hard to believe a man would go to such lengths if there wasn't even a possibility what he believed was true."

"You've established this person has mental health issues, correct?"

"Yes," Kate said, jumping back in. "I'm not sure of his exact diagnosis, but I know he's sought treatment. I spoke with his ex-wife, and she confirmed he'd been having paranoid episodes for the past couple of years."

"Andrew, you can understand why it would hurt Kate, a woman you admit has been nothing but honest with you, that you believed this person over her."

"Yes. I understand." His words were clipped, and Kate couldn't tell if it was from aggravation or shame.

"Kate, do you consider yourself an honest person?"

The question caught her off guard. She shifted in her seat. "Yes. I've never lied to Andrew. I've always been faithful to him."

"*To him.* By your own admission, your relationship with Andrew started when you were still dating Paul."

The couple looked at each other, searching for what, they didn't know. Kate turned back to Dr. Sutton.

"We were kids. My relationship with Paul was nothing more than a college fling. It's nothing like what I have with Andrew."

In the corner of her eye, Kate caught Andrew smiling. He quickly covered his mouth with his hand and looked away. She wondered if perhaps this was what he had been waiting to hear all along.

"I imagine you felt that way at the time. You've probably always felt that way. I wonder, if after Paul did what he did to your family, if you started to feel guilty. If you thought maybe you had brought this on yourself for how you acted back then."

Kate looked down. She didn't want to admit there was truth in Dr. Sutton's statement. She didn't want to admit that same line she'd heard caroling in her head since that night. *This is your fault. This is your fault. This is your fault.*

"What happened to your family isn't your fault," Dr. Sutton said, as if reading Kate's mind. "Nothing you did, whether it was last year or ten years or twenty years ago, justifies what Paul did. By all accounts, he has mental health issues and concocted this theory out of nothing, which put your family in real danger. But I wonder if maybe you think you deserved for Paul to come after you, and that's why you were so hurt by Andrew's actions. Because he was basically confirming your own fears."

Kate cut her eyes at Andrew. He was watching her intently, his eyes hopeful. Perhaps they were inching closer to the answers they'd come there to find.

"I don't regret what I did back then, but I regret hurting Paul. I hate feeling like what I did to him might have colored his relationships moving forward. That maybe he cared for me much more than I cared for him, and I didn't know it at the time. And I regret not telling Andrew after the first time I ran into him. Our interaction was innocent, nostalgic. But again, I think it meant something different to Paul. He had darker intentions. Maybe if I'd been more willing to admit how troubling his actions were, it wouldn't have happened."

Dr. Sutton nodded. Andrew remained silent, still staring at the floor. Kate pulled on the sleeves of her cardigan, wrapping it tighter around her body.

"I think you need to acknowledge the guilt Kate is already carrying with her," Dr. Sutton said to Andrew. "You have to be on her side. What you did with the paternity test made it seem like you were backing Paul's account of what happened, not your wife's."

"I understand. I know what I did was wrong, but I still wanted to tell you about it." He looked at Kate. "I don't want any secrets moving forward. That's why I told you about the test in the first place."

He reached for Kate's hand, but she didn't respond. He kept trying.

"I don't blame you for what happened, Kate. You didn't cause it. And if anything, you saved us that night. If it weren't for you…"

Kate jerked her head in his direction. She was watching his face, all the subtle movements. They were on the precipice of addressing everything that happened, and after so many months trying to block it out, Kate couldn't believe it was actually about to be breached.

"Explain what you mean. How did Kate save you?"

Andrew looked to Kate, like he expected her to answer. She didn't. She needed to hear him say it. His posture stiffened, and he took back his hand.

"I was in complete shock. I was dead asleep when the intruder broke in. It all feels like a dream, really. Still to this day. I'm not sure I even know what happened until after it was already over."

Kate's eyes narrowed, her mind traveling back to that night. Not the threat of Paul. Not the terror coursing through her bloodstream. Her mind revisited Andrew, comparing the man in pajamas to the man sitting next to her.

"Kate, what was your reaction when the intruder came in?"

They'd talked about what happened, but not exactly what either of them had done. Maybe that was what had been bothering Kate the most after all this time. Maybe that was why they were really here.

"I opened the door. I confronted him. I made sure Willow and Noah were okay."

"And Andrew?"

He looked down, opening his mouth but only breathing out sounds. Then finally, "Like I said, I was in shock. I don't even remember—"

"You did nothing."

Kate couldn't hold the words back. Not anymore. She couldn't help her husband carry on this charade any longer. Not after what he did to her with the paternity test. Not after he'd pouted and stewed and treated her like she had done something wrong this entire time. She'd been wanting to say those words for months but couldn't. Or perhaps wouldn't. Maybe she needed this. Maybe she needed this neutral space where she could express her memory of that night. Where she could express the truth.

Dr. Sutton's eyes bulged. "What was that, Kate?"

Kate locked eyes with Andrew, refused to look elsewhere. "You did nothing. We were both shocked. We were both afraid. But when that man came after me, came after our children, you just sat there. You froze."

"I… I didn't know what to do," Andrew stammered.

"I didn't know what to do!" Kate moved violently, pounding her own chest. "No one knows how to react in that situation. But I did something! I did whatever I had to do to keep our family safe, and you just sat there."

Dr. Sutton raised a palm. "I don't think we need to cast more blame—"

"No, she's right," Andrew said, cutting her off. "I was too afraid. I was too stunned."

"That's why you said Kate saved you. You don't feel like you did enough that night."

"I know I didn't do enough. I didn't do anything. And if Kate hadn't been there…"

Andrew's words fell away. He leaned over, sobbing loudly.

Dr. Sutton and Kate looked at each other. It was odd to have a man express his emotions so openly. Kate's man, her husband, her partner—the person who had proven to be so few of these things in the past few months.

"If I'd been the only person there that night, there's no telling what would have happened. I just wasn't capable of stepping up and defending my family, and that's a painful truth to reckon with," he sobbed. "That's why I've been shifting the blame to Kate, trying to block out my memories with silence and booze. I'm ashamed of what I did. If I can blame her for causing it, then I don't feel so guilty about doing nothing to stop it."

After several moments, Dr. Sutton spoke.

"What the both of you have been through is complicated. It's putting your marriage to the test. I believe you can overcome it, but I would recommend we continue counseling for the foreseeable future."

Kate looked to her left. Andrew was still sobbing. She wasn't sure if he'd acknowledged anything the therapist had said.

"I think that would be good," Kate said. She placed a hand on Andrew's shaking shoulder. "We can get through this."

And for the first time in months, Kate felt like she really wanted to.

CHAPTER 27

Now

After leaving the pharmacy, I take the scenic route back to the beach house, opting for narrow neighborhood streets instead of the highway. By the time I arrive at the rental, I've been gone more than an hour. I hope Willow is no longer sick, but a few pills will at least reduce her headache.

I've decided I'm going to tell Andrew I'm ready to return to Hidden Oaks. I realize his spontaneous decision to extend this trip was well-intentioned, but there are too many issues we need to address as a family, and this vacation, as ideal as the early days were, is only prolonging our denial. I'm still not convinced Paul hasn't followed us here; if he's determined to track us down wherever we go, we'll be more prepared to take him on in Hidden Oaks, where a familiar police department can help us.

As I exit the car, I can hear splashing on the other side of the tall security gate. Noah must be in good spirits if he's already in the pool. I walk inside and start fiddling with the pill bottle packaging. I need to find Willow and make sure she's okay.

I hear footsteps. I look up, expecting to see Andrew, but instead, there's a man I've never seen before standing in our kitchen.

My throat clenches shut, halting my ability to breathe. I take several steps back, stumbling into a wall. This man isn't Paul, but he's still a stranger, and he's inside our vacation home.

"I'm sorry," he says, holding out his hands. "I didn't mean to startle you."

"Who the hell are you?"

Andrew walks up and puts a hand on the man's shoulder. "Kate, it's okay. We didn't hear you come in."

My breath is still shallow after being startled. My eyes shift between Andrew and the man in front of me. "What's going on?"

Andrew appears calm. "Kate, this is Vincent. He's a member of the Second Chances group."

"I'm local to the area." Vincent smiles, his body language relaxed and inviting. He takes a step forward, holding out a hand for me to shake. His palm is thick and warm, his grip sturdy. "Sorry again for scaring you."

"It's fine. I just wasn't expecting to see someone, that's all." I tuck a strand of hair behind my ear, can feel my cheeks blushing from the embarrassment. Inside, my heart is still pounding against my chest maddeningly.

Vincent is a large man. He's well over six feet tall, his shoulders are broad, and he's got a slight paunch. He's wearing a buttoned-up linen shirt in a tropical design and cargo shorts that stop just past his knee. His physical stature is alarming at first, but when he smiles, as he is now, he appears kind.

"I hope you don't mind me dropping in on your family vacation," he says.

It is strange Andrew wouldn't tell me he'd invited someone over. I was gone at the store for an hour—it seems like a short amount of time to make plans in my absence.

"You say you're a member of Second Chances?"

"Yes, that's where I met Andrew."

"You're the first member I've met in person." I smile, but it feels forced. I'd been preparing to suggest we pack up and head home tonight, not host another visitor. I look to Andrew. "Where's Willow?"

"Sleeping," he says.

"Let me check in on her. Is Noah in the pool?"

"Went out there as soon as he finished his waffles. Vincent said he'd join us on the fishing trip this afternoon. He's more experienced than I am."

"First thing I did after retirement was invest in a little two-seater," Vincent says, puffing up his chest and crossing his arms. "I try to get out on the water any chance I get."

I nod, my cheeriness still feeling false. "I'd better check on Willow. Nice meeting you, Vincent."

Andrew, perhaps sensing my desire to speak with him, follows me.

"What's going on?" I whisper as soon as we turn the corner. "You never mentioned having one of your friends join us."

"I'm sorry to spring it on you. Thing is, I've been thinking about what you said this morning about Paul. As unlikely as it is that he might have found us, we can never be too safe, right? Vincent happens to live twenty minutes away from here. I thought, why not have him join us? Give us an extra set of eyes our final few days?"

I'm happy Andrew is at least taking my concerns from earlier seriously, but this feels intrusive. "I'm not sure I like the idea of some stranger bunking up with us on our vacation. I'm still on edge about finding the jammer. I'm not sure now is the time to be adding in distractions."

"He's not bunking up with us. He'll go back to his place at night. And he's not a distraction. If anything, he's an asset. He can protect us."

"But I don't know him. He's a stranger."

"I've invited him to stay for dinner. You can get to know him then. You'll see. We couldn't be in safer hands."

"How well do you even know him? What if he's not who he says he is? I know he's part of your group…"

"He's my best friend in the group. I know his face. Hell, I know everything about him. He's the guy we all turn to when we're feeling…" he pauses, tilts his head from side to side "… when we're feeling a little overwhelmed. I trust this guy with my life. I wouldn't bring him around my family otherwise." He looks around the corner, spying to see if anyone can hear us. "Besides, he's also an expert fisherman. I could use his help out on the water."

"Do you really think going back on the boat is the best idea?" I whisper. "What happened the other day—"

"It was an accident," he says. "I'm not going to let Noah near the edge of the boat. Vincent and I will do all the heavy lifting. I promise."

I look down. "Noah nearly drowned the other day, and I'm not ready to let him back out there."

"He's the one begging me to go. I think he wants to redeem himself. You can come with us if it would make you feel better."

"I can't." I look away, my body remembering the sensation of water breaking against my cheek, splashing over my head and up my nostrils. "Someone has to stay with Willow."

"Vincent knows what he's doing on the water. It will be fine."

You were supposed to know what you were doing on the water, I want to say, but I won't. Without waiting for a reply, Andrew turns and joins Vincent in the kitchen.

I press my lips together and inhale through my nose. There's no way I'll be able to convince Andrew to cut the trip short now that he's invited his friend to join us. The last thing I want to do is be rude to Vincent; I know from previous conversations with Andrew that he's been particularly helpful to him in recent months, but his presence serves as yet another distraction from our problems.

Willow's door is cracked open. The light pink walls look violet in the darkness, and the blackout curtains over the window have been pulled tight. Willow is under a bundle of blankets, the corner of one covering her eyes.

"Did you eat anything?" I whisper, not even sure if she's awake.

"I tried. My head is still killing me."

"Take this," I say, handing over the medicine.

She sits up in bed, takes a sip of the water on her nightstand. She swallows it down and exhales heavily. "How much trouble am I in?"

"A lot. But don't worry about that now. We'll discuss what happened once we get back home."

"That seems like forever away," she says, falling back on the mattress.

I echo her frustration. It's amazing how this escape has started to feel more like entrapment.

"Is Dad still mad at me?"

I think back to last night and Andrew's vitriolic tone as he lectured Willow. I'd like to think parenting a teenager pushes us all to our limits, but even I'd been taken aback.

"I think he's disappointed. You have to remember, after the year we've had, when we woke up in the middle of the night and couldn't find you, the worst came to our minds."

"I'm sorry." Her voice cracks. "You didn't deserve that, I know. Now I feel like I've ruined the trip."

"You've not ruined the trip," I say, placing a palm on her clammy forehead. "Although, I doubt you'll be up for another fishing trip today."

At the thought of it, she makes a gagging sound. I laugh.

"Get some rest. You should feel better by the afternoon but be prepared for some stiff consequences once we get home. There's still a few more days of vacation left."

Unfortunately, I think, as I exit the room.

CHAPTER 28

3 Months Ago

Kate sat at an outside table at Morning Maple, the best coffee shop on campus. She was in between her afternoon classes. It was her shortest break of the day, but she wanted to make time to meet with Detective Marsh.

The sun was peeking out beneath the clouds, the sky a perfect color of blue. In the distance, she heard birds chirping in between the lively chatter of college students at the neighboring tables. In many ways, it felt like the first day of spring, although the season had changed weeks ago.

Detective Marsh arrived. She was wearing navy slacks and a khaki blazer. Her hair was pulled back, and Kate noticed a pair of pearl earrings. She wasn't sure she'd noticed jewelry on her before.

Kate stood as she approached the table.

"Thanks for meeting with me," Detective Marsh said.

Kate smiled, waiting. She was used to seeing Detective Marsh at their weekly workout class, but she still felt nervous meeting her in this capacity. She feared Marsh had bad news.

"Are there updates in the case?" Kate asked. Her voice quivered, failed miserably at hiding her nerves.

"Not in the case, per se. But I do have some news, and I wanted to tell you in person. I'm leaving Hidden Oaks at the end of this month. I've taken a new job in a different state, which means I won't be working your case anymore."

"Oh." Kate looked down. She hadn't expected this to be the news, something so personal. And she felt a sense of loss. Detective Marsh had certainly gone above and beyond to make the Brooks family comfortable. Kate wasn't sure she'd have the same dynamic with another detective working the case.

"You know, I'm a hometown girl, but there's an opening in a bigger city, and I can't pass it up. This is my chance to see what else is out there."

"I understand. I wish you luck."

"I know we've already made an arrest, but the case isn't officially closed until after the trial. I hope, for your sake, it doesn't come to that. It appears Paul might be taking a deal."

"Okay."

"Either way, I know you'll want to stay updated. The person replacing me is named Detective Barnes. I would have asked him to meet with us today, but he's not here yet."

"Another transplant?"

"It would appear. I don't know the guy, but everyone from his old department has glowing reviews. I think you'll be in good hands, and I've already told him to make sure he keeps you updated on everything pertaining to the case."

"I appreciate that. And I appreciate everything you've done for us since that night."

"I want you and your family to know that even though I won't be here, we'll do everything within our power to make sure you feel safe."

Her words were meant to be reassuring, but the way she said it gave Kate pause. She feared maybe what Detective Marsh was trying to say was there were lots of ways this could still go wrong. There were ways Paul could cheat the system. That maybe this nightmare they had been trying to forget wasn't completely over.

That's paranoia, she quickly told herself. She took a deep breath, looking around. She was enjoying a beautiful spring day, and Paul was locked behind bars. He could only get to her in her mind. Nowhere else.

"Thank you for telling me."

Detective Marsh stared at her, unblinking, as though she was focusing on what she wanted to say next. "You've been through a lot, Kate. But you've come out on the other side. That's what matters." When Kate didn't respond, she continued, "Paul can't do anything to hurt you."

Those words echoed in Kate's head for hours after she left the coffee shop. That, and her bizarre sadness that Detective Marsh was leaving Hidden Oaks behind. She hadn't known her before that night, and yet, the past year had brought them close together. She didn't think any other detective could truly understand the terror she had felt that night, the lingering fears that followed her through her days. They weren't there to witness it, like Detective Marsh was.

Still, maybe it was a good thing, Kate reckoned. She had to stop depending on others to give her fulfillment and peace. She had to start relying on herself. The sooner she could step away from this incident in her mind, the sooner she could get back to feeling the way she once did.

I sound like Dr. Sutton, Kate thought. She was now reiterating the same message her therapist conveyed during their weekly sessions. Where Andrew had done his best to block out the events of that night, with his drinking and his secrecy, Kate had become obsessed. She'd let the event consume her, much like Paul had been consumed with ideas about Kate and Willow. It wasn't a comparison she wanted to make, but she couldn't deny it, either.

Dr. Sutton believed Kate needed to distance herself from the case. Stop with the weekly check-ins and Google searches. She especially thought Kate's meeting with Paul's ex-wife was unhealthy; she insisted Kate didn't need to be tracking down information about Paul, to fight fire with fire, in a sense. And yet, it didn't feel like that to Kate. It felt like she was simply trying to understand the intentions of a madman. It felt like she was preparing herself for another attack, if there ever was one.

Dr. Sutton did approve of Kate's self-defense classes. The weekly gym sessions boosted her confidence, made her feel more capable than she had nine short months ago, although she would now continue the classes without the guidance of Detective Marsh. Andrew also supported Kate's classes, admitting in their last session he'd noticed a glow in his wife that he'd not seen since college. Kate had blushed when he said that.

As she was driving home, Kate tried not to think about where they had been as a family or where they were now. She tried to focus on the future, on all the opportunities to come.

Inside the house, Andrew was sitting in front of the computer in the family den. He had headphones on but took them off when he saw his wife approaching.

"Good day?"

"Yeah, it was. Have you talked with Detective Marsh recently?"

"No," Andrew said. "Have you?"

"I met with her today. I thought maybe she would have reached out to you, too." She waited, but Andrew didn't respond. "She says we'll be dealing with a different detective from now on."

"Any particular reason why?"

"She's moving away. Got a new a job."

Andrew nodded and looked back at the computer. "Good for her."

Kate wandered behind him, bending down to kiss his cheek. These small moments of intimacy had finally returned to their relationship, letting them both know they were moving in the right direction. Andrew rubbed his cheek against hers. She noted the familiar website on his screen.

Much like Kate had her gym classes, Dr. Sutton suggested that Andrew also find some type of outlet, a form of group therapy, perhaps. Despite his initial resistance, Andrew had warmed to the idea, although meeting with people in real life irked him. Hidden Oaks was too small. Everyone knew everyone else, and it was no secret to anyone what the Brooks family had experienced in the past year.

No, Andrew thought he would prefer a group where he could remain more anonymous. He thought he'd be able to better open up that way, and Kate agreed. Dr. Sutton had forwarded him a list of online support groups for men, and Andrew had been sampling them. Lately, the one called Second Chances soaked up the most of his time.

After the first week, Kate realized how someone like Andrew could benefit from this type of interaction. He had no siblings. While he remained close with his parents, there was always a barrier between them. For whatever problem Andrew encountered, their solution was prayer. Faith had been embedded in him when he was younger, and while it was still within him, it wasn't as devout as it was with his parents. Prayer could do a lot of things, but it couldn't protect them from people like Paul Gunter.

Here Kate was again, thinking about Paul like he was out to get her. Like he wasn't killing time in a jail cell that very moment.

"I'm waiting for some of the guys to login for a quick video chat," Andrew said, drowning out her thoughts. "Maybe when you get back from the store, we could grab dinner?"

"I'd like that."

"Raj, good to see you again," Andrew said to the screen, sliding the headphones on. Kate was invisible to him now, and while she should have stepped away and given him privacy, she couldn't help but watch a few moments. Andrew's smile raised high into his cheeks. The lines in his forehead seemed to smooth. His laugh was genuine and youthful. Second Chances was good for him. And it was good for a couple to acknowledge they couldn't always be the answer for each other; sometimes answers exist elsewhere.

She left the room, wandering into the kitchen. She inspected the pantry and refrigerator, jotting down a quick list of essentials they'd need to make it through the rest of the week. It was only in the past couple of years Kate seemed to have these moments of quiet; now that Willow was driving, there were pockets throughout the day when she no longer had a child by her side. For a minute, she closed her eyes and envisioned what her life would be like with Andrew in the years to come, once both kids were out of the house. Empty nesters, but something about the thought made her feel fulfilled, not lonely.

Kate began gathering her things to go to the store. She walked back to the study, intending to knock on the door and let Andrew know she was headed out. She stopped when she heard a loud voice from the other side.

"You don't understand!" The voice was male, angry and unfamiliar. "That bitch thinks she's entitled to everything."

"You have to remain calm," Andrew responded.

"I've been calm. I've tried everything to reason with her, but she's got me by the balls and she knows it. She's found some rich boyfriend to help with her lawyer's fees. She knows I don't have any of that shit!"

"You can't act irrationally. You don't want to do anything that might jeopardize the custody arrangement."

"What else am I supposed to do? Sit back and let her take away my kids?"

Kate was listening intently, almost in a daze. It was like catching a bad scene in a television soap opera, but this was real life, some man she'd never met shouting about his problems to Andrew. Without realizing, Kate leaned forward, pressing on the door handle. There was a noticeable jangle. She tried to step back, but she was still close when Andrew opened the door. His cell phone was in his hands, the call obviously on speaker.

"Let me call you back," Andrew said, clicking off before there was a response. "I thought you were going to the store?"

"I... I was. That's what I was coming to tell you."

"Were you listening in on my phone call?"

"No. I mean, I wasn't trying to. I walked up and couldn't really stop myself. Was that Raj?"

Andrew scoffed. "No, I finished talking with him. It's just another guy from group. Trent."

Kate stared at him, waiting for him to reveal more, but that's all he said.

"He sounded so… angry."

"Yeah. He's in the middle of a nasty custody fight. I'm not sure how much you heard."

"Enough to make me uncomfortable." She cocked her head to the side. "Do all of you talk about your problems like this?"

"No, of course not." He put his hands on her shoulders. "I'm sorry you heard him ranting the way you did. Like I said, he's going through a lot right now. You caught him in a bad moment."

Kate couldn't imagine Andrew talking about any of them that way. She even felt pride about her husband, that she never had to worry about him going off the rails like that, but she didn't like the idea of him venting about their problems to people with such short fuses.

"I know you say the group is helping you, but I don't really like you talking to people who sound so… outraged."

"Look, I'm sorry. I understand what you're saying. You know I don't condone the way he was talking, and in the right moment, I'll tell him, too. Right now, I'm just letting him vent. That's what the group is really about. Voicing our feelings without fear of being judged. Once he calms down, he'll be able to make better decisions."

"Okay."

She trusted Andrew and had already witnessed how Second Chances had improved his demeanor. Maybe this angry phase was a necessary part of the process, one this Trent had just entered. She didn't want to judge Andrew, even if she still did have reservations about his friend. She'd never overheard Raj or Vincent speak so viciously. She decided not to let one bad apple spoil her idea about the bunch.

She wandered outside, having forgotten to check the mail before she arrived. Usually, Andrew was the one to check it, but the counter where he left her portion of the stack was empty. She was mesmerized by the way the clouds seemed to drift smoothly, filling the blue void.

Dana saw her from across the street and approached. "Have any plans this weekend? It's been ages since you've been over, and I'm dying to try this new recipe."

"That sounds lovely," Kate said, looking back at the house. "Maybe next week? Andrew's a little slammed with work."

"On a Saturday?" The words came out so quickly that Kate wondered if Dana had meant to say them aloud. Her friend quickly recovered. "I guess I can't say much. José works the same crazy hours."

Dana had started dating a guy who worked at the same company as Andrew. They met over holiday break. She'd been pestering Kate about going on a double date, but Kate kept pushing her off. She wanted to make sure her relationship with Andrew was mended before they started socializing with friends again.

"You look great by the way." Dana's eyes scanned Kate's body. "Do you think I'd look this good if I traded Doritos for half an hour on the elliptical every day?"

"Stop," Kate said, waving her off. Truth was, Dana already looked great. She was at least a foot taller than Kate, which made it easier to hide her weight.

But Kate couldn't deny that her weekly visits to the gym had improved her appearance. She noticed the changes in her body, the way outfits that once stretched across her middle now draped.

However, the biggest changes she noticed were internal. She felt less tired in the afternoons. More energetic in the mornings.

She opened the mailbox and sifted through the envelopes. At the bottom of the stack was a letter addressed only to her. She opened it.

Hi Kate. How's Willow?

The words terrified her. She fell to her knees, right there in the front yard, staring at the chicken scratch handwriting.

She wasn't sure how long she was there, her knees burrowing into the thick mud. She felt a hand on her shoulder. She looked up to see Dana.

"Kate, are you okay?"

"It's him." They were the only words she was able to form. She felt that terror from months earlier creeping back in, constricting her vocal cords.

"It's who?" Dana's head bobbed around. Looking to make sure the kids weren't here to witness this. Looking to see if Andrew was around to help. It's what women did. They addressed the initial crisis and each arising element all at the same time.

"It's Paul," Kate puffed out, after several deep breaths. "He's never going to leave us alone."

CHAPTER 29

Now

The boys come back just as I'm taking dinner out of the oven. I've paired our remaining chicken breasts with a simple vegetable medley and rice. Clearing out the fridge and cupboards gives me at least some hope that this vacation will be coming to an end soon.

"Smells delicious," Andrew says, kissing me on the cheek.

"Wish I could say the same for you." All three of them smell like sweat and rancid fish.

"I know. I'm going to hop in the shower. Vincent, you can use the hall bathroom if you'd like."

"Sure." He looks at me. "I hate to impose, but I also hate to smell like a chow line at the dinner table."

"It's not a problem," I say.

"Great. I've got an extra change of clothes in the car."

He walks outside. Noah comes up and gives me a hug. "How was fishing?"

"It was, like, the coolest ever. Vincent showed us all these tricks. You'll never guess how many fish we caught."

"Two?"

"Five!"

"My goodness! I don't know if we'll be here long enough to cook all of those."

"That's what Dad said. We threw some of them back but kept the biggest two. Dad took some pictures on his phone if you want to see."

"Wash up, and I'll take a look after dinner."

He wanders off just as Vincent walks back inside. I point him in the direction of the bathroom. While in the hallway, I poke my head into Willow's room.

"Feeling better?"

"Tons," she says, sitting up on the bed. "Really hungry."

"Dinner will be ready in ten. Dad has a friend over. He's taking a shower in the downstairs bath. I thought I'd give you a heads-up."

"Dad has a friend? And he's here?"

"He's one of the guys from his online group. His name is Vincent. He joined them on their fishing trip today."

She leans back on the bed, stuffing a headphone in her ear. Already, she's back to normal: lazy and disinterested.

As I'm leaving her room, I pass Andrew in the hall.

"Everything was okay?" Noah seemed happy when they returned, but I want to make sure.

"Yeah, it was great. I understand why you wanted to stay back with Willow, but I wish you could have seen the look on Noah's face. He was having the time of his life out there."

"Good," I say, and the nerves I have about Vincent and the water and all of it begin to settle.

One by one, everyone gathers around the table. I'm sure the boys worked up an appetite on the boat, and Willow will need something to soak up the juices in her stomach.

"I have to say I'm impressed you cook such elaborate meals while on vacation. Usually, we stick to frozen pizza and takeout," Vincent says.

"Kate is a fabulous chef," Andrew says, taking another bite of his food.

"Trust me, I don't do this every night. I enjoy cooking. I never feel like I get the time to do it as consistently as I'd like back home, when everyone is rushing around in a dozen different directions."

"Good food and family," Vincent says. "That's what it's about."

I take a sip of my wine. The kids remain silent as they eat.

"Tell us about you, Vincent. As I said, you're the only one of Andrew's online friends I've had the pleasure of meeting in person."

"Pretty boring guy, really. I'm retired. Big fisherman, but you already know that. On the weekends I work security at one of the pubs downtown. It keeps me busy and can be a good source of entertainment sometimes."

"What did you do before you retired?" I ask.

"He was a cop," Noah answers excitedly.

"Really?" I ask. Across the table, my eyes lock with Andrew's. That must be one of the reasons he asked him to come over. *He can protect us*, Andrew said.

"Part of me thought I'd never give it up, but my ticker isn't the best. I figured at some point I had to start living life on my own terms. When my pension was ready, I hightailed it out of there and never looked back."

"Is that why you joined Dad's group? Did you see a lot of messed up stuff when you were a cop or something?" Willow asks. It's the first time she's spoken.

"Willow, that's very personal," I say.

"What? We all know what his group is about. It's about helping people who've had problems." She looks to Andrew. "I'm sure Vincent knows what Dad has been through. What we've all been through."

"Yes," I say. "But that's between them—"

"Kate, it's okay," Vincent says, cutting me off. "I don't mind answering her questions."

"You don't have to," Andrew says sheepishly.

"She deserves to know," Vincent says. "Yes, I'm aware of what your family went through last summer. It must have been a terrifying incident. Sure, I've seen things as a cop, but I can't imagine having that level of violence targeted at my own family. I'm sorry you all had to experience it."

As usual, when I hear people talk about that night, I feel a thick lump in my throat. I look down and close my eyes, feel like I'm holding my breath.

"Vincent's experiences are different from mine," Andrew says. "We all enter the group for different reasons, but it's helpful to know that there are other men out there who are grappling with the same feelings. The fear and the stress and the resentment."

At that, my eyes flick up to Andrew. For a second, there's eye contact, but he breaks it and quickly looks away. I clear my throat.

"So, Vincent, why did you join the group?" I ask.

"Well, Willow is right. I did see some things on the job that bothered me over the years. Just before my retirement, my wife got sick. Cancer. It was devastating for me and the girls."

"You have children?" I ask.

"Two daughters. Sadie and Jenna." He stops, smiles. "After my wife's diagnosis, we fell apart. I'd like to think we were a happy family once. I know we were. But after she got sick, everything just started unraveling. You realize who keeps the world on its axis when something like that happens, let me tell you. Suddenly, we were griping and fighting all the time. The girls were acting out. I was angry, tired from running my wife back and forth to all her appointments and therapies. It's like we were running out of steam, and no matter how hard we tried, we couldn't get back to that happy place. What we were really doing was reacting out of fear. Fear of losing my wife, their mother. Fear of losing each other."

He stops talking, looks down at the table.

Andrew reaches out a hand and gently taps Vincent's arm, a calming gesture. "You don't have to continue, if you don't want to."

"No, it's good for me. You know it's good for me." He looks up at us again, a glimmer in his eyes. "It was a dark time for us. It forced me to really look inside myself and do the work. I had to figure out what would make me happy again, make us all happy again. Second Chances helped me do that. I'm telling you, in the midst of that dark place, I felt like the loneliest person in the world. When I found the group, it made me realize we all have dark periods in life. We all have greater desires for the future. They helped me find my way out of it when no one else could."

"That's comforting to hear," I say, feeling like it's my duty to say something. This man is a practical stranger yet he's pouring out his soul.

"The group was a huge comfort to me." He smiles, wiping under his eyes with his thick knuckles. "Now, I can honestly say I'm happier than I've ever been. I'm not held down anymore with all those negative feelings. All that darkness. None of us are. We're exactly where we're meant to be in life, and it's all thanks to guys like Andrew who helped me see my way out of it."

Vincent leans to the left and claps Andrew on the shoulder.

"Vincent's story was really inspiring to me," Andrew says, his voice quiet. "I remember having some of those same thoughts after… what happened. To know that this guy had gone through the same emotions and made it to the other side gave me hope."

"And your wife. Is she still sick?" Willow asks.

"She's healed. My girls have never been happier." He closes his eyes, tilts his head like he's listening to a distant melody. "I can almost see them now. We're back to the good 'ol days, and life has never been better."

"I'm happy the group has helped you," I say, reaching again for my wine glass.

"We all have issues we have to face, but as men we're told to hide those emotions. Be strong. Be the provider. Be the protector. As you can imagine, being a cop really hammers that message. Once I started expressing what I was feeling, my life changed for the better."

I look over to Andrew. He's watching Vincent as he speaks with bated breath, clinging to each word as it leaves his lips. It's like Vincent's words are a sermon, and Andrew is the sinner who needs to hear them. And yet, Andrew has failed to master the message. He's become more aware of his own desires, but he's having trouble voicing them. He's keeping them to himself instead of sharing. That's the last hurdle I'd like him to overcome in order to feel like we're going to be okay.

"Mom makes me talk to the counselor at school," Noah says, a desperate attempt to add to this very adult conversation. I would have asked the children to leave the table had I known how open Vincent was going to be. His emotions were so raw.

"That's good, little man." Vincent looks over at me and winks. "You should do what your mother says."

"I have to go, too," Willow says. "We all started talking to someone this year, after what happened."

"What happened that night changed you. It changed you as individuals. It changed you as a family. It's important you learn to look deep inside yourselves, pull out what really matters to each of you. So many people never do that in their lifetime, and I think it's the greatest tragedy of all."

I'm starting to feel uncomfortable, now that this conversation has circled back to our family and that night. Vincent has no qualms about opening up to strangers, but I remain guarded. I reach for my wine glass, but it's empty.

"Well," I say, standing. "I'm going to grab more wine and start clearing the table."

"Dad, can Willow and I rent that new *Avengers* movie?" Noah asks.

"Sure." Andrew smiles and sips the last of his wine.

"You sure do have a beautiful family," Vincent says, taking one more look around the table before we go our separate ways. Our eyes lock, and for a moment, even though he's rosy-cheeked and smiling, a shiver of fear shudders through my body.

CHAPTER 30

Now

I got in bed early but found it hard to sleep. My mind revisits Vincent and his story. Last night he preached about the importance of speaking your truth, and that's what he did, but something about his words haunt me, leave me with a bad aftertaste I can't quite describe.

When I do wake, I'm alone. The sun is shining in, and I can hear the unmistakable footsteps of people moving around the living room. I roll out of bed, grab my robe and wander into the kitchen to make a coffee.

I jump back when I see Vincent standing beside the stove.

"Did it again," he says, chuckling. "You're an easy one to spook."

I pull the sash of my robe tighter. "I wasn't expecting anyone. Back so soon?"

"Yeah, Andrew invited me over."

Vincent left last night after dinner. It ended up being an early night for all of us. Willow and Noah fell asleep on the sofa while watching their *Avengers* movie, and I went to sleep not long after. I remember Andrew climbing beneath the covers sometime late in the night.

"I hope you don't mind me crashing your family vacation," he added.

"The more the merrier." I force a smile. "Have you seen Andrew?"

"He's outside. I'm grabbing some snacks. We thought we might hang around the pool before we load up the boat."

"You're going fishing again?"

"Yeah. Andrew texted me early this morning. He said he wanted to get one more trip out of the boat before he has to take it back tomorrow."

"I see." I wander closer to the living room screen door, squinting to get a better view of the dock. I see the boat, but no Andrew in sight.

"Maybe you could join us this time?"

"I don't think so," I say, staring at the water. The waves look rougher than they did earlier in the week. "It's not really my thing."

Finally, I see Andrew emerge from the pool. Noah is swimming in the water behind him.

"Mom, have you seen my boots?" asks Willow, joining us from the hallway.

"Are you heading out on the boat, too?"

"It's the last chance," she says, quite obviously. "Might as well, right?"

"See, the whole family is coming," Vincent says, stuffing a bag of chips beneath his arm. "You should join us."

"I'm fine here. There's plenty to keep me busy."

"I found them," Willow says, crouching to reach her boots from under the table in the corner.

It's funny what activities she chooses to partake in. What's deemed cool or lame is ever-changing in her eyes. Behind me, Vincent walks through the sliding glass doors to the outside. I watch him. He walks confidently, and yet there is an air of aggression surrounding him I can't quite put my finger on. Perhaps it's the retired cop thing. How well do we really know him, I wonder? How well does Andrew know him? I look back to Willow. I shouldn't think these things, but I'm her mother and I can't help it.

"Say, why don't you stay back with me today? Let the boys have their fun fishing."

"They went without me yesterday."

"Yeah, but that's because you were sick. You stayed in your room all day. If you stay back, maybe we can do something together."

"Mom, we have plenty of time to hang out back home. My summer is pretty much over anyway thanks to the other night. This is my last chance to go out on the open ocean. If you're that worried, you should come."

"I promised Noah I'd take his fish to the market so we can have it for dinner tonight."

"I think everyone wants to hang around the pool for a little while. You know Dad will wait on you if you want to go."

Andrew walks inside rubbing a towel against the back of his head. "I guess you heard about the fishing trip this afternoon."

"Willow is already trying to persuade me."

"Your turn." She taps Andrew on the shoulder before walking toward her bedroom. "I'm going to put on my swimsuit."

"Are you thinking about it?" he asks.

"The close call with Noah is still on my mind. And the waves look even rougher today."

"We won't stay out long. Just enough to feel like we got our money's worth with the boat. Once you're out there and see how happy the kids are, you'll be glad you came."

"I have to get Noah's fish prepared for dinner."

"We'll wait on you. It's not a problem."

"I don't want to spoil—"

"You're not spoiling anything." He cups his hands on my cheeks and kisses my lips. "Please come. Nothing would make me happier than being out on the waves with the whole family."

He looks sincere. I think of how happy the kids are about another trip at sea. I hate to miss their excitement because of my own fears. Besides, Andrew has tried to step outside his comfort zone. Maybe that's what I should do, too.

"Let me run into town, and we'll go when I get back, okay? I'll text you to let you know when I'm headed back."

Andrew steps forward, pulling me closer to him. He kisses me. At first, it's gentle and expected, then it becomes more passionate. His lips move in sync with mine, his tongue tickling the inside of my mouth.

After a few seconds, I pull away with a giggle. "What's that for?"

"You know I love you, right?" Andrew's eyes are so blue. I can't quite describe the look on his face.

"Is everything okay?"

"Everything is perfect," he says, leaning in for another passionate kiss.

"Gross," Willow says as she walks up behind us. She slams the sliding glass door as she leaves.

CHAPTER 31

2 Months Ago

A month after receiving the first letter, Detective Barnes visited the Brooks family home. They had received four more since then.

Kate was nervous about his arrival. She'd made up some errands for Willow to run in town, convincing her to take her brother with her. She cleaned up the room, moving and replacing items nervously. Andrew watched her but didn't help. He sat on the sofa with crossed arms. They still hadn't said much about the letters to one another. There wasn't much they could say, really, other than they would address the issue together.

A car pulled into their driveway. Standing by the window, Kate watched as the man exited his vehicle and approached the front door. She wasn't sure what she'd been expecting, really—someone younger, fitter, smoother—but Detective Barnes was not that. His gray suit draped over his body awkwardly. Still, he appeared kind. He offered a firm handshake and accepted a glass of water before taking a seat in the living room.

"I believe Detective Marsh told you I'd be taking over your case."

"Yes, she did." Kate took a seat, clumsily. It was obvious how nervous she was.

"I apologize for not getting back with you sooner. It's been hectic what with the change of duties and all. I wanted to reach out concerning the letter you received from Paul. It was last month, right?"

"Yes."

"And have you received anything since?"

"Yes. Five in total," Andrew said. "I made copies and sent them over to your email."

"Thanks for that."

"I know he's in jail until the trial, but shouldn't the restraining order still be in place?" Kate asked.

"That's the problem," he said, this time his voice a bit more agitated. "We're having difficulty proving the letter came from Paul Gunter. He hasn't sent any correspondence through the jail mail system. And when we had another officer question him about the matter, he denied sending a letter."

"That's bullshit. You may not be able to prove he sent the letter, but he clearly did. Maybe he had someone else do it for him."

"All that is possible, ma'am. But it's the proving it that's difficult."

His trial hadn't even started, and already Kate felt she was up against reasonable doubt. Why was it they had to face the most monstrous side of Paul before he was taken seriously?

"The problem is we don't feel safe," Andrew chimed in. "How can we when this guy is able to contact us and you can't even prove it?"

"I don't want you to get discouraged. You're right. These letters are probably coming from Paul, we just need time to prove it," Barnes said, cutting back in. "If Paul is finding a way to contact you, we'll figure out how. And really, this will hurt him even more by the time we get to trial. It might make his sentencing more severe considering he's not following protocol. It could be a blessing in disguise. Receiving letters might be unsettling, but there's nothing he can do to physically harm your family as long as he's in jail."

And yet, Kate didn't believe that to be true. She *knew* it to be true, of course. There were countless barriers that kept Paul at a distance. And yet, reading that letter had made his presence feel as threatening as it had on the night he invaded their home.

"He can't hurt us," Kate repeated, for her own good rather than Detective Barnes'. She wasn't trying to prove she was listening, rather trying to make the words sink in.

*

"Kate?"

Andrew's voice startled her, and she jumped.

"What?"

"Are you okay?"

She'd been in bed the rest of the afternoon, ever since Detective Barnes told them there was nothing that could be done. Barnes believed they needed to sit back and wait for Paul to mess up, but Kate didn't like waiting around for the next threat. She felt helpless.

"Where did you put the letters?"

Andrew looked down, defeated. Perhaps he thought they'd be able to bypass this topic entirely. He was wrong.

"I don't know why you need to see them again."

"I just do."

He nodded. He balanced on the balls of his feet as he moved around some items on the top shelf of their closet. Then, he came over to the bed. He threw down a folder.

"They're in there." He exhaled. "I'm going to finish putting away the dishes."

He quickly exited the room, and Kate was grateful. She wasn't sure why she wanted to be alone when she read the letters, but she did.

Letter wasn't really the appropriate word, she realized. Letters were intimate, long-winded. What Paul had sent was, at best, a series of messages. At worst, a series of threats.

She looked at the first one she'd received.

Hi Kate. How's Willow?

Then the second one:

No response?

There were three more after that.

I'm watching you.

You can't ignore me.

And the most chilling:

I miss her. Does she still have my eyes?

That last one made her buckle. She could handle everything Paul was aiming at her, but targeting her daughter—her and Andrew's daughter, not his—was too much. She needed to be strong for Willow, for her entire family, she knew that, but in the solitude of the room, she wept. Maybe that's why secretly she'd wanted to be alone when she read the letters. She'd brought this upon her family, and she needed space for the guilt to consume her.

By the time Andrew returned from downstairs, Kate was rolled over on one side, her eyes closed. She waited until she felt him get in bed beside her before opening them again.

And she couldn't close them for many hours after that.

CHAPTER 32

Now

Andrew told me the name of the fish market he'd visited earlier in the week. The place smells exactly as you'd imagine, although you can tell from the windows and floors the owners try to make the rest of the space comfortable. They're backed up today, so it will be an hour before the meat is ready for pickup. Thankfully, the market is in a quaint part of the newly revitalized downtown area. There are several stores and restaurants within walking distance.

I stop at a few clothing stores, debating whether to buy Willow a sundress, but figure whatever I choose won't be her style. As I exit each store, I scan the sidewalks for Paul, wondering if he's after us, or if it's all in my mind. I eventually find a café and decide to wait there. I order a cranberry and chicken salad croissant and tea. Because of the warm weather, the patio area is packed with people, so I choose a booth inside. The air conditioner gusts against my back while a television blares national news in front of me.

I love spending time with my family, but I do value these rare moments alone. I don't think I've even watched television in the two weeks we've been here. I'm busy taking care of everyone else's needs.

"Kate?" A server walks to my table and drops off my drink. There aren't many people inside, so I wasn't hard to find.

"Thanks."

"Your sandwich will be out soon."

"Do you think you could turn up the television?"

"Sure. Seems like you're the only one paying it any attention."

It doesn't seem the world has changed much in the two weeks I've been disconnected. Politicians are still fighting. Celebrities are still hooking up and breaking up. With each passing day, there seems to be another tragedy. A bridge collapse in Maryland. In California, an entire family was found dead. Another mass shooting in Colorado. Right before the program cuts to commercial, there's a short segment about an army veteran who rehomes stray cats and dogs, as if to remind viewers the world isn't as bleak as it seems.

If anything, hearing these stories of tragedy remind me I'm not alone in my grief. I'm lucky my family got out of it alive, even if each day is an ongoing struggle to find normalcy. There could have been so many more horrible alternatives. Maybe Paul Gunter is my reminder to stay on my toes, never allow the protective field I've built around my family to fall.

My stomach rumbles when the waiter arrives with my sandwich. I'm just about to dig in when my phone rings with a call from Dana. Finally, a happy reminder of home.

"It feels so good to hear your voice," I say, genuinely.

"I thought you'd fallen off the face of the earth."

I go into telling her about Andrew's surprise extra week at the beach. I intentionally leave out the parts about Noah falling off the boat or Willow sneaking out of the house. I don't tell her I have reason to believe Paul Gunter has followed us here, either. I'd rather focus on the pleasant parts of the trip—the way I'd prefer for it to have been.

"I'm happy for you," she says. "If anyone deserves some time off, it's you guys."

"Thanks. For the most part, it's been relaxing." At least that much is true.

"And you both have plenty of time on your hands now."

"Eh, not that much longer. The kids return to school at the end of the month, and I'm only a week or two behind them."

"When's Andrew starting the new job?"

As she asks the question, I take a sip of my newly refilled tea. It's scalding, and I burn my tongue. I cough, wiping at my mouth with my napkin, before focusing again on Dana. I couldn't have heard her correctly.

"New job?"

"José told me last month. I was a little surprised it didn't come from you, but it seems we've not had much time to catch up since school let out."

I lean against the table and press two fingers between my brows. There must be some type of mistake.

"What exactly did José say?"

"Just that Andrew left the company last month. He told him he got a better offer and would be starting somewhere else soon. What is it?"

"I… I don't know. Andrew didn't tell me he left the company." I'm too shocked to be anything but honest.

"Oh." An awkward pause follows. "Maybe I misunderstood—"

"What else did José say?"

"That's it. He didn't tell him where he was going, but I know he's been out of the office the past few weeks. José mentioned all the changes they've made since Andrew left." She waits, then, "He told me about his replacement."

A replacement. His position has already been filled. This is a permanent decision, and it's the first I'm hearing of it.

"Thank you for telling me," I manage.

"Kate, I'm sorry. I didn't realize you didn't know about this. Like I said, we've not talked. I'm sure Andrew has a reason—"

"Andrew always has a reason," I cut her off. "But he doesn't care to fill me in on it."

"Please, don't let this ruin your trip. I feel terrible."

If she only knew about Noah's scare and Willow's antics, and Aster's visit before that. The dinner where Andrew asked us to relive one of the worst moments of our lives. This vacation is slowly disintegrating, and it doesn't feel like there's anything I can do about it.

"Tell me, what are you guys doing today?" Her voice is forced and happy, trying her best to cheer me up from miles away.

My eyes fill with tears as I look up at the television. The news program is back on and the presenter is going on and on about the family that was murdered, calling it the Rogers Family Massacre. She quickly switches to talking about the most recent mass shooting. My stomach clenches, thinking of the petty stuff I allow to cloud my day; life could be so, so much worse.

"I'm cooking Noah's fish for dinner. The kids have talked about going fishing."

"Do that, okay? Enjoy your time together. We'll talk more when you get back."

I hang up the phone, my mind drifting as another infomercial fills the screen.

CHAPTER 33

Now

I pick up the fish from the market and rush back to the house. It doesn't feel like I can get there fast enough. I still can't figure out why he lied to me. It's beyond lying. Did he think I wouldn't find out? Or was he not even concerned about the embarrassment I might feel to learn from someone other than him that he was unemployed? Besides, what has he been doing the past month? He's left and returned to the house at normal hours, and he often claims to be busy working. He's gone out of his way to deceive me.

When I arrive, everyone is still at the pool. I march to the sliding glass door and pull it wide.

"Andrew! We need to talk. Now."

I couldn't alter the shrill tone of my voice if I tried.

He hurries inside, drops of water dripping on the tile floor where he stands. "Is everything okay?"

"Shut the door."

He obeys, pulling the blinds so no one can look inside. "Kate, you're scaring me. Is everything okay?" Then, as though the answer is simple, he purses his lips. "Did you see Paul again?"

"No." In this moment, the accusation seems ridiculous. Paul could quite possibly be a figment of my own paranoid imagination, but the situation with Andrew is something I can't ignore. "Dana called. She told me José said you're not working for the company anymore."

I hold eye contact, but his expression is blank. Finally, he says, "He doesn't know the specifics."

"Then please. Tell me."

"I left the company last month."

"And you didn't tell me?"

"The last thing I wanted to do was upset you before our vacation."

"What about the weeks between then and now? You left each morning, returned at night like you normally would. What were you doing during that time, other than actively hiding the fact you'd quit your job?"

"I just kept myself busy. It's not like I lost everything overnight. I still had some loose ends that needed tying up. Sometimes I'd meet up with some of the guys from Second Chances to talk about it."

"Your friends online know about this? But you didn't tell me?"

"Don't talk about it with that condescending voice."

"I'm sorry, Andrew, but I feel blindsided. What were you thinking? What could have possibly possessed you to quit your job?"

"I was just sick of it. The year's been difficult enough. We were just starting to get back to a place where things were better. I needed to eliminate anything that was weighing me down, and at the top of that list was my boss' crap."

"You've never liked your boss but if you wanted to leave the company, it's something we should have talked about together. We could have set up a plan, one that definitely wouldn't have included a two-week vacation. Why do this now?"

"If this year has done anything for me, it's put things into perspective. I can always find another job. I'm not going to let something like that ruin my time with you and the kids."

"What about the perspective of being responsible? We have kids. Bills. You can't just cut our income in half on a whim!"

"Do you think in the last moments of a person's life, they're thinking about their mortgage? Their bills? They're thinking about their family. Loved ones. Happiness. That's what life is about, Kate. Nothing else matters."

The air in the room turns thick, like it's squeezing into my lungs. I stare at Andrew.

"No one is talking about death. I'm talking about life. We can't live without a house. We can't live without food and electricity and money. Why are we here pretending like everything is okay?"

"Because it is." He clasps my hands between his. "We have each other and the kids. That's what this week is about."

My cheeks are flushed, my eyes brimming with tears. I'm angry with Andrew for his impulsivity, hurt by his deception. But in this moment, I'm also concerned about his state of mind.

"You think you're making positive changes, Andrew, but all you're doing is pushing this family apart."

"Don't say that." He sounds wounded. "You have to believe me when I say that's the last thing I want to do."

"You're not being there for us the way we need you to. You weren't there for Noah when he needed you. You tried confronting Willow, but all that did was shame her. Now this. I don't know what's gotten into you, but you can't bring us closer together by trying to take control of everything."

"I thought that's what you wanted me to do. Be a man."

"Right now you're acting like a very selfish man. Like my dad." The slip was so sudden, so honest. "You're not acting like the man I fell in love with."

"Yeah, well a lot has changed since then." He laughs. "Really, the last thing I want is to go over this today. Can we please just forget about it? Let's just go out on the boat, enjoy our time together."

"No." I laugh, cruelly. "I'm not going on the boat with you."

"But you said—"

"That was before, okay? I've never been a fan of the water. You know that, and yet you pressure me to go anyway. I'm staying back."

"Kate, you can't. Please don't ruin this."

"Don't you dare say I'm the one ruining anything. I'm the one trying to put all the pieces back together. You don't get to lie to me for the past month and then say I'm ruining what we have."

The sliding door swooshes open, and a large hand pushes back the curtains. Vincent stands in the doorway. He looks around the room, his gaze landing on both of us. "If we're going to go, we best do it now. The storm will be here before we know it."

Andrew nods, then looks back at me. His voice is sheepish. "Kate, please. Come with us."

"No." I turn, careful not to look either Andrew or Vincent in the eyes.

CHAPTER 34

Now

I storm into the bathroom, locking the door behind me. My anger has exhausted me, it seems, with my sweaty skin and flushed cheeks and labored breath. I turn on the sink and splash water onto my face, hoping the cold temperature will level out my emotions.

I can't believe Andrew would quit his job without telling me, then try to justify his actions. In all the ways he's acted selfishly since the invasion, this is the most outrageous. How could he leave his job, forfeit half our income, without even running it by me? Worse, he's paraded around for the entire time we've been on vacation as though he has nothing to hide. He's even talked about completing work while we've been here; he's completely gone out of his way to deceive me. When I finally look in the mirror, I see a tired, haggard reflection, a woman who is on the brink of losing what little patience she has left.

I exit the bathroom, jumping back in an instant when I realize there's another person lurking in the hallway. It's Vincent, seemingly waiting for his turn to use the hall bathroom.

"You scared me," I say, clapping a hand over my chest to calm my beating heart.

"I have to stop making a habit of that." He smiles.

He does have an almost phantom-like quality. Ever since he arrived at the house, he's seemed to appear in quiet, unsuspecting moments, like a ghost. I move to the left, giving him access to the bathroom, but he stands still.

"I couldn't help overhearing your argument with Andrew. I wanted to make sure you're all right."

"I'm fine, Vincent," I say coldly. Unlike Andrew, I'm not used to sharing my emotions with strangers, and I resent the fact Vincent knows as much as he does about our lives. "You don't have any reason to worry about me."

"I hope you know that everything Andrew has done in the past few weeks has been to make himself happier so he can enjoy more time with his family. He's not making any of these rash decisions to upset you."

A ripple of anger returns. Who does this man think he is to talk to me about my family? My marriage?

"If you don't mind, it's a personal matter and I don't wish to speak about it."

"I know, I know." He looks down, as though he's seriously considering what I've just said. "You're going through a sensitive situation, but that's part of what Second Chances is about. All these feelings and issues we've been told we're not supposed to think about, we can share with each other."

"So, you knew that Andrew had left his job?"

"Yes, I did."

I cross my arms over my body. "And did you encourage him not to tell me?"

"No, nothing like that. The group isn't about encouraging people to act one way or another. It's about allowing people the freedom to act on what they're really feeling inside." His gaze rises over my shoulder, staring away from me. "When I first joined, I was the worst about keeping my emotions inside—to the point I was on the verge of bursting. Once I started being honest with myself, my entire life changed. And I've found a new purpose, encouraging other men, like Andrew, to follow the same path. Get the most out of life in the small amount of time we're here. I can honestly say I've gone my entire life without realizing my purpose, until now."

I would label Vincent as patronizing, but I think he's so lost in his own spiel he doesn't realize how he comes off. He believes what he's saying, every part of it. I can tell.

"I appreciate your friendship with Andrew," I say, stumbling to find a proper end to this conversation. "But there are certain things I need to work out with *him*. If you'll excuse me."

I push past him, trying to enter my bedroom.

"Kate, I wish you would join us on the boat today." His voice is sterner this time.

"I don't think so—" I try to shut the bedroom door, but he holds out an arm to stop me.

"Please, Kate. Do this for your family. Give them this memory."

I open the door wider, pushing my body forward. "No," I say. I hold eye contact until he nods and walks away.

With the door shut, my heart is racing again. That confrontation was unexpected, and I feel chilled. Did he think a few minutes of conversation would change my mind about the boat? Especially having just found out about Andrew's betrayal.

Andrew said he invited Vincent over these last few days to protect us from Paul, but after that conversation, I wonder if Andrew is being too trusting. How well does he know Vincent, or any of these men for that matter? What if he's being played? That brief interaction made me feel like I was talking to a con man, not a protector.

My mind thinks back to the jammer. We found it the night before Vincent came over. What if he planted it there earlier in the week, and his plan all along was to reach out to us? I can't think of what his motive would be, unless… unless he somehow has a connection to Paul. It's a far-fetched theory, but who else would have enough access to do Paul's bidding? Paul is smart enough to know how risky it is for him to contact us. He's been making threats in his letters for months—since right around the time Andrew joined Second Chances. What if this friendship has been a fraud from the start, and Vincent isn't who he says he is?

I rush to the back patio, hoping to catch Andrew before they take out the boat. It's too late; they're already a few feet away from the dock, sailing toward the horizon. I wave my arms, but it's useless. No one is looking back, and even if they did, they wouldn't have any reason to think I'm alarmed.

If Vincent is helping Paul, I don't believe he'd do anything to my family without me there. At this point, I think Paul is as determined to punish me as he is to take Willow. What I need to do is find some sort of proof that Vincent isn't who he says he is. But how?

Looking around the condo, there's no trace Vincent has been inside. He's not left a bag of any sort. The only item I have that might belong to him is the jammer. I go back into the bedroom, retrieving it from the nightstand. I inspect it, much closer than I did the first time I found it. It's mostly nondescript, so I type the brand name, West Coast Surveillance, into Andrew's computer. I scroll through the company website, seeing if there's anything that might tell me more about who purchased the unit, if it can only be bought by police officers, perhaps. Anything that might be connected to Vincent.

I click on the tab that reads customer support. *Have a problem with your device?* the advert reads. *Enter the item number and someone from our management department will reach out to you shortly.*

I look at the bottom of the device, and, sure enough, there's an eight-digit number. I type the code into the form online and provide my email address as a contact. It's a long shot, but if I can prove this device was planted by Vincent, maybe Andrew will understand what a potential threat he might be.

I press send on my request and wait.

CHAPTER 35

1 Month Ago

As promised, Detective Barnes continued to contact the Brooks family, usually via email. After a month passed, he asked if he could come by their house to speak to them in person.

He arrived shortly after lunch. The kids had been coaxed into going out. Andrew and Kate were the only ones at home, anxiously waiting to hear what their visitor had to say.

"You're probably wondering why I asked to visit." Barnes cleared his throat, and Kate picked up on a slight stutter. *He's still new*, she told herself. At least to Hidden Oaks. He must have felt as much an outsider as he looked.

"I assumed it was about the letters we received," Kate said. She looked over at Andrew for support, but his gaze was focused on the carpet.

"Yes, your husband has given me copies of those." He glanced at Andrew, then back at Kate. "We still can't confirm how Paul is getting those letters delivered, but that's not what I'm here about."

"Is there something else?" Andrew asked. He was fully attentive now, leaned over with his elbows balancing on his legs.

"We've had a setback when it comes to the trial," Barnes said. "The judge has granted Paul bail. The trial date hasn't changed, but he'll no longer be in jail while awaiting his court date."

"What?" Kate felt her body jolting forward, her volume raising. "He's getting out of jail?"

"He's getting out of jail, but not out of these charges. There will still be a trial, but given the nature of—"

"The nature of his crimes is precisely why Detective Marsh said this wouldn't be a possibility. She promised he would remain behind bars until his conviction."

"He's being charged with a violent crime, yes. But this is also his first violent offense. His lawyers were able to pull it off, and there's nothing I, or anyone else in the department, could have done to stop it."

Kate sat back. How desperately she wished Detective Marsh were here. Perhaps what Barnes said was true, that even she wouldn't have been able to stop a judge from making this decision, but she believed Marsh would have done everything in her ability to keep it from happening. And if she still couldn't, Kate would have accepted the news better from her, as opposed to this stranger.

"The letters he's been sending violate the order of protection we have against him. Surely if the judge knew about that he wouldn't have allowed him out on bail." Andrew's voice was calm. Kate, in the midst of her emotional reaction, hadn't thought of this. She could only envision the looming danger.

"You're right, and we did let the attorneys know you were receiving letters. The problem is, we still can't prove whether or not the person who sent the letters is Paul."

"I can't believe this." She was standing now, looking out the window, her arms crossed over her body. Very similar to her stance on that day back in September when Detective Marsh had first dropped Paul's name.

"I'm sorry I have to share this news. I know how difficult this must be for you." He paused. "The good news is Paul Gunter hasn't been released yet. The bail amount is high, considering the magnitude of his charges. I'd say it'll be another week or two before he's out. Maybe three."

Kate looked down. Barnes might have assumed this news would make them feel better, but all it did was start a timer in Kate's head, each second counting down to the point when they would no longer feel safe.

"Will you let us know when he's out?" Andrew asked.

"Of course. I'll stay in contact." He stood. "And please, let me know if you receive any more letters. They could make a difference in whether or not he's actually released."

"I'm no longer worried about the letters," Kate said under breath, her back to both men.

"I'm sorry this isn't what you want to hear. You'll contact me if you need anything?"

This question was to both of them, but only Andrew answered. Kate was still staring out the window as Barnes left. She watched him walk to his car, slide behind the driver's seat and drive away.

Andrew came up behind her. He put a hand on her shoulder. "Are you okay?"

"No, I'm not. This is the worst thing that could happen."

Perhaps that wasn't true. Paul could do worse things to them. He'd already tried, but knowing he would be released from prison meant he'd have the opportunity to hurt them again. Kate didn't think she could live under that threat.

"I can't cope with him being out. It wasn't supposed to be this way. What will we tell the kids?"

"Maybe we don't have to tell them anything."

"Are you crazy? They have to be on the look out for him. For anything suspicious. He's already tried seeing Willow in person."

"I'm not suggesting we lie to them." He looked down, rubbing the skin underneath his jaw. "Maybe we could just distract them. Get them out of town for a bit."

"We can't run away from this forever."

"Not forever. But it's summer. Maybe some time away together would do some good. For all of us."

"Like a vacation?"

"Yes, a vacation," Andrew said, his voice optimistic.

They hadn't talked about a vacation all year. It didn't seem right. The vacation they'd taken just weeks before the attack was the last time Kate remembered her family being truly happy. She wondered if Andrew thought the same.

"When would we even go? You've been so busy with work."

"I've been busy trying to close this account, which should happen at the end of the month. It's perfect timing, really. We could leave town right before—"

His voice trailed away, but Kate knew what he wouldn't say. Right before Paul was released, if Detective Barnes' timeline checked out.

"Just think about it," Andrew said, sitting beside her on the bed. He placed his hands on her shoulders and began to rub. "We can sit around here, driving ourselves crazy. Losing sleep at night. Looking over our shoulders. Or we can enjoy a few days at the beach. Drinks by the dock. Nights where the kids take off, and we're left to our own devices."

Kate looked at him and couldn't help but smile. He seemed joyful, happier than she could remember in a long time. She didn't have it in her to shoot him down, even though her own body was filling with dread. He was trying, which is all she had asked him to do. Maybe, instead of living and dying in her own head, she should try back.

"We'll talk about it," she said, even if she didn't feel fully committed. "If there are any places open."

"There are always places available," Andrew said, climbing the stairs that led to their bedroom.

She imagined he was searching for rentals on his computer. Their usual hotel would be booked. Rather than join him, Kate wandered into the kitchen. She didn't want her own lack of enthusiasm to dampen his. Both children were back now and in the yard, and she watched them from the kitchen window. Noah was shooting a basketball, and Willow was swaying in a hammock, her familiar earbuds in.

Her children, she realized, were content wherever they went, as long as they felt safe and protected. Her children could sense that happiness in their own mother, picking up on her feelings like vibrations. When she was afraid and vulnerable, they sensed it. When she was confident and at peace, they sensed that too. It wasn't Kate's fault she'd lost her sense of security in the past year, but she was the only person responsible for finding it again. And if she needed just a little more time to do it, if she needed to find that peace in a different setting, so be it.

She went upstairs to help Andrew weigh the pros and cons of the rentals he had selected.

CHAPTER 36

Now

I'm pacing across the living room. Not even ten minutes after I send the request, my phone buzzes, but it's not an email, it's a phone call. I answer, and am surprised to hear Detective Marsh's voice.

"Sorry it's been so long," she says. "I've been meaning to check in with you since the move, but life has been pretty hectic. As I'm sure you noticed, my phone number has changed."

"Not a problem," I say. I've been trying to reach Detective Marsh since I first got word Paul was being released. Detective Barnes has been forthcoming, but Marsh has a way of putting me at ease. If she tells me there's no way Paul Gunter will be able to reach us, I might believe her.

I feel my chest flutter with anxiety. "I don't want to bother you. I realize this is no longer your case."

"If you were a bother, I wouldn't have called back." She sounds sincere. "What's going on?"

I take a deep breath, holding the air a few seconds before slowly exhaling. "I've been struggling ever since we learned Paul was released. When I think our lives are back to normal, we learn he's out there again. It's brought up all those old feelings."

There's a pause. "Kate, I'm sorry. I think—"

"I know, I know. I'm in my own head. There are tons of procedures in place to keep him away from us, but life was a lot easier when I knew he was still behind bars. Knowing he's back on the streets—I don't feel safe anymore. We're on vacation, and I keep thinking I see him. And we've been finding things in our house, things I think were left by Paul. I know it's out there, and I don't have any proof, but I think Paul has followed us here."

Another pause. Then, "What makes you think Paul Gunter has been released?"

I squint in confusion.

"Detective Barnes told us Paul was released two weeks ago."

"I looked up the status of your case before I called you, just in case there were any updates." Marsh exhales. "Paul Gunter is still in jail. His request for bail was denied. He'll be there until the trial later this fall."

I lean forward, raking three fingers against my forehead. "That can't be right. Detective Barnes told us. We've had multiple conversations about it. The whole reason we planned this vacation is because we didn't want to be in Hidden Oaks when Paul was released."

"Tell you what, let me put you on hold while I make a quick call." It sounds like she's playing along, but I can tell her voice is strained.

"Please. I don't understand. Surely—"

"Kate, it makes perfect sense that Paul's release would upset you. That's why I want to get the facts. Give me a minute."

There's dead air on the line, but the call is still connected.

This wasn't the information I was expecting, and Marsh's response has spurred a reaction in my body, my hands shaking, and my toes clenched. I have to remind myself to breathe, otherwise I hold in all the air until my head feels fizzy.

There's no way what Detective Barnes told us could have been misunderstood. It's impossible. Paul's release was the basis for this entire vacation. It's what we've dreaded most about returning home. It caused the backslide we've experienced as a family in the past month, my more present anxiety and Andrew's obvious insecurity.

And it wasn't only one conversation with Detective Barnes. We had multiple discussions. Barnes has communicated with Andrew much more, but I've seen him in person at least twice.

If Paul isn't being released, then why would Barnes insist otherwise? Why has everything felt as though it were crumbling this past month? Why are we even here?

"Kate, are you still there?" Marsh is back on the line.

"Yes."

"Tell me one more time," she begins, her voice slow like she's reciting an oral exam. "Who was it that told you Paul was being released?"

"Detective Barnes," I answer back. "You told us that he would be taking over our case once you were transferred. He reached out a month or so after you left, then another month after that to tell us Paul was being released."

"Problem is, I just spoke with Detective Barnes. He told me he's not spoken to you at all. Or your husband. He said he's had trouble contacting you."

My shoulders drop and I raise a hand in frustration. "That's not right. I'm telling you, he told us about Paul's release numerous times. Both Andrew and I met him."

"What's Detective Barnes look like?" she asks, her words clipped.

"Short. Scrawny. Dark blond hair."

"I met Barnes before he took over my job, and he doesn't fit your description in the least. He's tall, like basketball player tall. He's bald, certainly not blond. I'm not sure who you talked to, but it wasn't Barnes."

The thumping in my chest picks up pace. "I don't understand. Why would someone pretend to be him?"

"Don't know that either. But I can tell you this, Paul Gunter is definitely still in jail. He hasn't been released, and the minute the idea is even brought up, you'll be the first notified."

I should be relieved Paul is incarcerated, and I am, but I can't get over this deception. "Don't you think it's odd that someone would try to impersonate a cop?"

"Odd and illegal. I'm going to write down everything you've told me and forward it over to Hidden Oaks PD. And I'll give Barnes your number and make sure he calls you directly. You two should probably go over all of this together."

"Do you think Paul is behind this? Do you think he's hired someone to keep an eye on us for him?"

"It's a long shot," she says, then adds, "but it's a possibility. That's why you need to talk with Barnes. Either someone is trying to fool you or there's some guy walking around claiming to be him."

"None of this makes sense—"

"Did you say you're out of town right now?" she cuts me off, but not to be rude. This is how she operates when she's trying to collect as much information as possible. I remember from when she was on our case. She's more disturbed by this situation with the fake Detective Barnes than she wants to let on.

"Yes. We rented a beach house a few hours away."

"Good news is, Paul is still behind bars, so you don't have to worry about him when you return home."

I may no longer have Paul to worry about, but I'm fearing something. What, I don't know.

CHAPTER 37

Now

The house is quiet. The cool air in the bedroom prickles at my shoulders as I charge up Andrew's computer for a second time. I distinctly remember him telling me he'd received emails from Detective Barnes, updates about Paul's release date. This might be my best chance at figuring out who is impersonating the new detective. If I can find written proof, it might lead me toward something.

I immediately click on his email icon, scrolling through his most recent messages. Almost all of them are from names I don't recognize. Nothing in his recent inbox looks like it was sent by a Detective Barnes.

In the search bar, I type Barnes, hoping something will pop up. Maybe he's moved those messages to a separate folder, or they're stored somewhere else on his computer. The search produces results, but the name "Barnes" is only found in the body of messages, not as a sender or recipient.

I click on the first one that highlights the name. It's an email between Andrew and a man named Trent.

I've told her Detective Barnes contacted me with the exact dates. We've got the place booked for the first two weeks in August.

Does she need another visit from Barnes? Trent asks.

No, Andrew says. *I think we're good.*

What the hell is this? Who is Trent, and why is Andrew talking to him about Detective Barnes? The name Trent sounds familiar, but I can't remember how I know him. I don't think it's one of his co-workers, and it's definitely not someone we know mutually. Suddenly, there's a flash of memory. The person who I'd once heard screaming on the other end of the phone. Not at Andrew, but to him, venting about his ex-wife. I'd been taken aback by the harshness in his voice. That's why I remember.

Trent. He's a member of Second Chances.

I click on his name. There are dozens of emails between them. And there's several more that discuss Detective Barnes.

His name is Detective Barnes, Andrew says in one. *He's taking over the case. This could be the perfect opportunity.*

I don't know, Trent replies. *I'm not comfortable impersonating a cop.*

It's just a couple of phone calls. Maybe a visit by the house. Vincent thinks it's the best course of action.

That seems really personal, man. I don't know if I can pull it off.

Sure you can. I think she might have seen Rog onscreen, and Vincent can't really be seen right now, Andrew responds.

As my eyes scan their correspondence, my heart beats faster. I cover my mouth in shock but find it impossible to look away from the screen. For whatever reason, it appears Andrew asked one of his friends from Second Chances to impersonate a police officer. Why? To fool me? Maybe he planned this entire trip as a way to finally prove to me he can be a protector, so he can be the hero for once. Maybe he needed me to think Paul Gunter was released in order to do that. And what does Vincent have to do with any of this? Was it his idea?

At the end of the email, there's a link that says SC Private Chat. I click on it, but I'm denied access. It seems whatever has been discussed on this forum has already been erased. That doesn't dampen my desire to get to the bottom of this, though. Something strange is happening, and I'm convinced Vincent is behind it.

I check the clock in the corner of the room. If they stick to the schedule, Andrew and the others won't be back for another hour, at least.

That gives me plenty of time to find out everything I can about Andrew's friends.

CHAPTER 38

Now

This entire time, I believed Second Chances was helping Andrew, not filling his head with twisted ideas. I don't trust Vincent and I feel a wave of nausea setting in at the idea he's currently at sea with my children. Since the first day we met, I questioned who he really was, but Andrew seemed so convinced he was here to help us. I don't buy that anymore; he's encouraged Andrew to withhold information from me, openly lie. That's not the husband I know, and I can't help thinking he's been duped. It seems as though Vincent is building up toward something, though what I don't know.

I wonder if Paul is still orchestrating this somehow; maybe he knew there was no way he could be released, so he's instructed Vincent and this Trent character to keep tabs on us. Andrew thinks he's bonding with like-minded men, but this could be yet another ruse Paul has arranged.

I need to know more about the third member of the gang. I've heard Andrew talk about him before, but I always thought he was saying the name Raj. Turns out they call him "Rog"—short for Rogers. I rush back to the computer, trying to see if any of the messages reveal his first name. It doesn't take much searching through the history to find it: Cal Rogers.

I type the name into the computer. For some reason, it sounds more familiar than it should. Unfortunately, the online nature of the group means these people could be based anywhere; they're not necessarily in Hidden Oaks, or even our state.

At the top of the page, there are numerous links to various LinkedIn users named Cal Rogers.

Below that, are recent news articles. One catches my eye, and I click it.

Rogers Family Massacre.

Isn't that what the television reporter was talking about at the café?

It can't be the same Cal Rogers. Andrew wouldn't be friends with a person like that.

I scroll through hurriedly, hoping there will be a picture attached. If I see his face, I'll be able to tell if I recognize him from Andrew's group chats. Finally, I find one. It's a family of four. The wife has blonde hair cut just above her shoulders. Her children are standing in front of her: both the boy and the girl have dark hair and eyes.

Behind them, stands their father. Cal Rogers.

I know I've seen him before. I walked in on one of his video chats with Andrew. I only caught a glimpse of him, but it was enough to know I'm staring at a photo of the same man now.

What Went Wrong?

Authorities are seeking information about what might have taken place inside the Rogers household this past Friday night. Daphne Rogers, 48, was found on Sunday afternoon beside her two children, Zachary, 17, and Rose, 16. All family members died from a single gunshot wound to the head. Cal Rogers, 47, was found in the family's basement. He also died from a gunshot wound, although several sources are reporting that his injury may have been self-inflicted.

"I just don't understand," says Yvonne Westbrook, their neighbor across the street. "They were a perfectly normal family. There were never any signs of problems. I don't get how something like this could happen."

When asked how she would describe Cal Rogers, Westbrook said he was "quiet, shy, but always involved with his family." No one in the family had criminal records, and there were never any suspicions of domestic violence. Although Cal Rogers reportedly lost his job last month, a close friend says the family was recovering and doing better than ever.

"It just doesn't make sense," said our source. "You don't expect something like that to happen to a family like this."

If you have any information about the Rogers family, please contact San Diego PD.

My eyes find Cal Rogers' face. He's smiling, a hand placed on the shoulder of each child. He's wearing a belt and tie and glasses. He doesn't look like a killer. Doesn't look like the type of person who could murder his whole family and then kill himself. And yet, the article suggests that's the working theory.

My body shivers. I'm sickened that Andrew was ever cordial with Cal Rogers. How could he be connected to someone capable of committing such a heinous crime? Then again, as Cal's own neighbors attest, there was no way of predicting he was so fragile.

The men in the group should have known. They are being open with each other in a way they feel they can't with the people in their lives. This camaraderie is supposed to help them, not push them in the opposite direction.

I grab my cell phone and try calling Willow, then Noah. Both their phones go straight to voicemail. They're too far out at sea. My own phone is about to die, so I plug it into the charger in the living room. Back at the computer, I retrace the messages, trying to see if there's anything else that might make sense of what happened to the Rogers family. I halt when I stumble across Vincent's full name: Vincent Leroy Fowler.

I type it into the computer, curious to see what comes up.

The page fills with recent news articles, nothing else.

Police Name Fowler Person of Interest in Family Murders

Police are still asking for any information that might lead to the whereabouts of Vincent Leroy Fowler. It's been over a month since investigators tried to find him in the wake of his family's murder.

I clasp a hand over my open mouth, continuing to read.

His wife and teenage daughters were murdered inside their home. It wasn't until the local high school conducted a welfare check that the bodies were discovered. No one has had any contact with Vincent Fowler since that time.

"They were two very sweet girls," Sherriff Hickey says. "And by all accounts, Melissa Fowler loved her family. We don't know what happened behind closed doors that night, but we're wanting to talk with Vincent Fowler so we can find out."

Below the article is a picture of Vincent. He looks crueler than he does in person. Dangerous. There's also some noticeable changes. The beard and head of hair he sports in the picture are gone now, just as his suit has been replaced with tourist-wear. I'm surprised he could have avoided detection from the police this long, but it's been over two months since that article was written, and he's clearly free.

A new terror takes over me. What if Cal Rogers wasn't involved in his family's murder after all? What if Vincent was responsible? If he has the gall to hurt his own family, what would stop him from destroying someone else's? I think back to what Vincent said earlier. About finding his purpose, a way to help other men. Whether he's working with Paul or not, it appears Andrew has underestimated the danger of the man he's invited into our lives.

A notification flashes on the computer. I've received an email. It's an automated response from the jammer business, West Coast Surveillance.

Dear Customer,

Thank you for your inquiry. We've looked up your purchase information, and a customer representative will contact you shortly.

Product Number: 80097564
Customer Name: V. Fowler

"Knock, knock."

I jump back in my seat. The fear grips tighter when I see Vincent standing in the doorway.

CHAPTER 39

Now

I stand, hurriedly, looking out the window. There's a momentary rush of relief when I see Noah and Willow still standing on the boat. They're safe, for now.

I look back at Vincent and try to smile, even though the thought of being near him makes me tremble. "You're back."

"The storm is settling in." He points outside. My gaze follows his finger, and now I see the dark, rolling clouds spreading across the sky, like thick billows of smoke.

"Say, you okay?" Vincent asks. "You look a little pale."

"Yeah. Yes." I inhale deeply through my nose, trying desperately to relax my posture. "I'm fine."

He stares at me a beat longer, then walks back into the hallway.

I hurry back over to the computer and exit Andrew's email. I thought they wouldn't be back for at least another half hour, although time now seems an impossible concept to grasp. I can see through the window that Andrew and the children are still on the dock, trying to cover all the equipment before the storm sets in.

I race down the hallway to the living room where I'd left my phone on the charger. I need to call the police, even if I'm forced to hang up. They'll at least trace the call and send someone to check the address, and I'll have a way of getting the kids away from Vincent.

Beside the sofa, where I'd left it only moments ago, only the charger remains.

My phone is gone.

I hear footsteps wandering through the house. It must be Vincent, and he must have taken my phone.

I hurry back to the laptop in the other room, hoping I can pull up my own email. I can message Detective Marsh or Aster, or maybe there's even a way to alert the local police. Whatever I do, I need to do it quickly.

I'm typing in my password when the lights around me go off. We've lost power. *Shit*, I think, but at least the computer still has a charge. I try typing in the password and refreshing the page, but nothing loads. Nothing will load. The internet connection is lost.

The hairs on my skin stand on end, and there's a coldness seeping into my lungs, dispersing throughout my body like frost. *This can't be happening*, I think.

There's no way out. I have no phone. No electricity. No internet.

And my children are under the same roof as a man prepared to do the unthinkable.

I run outside to the dock. Willow and Noah are both on the boat. I'm determined to take them and leave this house immediately. Then I catch sight of Andrew, and my heart stalls. He doesn't know what Vincent's intentions are, that he's already responsible for the deaths of Cal Rogers and his family. It pains me to tell him that his plan to keep us safe has backfired, but I don't have a choice; if we don't get out of here now, we may not have another chance.

"You missed a beautiful day at sea," Andrew says, stepping onto the dock. "Although we did have a few casualties. The bag containing our phones went overboard."

"Which is, like, the worst thing that could happen," Willow says, her arms crossed over her body.

"No phones until we get back home," Noah says.

I slowly catch on to what's happening here. Vincent has found a way to disconnect us from everyone, and I shudder.

Andrew catches sight of my face. "Everything okay?"

"We need to get the children out of here right now. We need to leave."

"I need to wash up," says Willow.

Noah, behind her, says, "And I'm starving."

"Stop right there," I shout after them. There's an urgency in my voice that makes them halt immediately. "Don't go inside yet."

"Mom, it's about to storm," says Willow.

"I don't care. Just listen to me."

"Kate, what's going on?" Andrew sounds alarmed.

I've found out so much in the past hour, I don't have time to explain everything.

"We need to leave the house right now. We have to get away from Vincent," I whisper to Andrew so the kids won't hear.

"What are you talking about? We've been with him all day. He offered to cook dinner."

"Everything Vincent has told us about his family is a lie. His family was murdered, Andrew. And the police think he's responsible." I feel like I should pause, give him time to process, but each passing second is a threat to our safety. "You know your friend Cal? He's dead. His family, too. I think Vincent might have been involved."

Andrew squints and cocks his head to the side. "Kate, what are you talking about?"

"I know it sounds crazy, but there are articles that prove what I'm saying. The police assume he's on the run, and they're searching for him. I even looked up the jammer we found in the garage. It was registered in Vincent's name. *He* brought it into our house, not Paul." I don't tell him I believe Paul might be somehow pulling the strings from behind bars.

Andrew places his hands on my shoulders. "You're saying Cal is dead? And his entire family?"

"Yes. And I think Vincent is somehow at fault. It's too much a coincidence that his own family is dead, too. And now he's here with us. I'm afraid we're in danger."

"Mom, come on." Willow is irritated. "It's starting to rain."

Andrew ignores Willow. We both turn back and look at the house. The windows are dark because the power has been cut, and the howling wind is bending the leaves of the plants on the patio.

"The keys are inside. I'll come up with some excuse to get you out of the house. You take the kids somewhere safe. Somewhere public. He won't be as suspicious if I stay behind."

"But what if he hurts you?"

"All that matters is getting you and the kids away from him. If you're right, and he is here to hurt us, we need to stay one step ahead of him."

I'm elated he's not dismissing my concerns. The four of us walk up the ramp, droplets of rain sprinkling our shoulders. We enter the house together. Willow first, Andrew bringing up the rear.

Without electricity, the house is dark. Vincent has lit several candles, scattering them around the kitchen like little prayers.

"I hope you don't mind." He nods to the platter on the counter. "I spotted Noah's fish in the fridge. If we hurry, I might be able to bake it on the grill outside."

"What about the power?" Noah asks, looking around the dark room.

"Looks like a charcoal grill. We might have to eat in the dark, but at least we can have a good meal," Vincent says, not even a hint of something sinister in his voice. "You missed a lovely day of fishing, Kate. I don't know if Andrew told you, but I wanted to cook dinner tonight. It's my way of thanking you for being so welcoming to me the past couple of days."

"That's very kind, Vincent." I wander over to the island and look for the car keys. They aren't there. "I'm just going to run a quick errand first."

"Oh?"

"Yeah, Kate wanted to snap a picture of the kids," Andrew says, gently placing his jacket on the counter. "Before we leave."

"Here's an idea," Vincent says. "Why don't I take a picture of the four of you?"

"That's nice, really," I say, still looking around the living room for the keys. "You should get busy cooking. It won't take us long."

I go into the bedroom, looking on the dressers and inside drawers.

"Willow? Noah?" I call into the other room. "Either of you seen my keys?"

"No," they shout back in unison.

I walk back to the living room to find Andrew sitting on the sofa. He looks deflated with his shoulders hunched and his gaze on the floor.

"I really need to find the keys," I say under my breath. By now the kids have gone to their rooms. We're the only two in the living room, although Vincent stands in the kitchen within earshot.

"I don't know where they are." Andrew looks up at me. "I'm sure the kids have misplaced them."

They're gone. Just like our cell phones. This is deliberate.

"What are we going to do?" I whisper desperately.

"I'll see if I left them on the boat." He stands quickly and exits the room. Without saying anything, Vincent follows him outside, and I fear he's aware that I'm on to whatever he's planning.

We're alone, but only for a minute. I march down the hallway. Willow is about to enter the bathroom when I jerk her arm, pulling her into Noah's room.

"Mom, what's your problem?"

"I need you both to listen to me," I say, making my voice as serious and clear as possible. "We need to get out of here. Now."

"Is something wrong?" asks Noah.

"Yes. We're not safe. I don't have time to explain. You need to come with me now, and whatever I say you need to do, you do it. Okay?"

My delivery must have worked because there isn't the angsty rebuttal I'm used to receiving. They both nod, then look at each other in mild confusion.

"Let's go. Now."

They follow me into the hallway. As we pass the living room, I look at the sliding glass doors. There's no sight of either Vincent or Andrew. We make it to the front door and open it.

Vincent is standing on the other side. We all jump.

"Did you find your keys?" he asks, offering up that loaded smile.

"We're just going to walk down to the nearest pier. Snap a few photos there."

My words are clipped, my panic threatening to break. I don't like being this close to him, and I'm frightened Andrew is nowhere to be found. What if Vincent has already hurt him?

Vincent takes a step closer, forcing us back inside. "I don't think you're going to want to do that. The wind is already picking up, and it's starting to rain. It's going to be one hell of a storm."

"We won't—"

"Let's get this dinner started," Vincent says, cutting me off. "I know the kids must be starving."

Across the room, the sliding glass door opens, and Andrew walks inside. He looks pasty, his hair wind-swept, his shoulders damp from the falling rain, but he's alive.

"I'm sorry, Kate," he says calmly. "Looks like we're stuck here."

There's something different about Andrew. The look he's giving me now isn't one of fear, but defiance.

In that moment, it hits me. Vincent might be here to hurt us, but Andrew is complicit.

Vincent, now fully inside, closes the front door.

He clicks the lock.

CHAPTER 40

Andrew

Andrew never knew his purpose, and yet finding one's path was something that was drilled into him at a young age. His father preached these ideals from the pulpit every Sunday, and in smaller, more intimate sessions around the dinner table during the rest of the week. Andrew didn't disbelieve his father; he had a relationship with God, but it never felt as intimate as the one his father claimed to have. It was more avuncular, clearly there, but somewhat disconnected.

He longed for a deeper connection with the world around him. After his lonely childhood as the minister's son, he was happy to take on the role of brother. His fraternity fostered friendships he'd never had before. For the first time, he found himself on the cusp of belonging. He rejoiced in the brotherhood.

And yet, Andrew knew he was always a little different. He was a beta, a helper, a friend of. Most of the time, he watched festivities from the sidelines, but this didn't leave him bitter. Detachment wasn't an unfamiliar feeling.

He sometimes wondered if he inherited this docility from his mother. Marsha Brooks was a kind woman, gifted musically, but she was also extremely submissive. She didn't form her own opinions, instead allowing Simon Brooks and the gospel to lead her way.

That was what first attracted Andrew to Kate: she was so wildly different from the parents he'd known. She was full of opinions, passions that were impossible to thwart. She was also religious (a requirement, Andrew admitted, for any future wife) but she had other callings that made her well-rounded, and it was these characteristics that left Andrew mesmerized.

He couldn't believe he'd actually caught her attention. He had some experience with girls, usually the drunken cast-offs of his fraternity buddies, but nothing serious, no one who ever penetrated his soul the way Kate did. Everyone knew she was dating another fraternity brother at the time, but Kate didn't seem to care. And the more Andrew got to know her, the more obvious it became that Paul Gunter was not a good match for her. What they had couldn't hold a flame to what he was building with Kate.

And so, their relationship progressed at lightning speed. In many ways, Kate became his new religion. She fulfilled him in a way no message or sermon ever had, and he was humbled to be in her presence. Then, the pregnancy. Andrew had to hide his elation. It wasn't hard; all he had to do was think of his parents' reaction when they learned he'd conceived a child out of wedlock. Even with that stumble, he knew his parents would welcome Kate with open arms. They'd be as transfixed by her as he was.

Their wedding was small and intimate, all pictures taken before the baby started to show. By the time Willow was born, they were a happy family. His parents loved Kate, and Andrew adored Kate's mother, although his relationship with his father-in-law always felt somewhat removed; he reminded him too much of some of his alpha fraternity brothers. The ability for everyone to get along was an added bonus, but the true prize was his future with Kate, and he didn't believe either one of them could have been happier.

Parenthood produced some challenges; they were still so young themselves. And he knew Kate had made bigger sacrifices. She'd forfeited her scholarship, had less time to write with each passing day. She said she didn't mind, but he could see the responsibilities weighing on her, slowly stripping away the vibrant woman he'd once known.

By the time Noah was born, they'd each settled into their new roles. He thought they'd accepted the choices they'd made as easily as they'd forgotten the ones they didn't. *This is life*, he told himself. Again, with a smile, *This is our life together.*

And then there was that night in August.

It had been Andrew's greatest failure, a loss he believed he would never recover from. Somewhere, in between the years and responsibilities, he'd lost it: the ability to take care of his family. Worse, he feared maybe he'd never had it at all.

And to top it off, the man who had attacked him was his former frat brother, Kate's ex-lover. He'd stormed back into their lives, as if to say, *you never deserved this. You never deserved them.*

A person always thinks they know how they'll react in certain situations—what he or she might do, what he or she might say. Truthfully, Andrew had never considered what would happen if an intruder entered his home in the middle of the night, and perhaps that was his first flaw. He hadn't prepared. But he did believe he would be able to protect his family when they needed him most, and at that, he had failed.

He tried to block out images from that night, ignore his own disappointment with himself. When that didn't work, he tried drowning out his thoughts with booze, but that too was an ineffective balm. The alcohol's warm effects were only temporary—when they relented, he was blindingly more aware of just how incapable he was.

And yet, he couldn't voice any of his regrets and fears; the latter seemed to grow in size every day. Fear that he wouldn't be able to protect Willow. Fear that Noah would end up just like him, a coward. Fear Kate would lose respect for him. He was no better equipped to help his family now than he was the night of the invasion.

Sweet, dewy Noah. He was like his father, maybe too much. Already he was being tormented by peers, singled out for not being brave enough. Andrew remembered those tortured feelings, and the only thing worse was imagining his son receiving such treatment now.

In an attempt to distance herself from that night, Willow was trying to grow up. His little girl was gone. Overnight, it seemed. Worse, she was dressing like a skank, pressing boundaries with her mother, giving Kate one more thing to worry about. She was spiraling and all because Andrew had failed to make her feel secure, as a father should.

Then again, was he her father? Paul Gunter didn't think so. Andrew remembered Paul in flashes; the two had never been close. Those glimpses in memory had stretched since the attack; he now had a clear image in his mind of someone loud, vocal, impulsive. The type who would break into another man's house, but would also fiercely defend what mattered to him—had that not been his true motive in the first place?

Kate insisted Paul couldn't be Willow's father, and he wanted to believe her. She could have had Paul or any other man of her choosing—she went with Andrew. Why? He wondered that then, and even more now. The short answer was love, but that alone wasn't a renewable resource, was it? Love was conditional, able to be altered by its environment. Maybe Kate, with her smart, strategic brain, had picked Andrew because he was the safer choice.

Sometimes, in his darkest moments, Andrew believed his family would be better off without him, but then he'd think about their lives after he was gone. They'd already suffered one trauma—losing their father and husband would only exacerbate those issues. Besides, he believed suicide was a selfish act, had been taught it was the greatest sin. If only there was a way he could protect his family, find happiness within himself, and put all these dark feelings behind him.

Something inside Andrew appeared to be fighting for attention, a sensation no greater than a whisper. As the months passed, the calling spoke louder, combining with his paranoia and insecurity, until it became a deafening howl he was too weak to ignore.

He was desperate for guidance, for a connection that he'd failed his entire life to create.

He was trapped on a vicious carousel of self-pity, until he found Second Chances, and the ride, at last, came to a halt.

CHAPTER 41

Now

The storm is fully upon us, darkening the skies and enhancing the dim shadows in the room. It feels like night, the flickering candles scattered across the living room and kitchen resembling a vigil. By now Willow and Noah sense the tension in the room, although they still aren't sure why I'm so alarmed.

"Let's sit at the table," Andrew says. He walks up, putting a hand on each child's shoulder. They obey, each picking a chair on opposite ends. They must be torn, wondering why I'm adamant about leaving while their father insists we stay. I sit between them at the head of the table, which leaves a clear view of Vincent in the kitchen.

Andrew takes a seat across from me. When I look at him, it's as though I'm seeing him for the first time. A stranger, in the form of my husband.

I recall everything I've uncovered up until now. The articles about the Rogers family didn't mention anything about a possible culprit; they believe Cal had murdered his family.

And although the jammer was registered in Vincent's name, it was stored in a bag from Hidden Oaks, our hometown.

Vincent isn't here to harm Andrew; the men from Second Chances are helping each other. It's no coincidence that two of his closest friends have lost their families, albeit in different ways. If the media theory is correct, Cal Rogers seems to have killed himself after his family's murder, and Vincent is very much alive and on the run.

I remember the messages exchanged between Andrew and Trent. It wasn't Vincent encouraging Trent to impersonate a cop, it was Andrew. He was pulling him into a scheme to fool me. He asked Trent to play the role of Detective Barnes. His sole purpose was to tell me that Paul was released from jail, but why? It wasn't even true.

I repeat the words back to myself, but this time they take on new meaning.

It wasn't even true.

Andrew wanted me to believe that Paul was being released. He wanted me to think our family was in danger because it would drive us away from Hidden Oaks and somewhere else. Here.

I think back to the other events of the past month that don't add up. Andrew quit his job and refused to tell me.

Who's thinking about their mortgage and bills before they die?

The letters started arriving at the house shortly before we received the news that Paul would be released. And I think back to how he reacted with Noah on the boat the other day. It was more than inaction. On the night of the invasion, he'd done nothing out of fear. On the boat, his delay seemed intentional. Maybe he'd meant to harm us then but backed out. And now Vincent is here to make sure Andrew carries out his original plan.

"Does it storm like this often?" Noah asks, breaking my thoughts, reminding me my children are part of this terrifying situation.

"We get a good one every now and then." Vincent winks. "Nothing too scary."

"Anyone thirsty?" Andrew walks into the kitchen and begins filling a pitcher of water.

"Nothing like some good food to eat while you're waiting out the storm," Vincent says, turning back to the fridge. "I think you'll enjoy this. It's a family recipe."

"How is your family?" I ask Vincent, trying to squeeze out more information.

He pauses, his back still to me, then continues messing with the platter.

"They're getting so old, no one has time for 'ol Dad anymore."

"It seems like you've been with us nonstop the past two days," I say dryly. "I'm sure they miss you."

"It's not often I get to meet up with one of the guys from Second Chances, and I didn't want to pass up the opportunity. People underestimate the power of a brotherhood. Through our greatest weaknesses, we've found strength in each other. That's what makes this group special."

"Have you spent time with any of the other members and their families?"

"Some."

I picture the Rogers family, their beautiful children reduced to nothing but an old family photograph in the newspaper. Was Vincent with Cal Rogers during his last moments, or was he simply the puppeteer, pulling strings from a safe distance?

"Mom, are you okay?" Willow asks. Her voice is low, but we're all too close for her words to go unheard.

"I'm fine," I say, keeping my eyes wide, hoping my smart girl is able to sense something in my expression.

"Mom is just bummed she missed out on the fun today," Andrew says, and for a minute, it sounds like he's back to normal. Is that why Vincent and Andrew were so insistent about me joining them? Did they plan to hurt us then? *Kill us then*, my mind corrects itself. After all, the Rogers and Fowler families aren't just hurt; they're dead.

"I actually have some news," I say. "I spoke with Detective Marsh."

"Really?" Andrew's voice climbs an octave.

"I'd tried reaching out to her before we came on vacation. She just now managed to get back to me. I wanted to ask her more details about Paul's case. She assured me Paul Gunter is still behind bars and will remain there a long, long time."

Both the children tense up. They're not used to hearing me say his name. They also have no reason to suspect Paul is anywhere else; we kept the news of his release from them. But now Andrew knows I'm aware of the ruse, and Vincent, too.

"And this is odd," I continue. "Turns out the person we've been communicating with over the past few months isn't actually Detective Barnes. Someone was pretending to be him and giving us false information."

"Why would someone do that?" asks Noah.

"I don't know."

Andrew's expression has fallen, and his shoulders are slumped. I know too much for him to offer up an easy explanation.

"Do you think this Paul guy had one of his friends try to scare us?" asks Willow.

"Something like that." This time, I lock eyes with Andrew. I see the shame on his face, the disappointment that his plan has been found out.

"Kate, I think you're jumping to conclusions," Andrew says.

"I don't think I am. I think I've got just about everything figured out."

"We're here, okay?" Andrew begins to pace about the room. "We're safe as long as we're together. That's all that matters."

"We need to go home," I say calmly. "There's nothing to fear there."

And there's everything to fear here, I think. Vincent's presence on our trip isn't coincidental. Nothing about our lives in recent months has been a coincidence. It's all been carefully orchestrated by Andrew, with the help of his friends, and I don't want to stick around to find out the rest.

"We can't do that." This time Andrew's voice is condescending and direct. "No keys. No phones. We're stuck here."

He's reminding me there's no escape. My chest rises and falls rapidly. I can feel a powerful wave trying to overwhelm me. There is danger in this room, swarming around my children and me. I have to find a way out of here. My eyes dart between Andrew and Vincent. I'm not sure how we can escape.

Then there's a knock on the door.

CHAPTER 42

Andrew

The men from Second Chances provided a different type of brotherhood, a more united form of family. Even though he'd not met any of them in person, it was frightening how easy it was to connect. Sure, their specific situations were different, their catalysts were unique, but the feelings—those were all the same.

Cal Rogers had failed his family. As much as he tried to blame his employer for his problems, eventually he admitted he was the one at fault. He'd mishandled his responsibilities at work, lost large sums of money. All this led to his eventual firing, which was the ultimate failure. He'd let his family down. His wife, Daphne, hadn't worked for the entirety of their marriage. Her greatest concerns revolved around whether they should landscape the front lawn or backyard first (in her mind, both would get done), and she prided herself on being the envy of her friends.

And their children were on the cusp of their own adulthood. Rose, her sweet sixteen approaching, would be needing a car soon. Their oldest, Zachary, was expecting a newer model to celebrate his acceptance into college. They had been begging him for a tour around Europe, prom dresses, sports equipment—all things that would be impossible to fund without Rogers' almighty salary. How could he explain to his family, who had so blindly followed his lead throughout their lives, that he could no longer afford these things? That they might have to sell their home (Daphne's true pride and joy) just to make ends meet? When he thought of the inevitable disappointments they'd face, the pious sneers they'd receive from former friends and neighbors, it sounded dramatic, but he'd very much rather die than put his family through that.

Trent's dilemma was more typical. His marriage was falling apart, his wife making their fight for custody an increasing struggle, but, like Cal, he stood witness as the life he knew, the family he loved, slipped through his fingers.

The divorce wasn't his fault. Stacey wouldn't stop hounding him. She refused to be happy with their life. She always wanted more, bigger, better. Trent hadn't grown up with much, just enough to let him know what really mattered in life. It wasn't your address. It wasn't how much money you had stashed away in a pension. It was family. Sure, Stacey was no longer in the picture. But his children? He couldn't go on without them.

Yet, it seemed that Stacey's new mission in life, now that she'd found a wealthier man and moved into a fancier neighborhood, was to eliminate Trent. She wanted to expel him. The worst part of it all was that she was winning this battle. Trent lacked education, an established career, the right connections. None of this had seemed to matter when Stacey agreed to marry him, back when she was begging him to knock her up and start playing house. Now that she had everything she wanted—all the things he couldn't provide—she wanted to leave him in the dust. It just wasn't fair.

Andrew listened to the men from Second Chances, connecting with some more than others. Perhaps what was most bizarre, what was really frightening, was how easy it was for him to relate to them. He hadn't walked the same path as Trent or Cal or the others, and yet he shared their sense of loss. Like theirs, his life had spun out of his control, thrusting him onto a different, darker path, one that seemed impossible to navigate on his own.

In the depths of that darkness, Vincent seemed to represent a light. A different way of looking at their situations. A theory, which at first felt like an outrageous suggestion, which slowly started to make sense. Life had numbed them, he said. Their wives and their kids had dulled their senses. Generations were being watered down, losing the strength that once made them capable of protection and control. There was only one way to get that control back: seize it. Carpe that effing diem and stop feeling sorry for yourself. If you didn't like how your life was unfolding, then damn well change it.

And if you didn't like the people joining you on your journey, well, that was changeable, too. For some men, like Vincent, it was fitting to leave their families behind and start over.

For others, like Cal and Andrew, their bravest action would be to stand by their families until the end, protect them as they ventured into the dark.

CHAPTER 43

Now

Vincent and Andrew look at each other. For a long, horrible moment, I fear they've invited others over. We're already at a disadvantage, the three of us obeying the dominating presence they hold over us. If more of their friends arrive, we may not have any hope at all.

Those thoughts scurry away when I recognize the look of confusion on their faces. Vincent and Andrew are as surprised to have a visitor as I am, which is a good sign.

There's a second knock, this time louder. Vincent gives a subtle nod, and Andrew goes to the front door and answers it.

"Sorry to bother you…"

The voice outside sounds both familiar and strange. I stand quickly, before Vincent can stop me, and position myself behind Andrew. I immediately recognize the person standing on our front porch as Dan, the man from the restaurant. He's wearing a dark raincoat with the hood over his head, droplets of rain sliding down the slick material.

"Hello, Dan," I say, my voice deliberately cheerful. "Andrew, this is Jan's husband. Remember me telling you about them?"

"Of course." He tries to sound friendly, but I can hear his irritation. "I believe I met your wife the other night."

"Yes, that's actually why I wanted to stop by. I feel awful about the whole thing, our girls getting your daughter in trouble like that. I pass your place on my way home, and I thought I'd swing by and introduce myself. Apologize on behalf of my daughters."

"It's not a problem," Andrew says.

"Kids will be kids. We understand that. We don't blame you or your girls," I say.

I have to think of a way to keep the conversation going. This could be my only opportunity to flee the house, or at least signal for help. I can't tell Dan what's actually going on here, not with Vincent so close to my children inside.

"I can promise you our girls don't give us much trouble, and I'm sorry we brought Willow back to you in such a state."

"We're just happy she came home safe," I say. "It seems like our daughter was in good hands."

Our daughter. Safe. I'm hoping these reminders will trigger something in Andrew and prevent him from doing whatever it is he has planned.

"Really, Dan, Willow is the one who should be apologizing to you. Come in and I'll let you speak with her."

"That's not necessary," Dan says. He seems embarrassed to be put on the spot, but I need to keep him here as long as possible. The minute he leaves, we'll be back in danger.

"Maybe it's not best to keep dragging this out," Andrew says, his voice a warning.

I ignore him. "Willow? Come here, please."

She slowly walks to meet us at the door, her eyes cutting across the kitchen at Vincent. She's picked up on the fact I'm agitated, that something is brewing beneath the surface.

"Do you remember Dan?" I ask.

"Yes." She looks down in shame.

"He came over to apologize about the other night. I told him you're the one who should be sorry."

"I am sorry," she says sheepishly, looking at me with questions in her eyes.

Andrew, still gripping the front door, looks like he's beginning to sweat. He's impatient. I can only drag this out for so much longer.

"We'll be heading home soon," I say. "Maybe Willow could come over and say goodbye to the girls?" If I can only get her out of the house, she'll remember what I told her earlier, and I trust she'll get someone else involved.

Andrew takes a step forward, creating a barrier between us and Dan. "I don't think that's a good idea. We were just about to sit down for dinner."

Dan looks at Andrew uneasily. "Right. Probably best not to get out in this mess anyway. I'm about to go home and call it a night."

Inside, the flame of hope is dwindling. We can't be left alone with Vincent and Andrew.

"It looks pretty dark in there," Dan says, moving his head to look beyond us.

"The power is out," says Andrew.

"Yeah, it gets tricky when these storms roll in. Say, I could probably look at your fuse box. I've picked up a few tricks over the years that might help."

"That's not—"

"That would be wonderful," I say, interrupting Andrew before he can finish. I place an arm on his shoulder and shove him out of the doorway. "Come on in."

Andrew, defeated, steps back so Dan can walk inside. He stands there a moment before closing the door. Noah is still seated at the table. Dan gives him a friendly wave. As we turn the corner, he catches sight of Vincent in the kitchen.

"Hello," Dan says. "Sorry to interrupt."

"Not a problem." Vincent marches over and gives Dan a hand-shake. He smiles. "I'm trying my best to prepare dinner, without the luxury of electricity at the moment."

"I'd say that's a struggle. Hopefully I can help you with that." He starts to walk forward, then turns back. "Say, you look familiar. Have we met before?"

"Are you local?"

"Yes. My wife and I both work at the hospital. Maybe I know you from there?"

"He used to be a cop," Noah says from the table.

"Could have been that then. You look so familiar."

"I moved to the area about six months ago. Maybe we've crossed paths before," Vincent says.

"Must be," Dan says. "I never forget a face."

Vincent offers another smile and returns to the stove.

"I'll show you the fuse box," I say, nudging him in the direction of the garage.

"Sure."

He follows me, and Andrew follows him. Right now, my plan is to simply extend his presence in the house for as long as possible. As we enter the garage, a flashlight leading our way, I squint in search of a paper or pen. Something I could write a message on. Of course, even that would be hard to do with Andrew so close.

"Here we go," Dan says, opening the lid of the breaker box. "Sometimes the system gets overwhelmed. You can give it a little flick, and the power will come back on. Care to hold the light up for me?"

I dangle it overhead. Beside me, Andrew stands with his arms folded. I hear the impatient tapping of his foot on the concrete.

"Dad?" It's Willow calling from the other room. "I need your help with something."

"In a minute." His tone is so harsh that Dan and I reflexively look over our shoulders.

"I can't get into the bathroom," she calls. "The door is jammed."

"Just a minute."

"Please, it's an emergency!"

"You better go help her," I whisper.

Andrew looks at Dan who is busy fiddling with the breaker box, then he stomps back into the house, leaving us alone in the dark.

"I think I found your problem," Dan says. "It looks like someone accidently flicked the main switch. This should fix—"

I stop his hand from touching the box and pull the flashlight close to my face.

"Dan, I need you to listen to me," I whisper. "That man in there, his name is Vincent Fowler. He's dangerous. I believe he wants to hurt our family, and I think Andrew might somehow be involved."

"Kate, what are you—"

"Vincent is on the run. I believe he plans on hurting us, and I'm scared. They've taken our phones. They've cut the power. I need you to leave here and call the police. Can you do that?"

"Sure." He nods, but he looks shaken. His eyes wide and watery.

I hear footsteps and shine my light back on the box.

"Fix the lights, and then leave."

He nods. He flicks the switch, and the room illuminates. When I turn, I see Andrew standing in the doorway.

I smile. "See? That was easy."

"Thank you, Dan," Andrew says as unenthusiastically as possible.

We walk back into the living room. Noah and Willow are still sitting at the dining room table. Vincent is in the kitchen chopping something on a cutting block. When he sees us, his face lights up like the room around us.

"Let there be light," he says, in a mock roar.

"Just a simple fix," Dan says. I can tell he's trying hard to disguise his nervousness.

"It makes it much easier to cook now," says Vincent. "Thank you for your time."

If Dan calls the police right away, someone should arrive within the next ten minutes. And if that doesn't pan out, now that the power is back on, I might have a chance at sneaking back to the computer and sending a message.

"Well, I suppose I should get going. This storm might knock it out again, but at least you have power for the time being." He holds out a hand to shake Andrew's, and I'm suddenly impressed at his ability to maintain composure. "Nice to meet you."

Andrew shakes his hand and nods.

"Thanks again for all your help," Vincent says, as Dan passes the kitchen en route to the front door.

"Nice meeting you, Vincent," Dan says. "Maybe I'll see you around."

My stomach clenches when I realize Vincent never said his name. Thankfully, he doesn't seem to pick up on the snafu. His gaze never leaves the counter as he continues chopping.

Dan's hand is on the doorknob when Vincent speaks.

"One more thing," he says, moving quickly around the corner.

Dan pauses, turning to see what he wants.

It's then that I see the knife in Vincent's hand. He plunges the blade into Dan's stomach, pulls back, before punching another vicious stab.

Dan's eyes are wide, flooded with equal parts fear and surprise. Vincent steps away from him, leaving Dan to sink to his knees, before collapsing on the floor.

Then, like I'm reliving that terrifying night from a year ago, I hear Willow scream.

CHAPTER 44

Vincent

Vincent hadn't always been an angry person.

In fact, he started his journey in life defending others. It was what inspired him to go into law enforcement. What better way to protect your community and those who mattered most to you than to sacrifice yourself on the front lines?

As time passed, he started to feel less like a hero, more like a cog in the machine. He never climbed the ranks like some of his peers—why he never really knew. Twenty years in, he was still getting the same respect as those who were fresh out of the academy. It didn't sit well with him, this feeling of being overlooked. He'd reached a point where the opportunities to branch out had passed him by. He was counting down the years to retirement, and after that, the years until his life would be over. He could almost hear the time passing with loud, vibrating ticks.

Likewise, his family life was deteriorating as quickly as his wife's health. He missed the days of coming home after a long shift to a chatty wife and a warm meal. He missed being fawned over by his two young girls; in their eyes, he was always a king. The cancer stole away his wife's energy just as age had stolen his daughters' admiration for him. He was no more important at home than he was on the job.

And then, just when he thought his life had started a downward spiral, he met Trixie. She was ten years his junior, the newest receptionist at the call center downtown. They started talking during his weekly patrols. At first it was nothing, but as their conversations became more flirtatious, Vincent found himself riding a feeling he'd not had in years, a sensation he'd long believed he'd never find again.

Trixie, without ever knowing it, gave Vincent new possibilities. He was alive, perhaps for the first time ever. And then, as quickly as that fire burned, it was extinguished. He'd return home to his sickly wife who grew angrier by the day. His oldest daughter was ditching school to get high. His youngest daughter was spending too much time with older boys. He'd found condoms in her room. Vincent was the toughest guy on the force at one time, and now he couldn't even control his own daughters, couldn't put a smile on his wife's face. Was this why he'd never risen in the ranks? During some of his lowest moments, he thought it might be.

He held onto that different side of his life. The bright side. The Trixie side. Of course, Trixie didn't know he was still married or that he had two teenage daughters. When he was busy living that other life, it was like the one he'd spent the past two decades in didn't exist. As time passed, he was less and less ashamed to admit that it didn't bother him. Sometimes it was nice to picture a life without them.

And then, he wasn't even sure when, he stopped imagining; he started planning. What he would do if he no longer had to interrupt his schedule with treatments and doctors' visits. If he didn't have to lie awake at night fearing one of his daughters might get knocked up or wasted. He pictured a life where he was no longer on patrol, rather in control. He'd have days to do what he wanted. A boat to go fishing. He'd have Trixie. And the more he thought about it, the easier it felt it might be on all of them—especially him.

He quit his job and cashed out his retirement fund. He used the money to whisk Trixie away up the coast. They found a cozy little rental by the sea, put the place in her name. For an entire weekend, they stayed there. It was the most rewarding three days of his life. They could be together here, forever.

When the weekend was over, he left Trixie drunk and sticky in their new bed. He got in his car—a new one he'd bought in cash the week before—and returned home. He used his key to walk in the front door of his house. He used the scissors in the kitchen to cut the phone lines. And he retrieved his gun.

He went upstairs. First, to his oldest daughter's room, where he held a pillow over her head and pulled the trigger. His youngest daughter, having heard the sound, stirred briefly when he entered her room. He shot her before she was able to piece together that her own father was pulling the trigger.

His wife was too zoned out from the meds to be bothered by the sounds. She was still asleep, deep and heavy, when he put the pillow over her face.

What he did wasn't easy. And he wasn't particularly proud of it, but he didn't regret his actions. They were necessary. He didn't know until that moment, when he stood in the quiet house, the blood of his family splattered across his chest, that he'd been suffering all those years. He'd been suffocating, slowly, and now it was as though he was breathing for the first time. Deep, replenishing gulps.

Vincent had never been a religious man. He liked to believe his family was in a better place, but he knew without a doubt he was.

And that was all that mattered.

CHAPTER 45

Now

I run to Willow.

I pull her in for an embrace, turning her body so she doesn't have to see Dan on the floor. Noah is standing in front of his seat, staring at the scene, stupefied. I grab him, forcing him to turn around, too. They whimper against my chest, and for a moment, remind me of much smaller children.

"Vincent!" Andrew scolds. "What did you do?"

"He didn't leave me any choice," Vincent says, wiping the knife clean with the edge of his shirt. His eyes land on me. "Kate pulled him into something he had no business being a part of."

"Why did you do that?" Willow shouts, her voice thick with fury.

Vincent takes a step closer. We all flinch, but he stops just in front of us. His brow is free from any creases.

"I'm sorry you had to see that," he says, his eyes bouncing between Willow and Noah, ignoring me. "I promise. Neither of you have a reason to be afraid."

I pull them behind me, so that I'm now only inches away from Vincent's face.

"Let us leave. We won't tell anyone what happened here. We won't tell anyone we've seen you."

Vincent's eyes lock on mine, but they're dark, vacant. I can almost see my reflection in his pupils. The left side of his mouth ticks upward, and he scoffs.

"None of this is about me." He turns, walking back to the kitchen. "This is about your family."

I look to Andrew. The expression on his face is hard to read. There's a mixture of disgust and triumph. Nothing is going to plan, but all these mistakes will be ending soon.

"What is he talking about, Dad?" Noah asks, his voice weak.

"I wanted to come here to protect you," Andrew says. "To keep us together as a family."

"The way Vincent kept his family together?" I cut my eyes across the room.

"Everything you've experienced the last year, you have to believe me when I say I understand. I was right there with you. With Andrew," Vincent says. "There was a time when I felt like I was losing my own family. The world was taking them away from me, and there was nothing I could do to stop it. My girls were trying to heal themselves with boys and parties. My wife all but shut me out because her sickness had taken over. And there was nothing I could do about any of it. I couldn't make my girls see the error of their ways. I couldn't cure my wife's disease.

"Then I realized I did have some control. I could do what they were unable to do for themselves. I could put them at peace."

He won't say the words, but I know what that *peace* means: he murdered his family.

"You're still here. You didn't do anything for them, only for yourself. And now you're trying to justify your actions by encouraging others to make the same horrible mistakes you did."

"There's no right or wrong way to make sense of this, Kate." He raises his hands in front of me. "Each family has their own path. My girls are in a far better place than they were here. I don't deserve the peace they have now."

"What the hell is he talking about?" Willow cries.

I shush her, patting her head like I did when she was a child. "You don't have any business being here," I say to Vincent. "You think you're helping Andrew, but you're not. You're taking advantage of him, filling his head with ideas he'd never consider on his own."

Beside him, Andrew stares at the ground.

Vincent looks at him. "Is that true? Do you not want any of this? All I've ever tried to do is help you."

Andrew is silent, then slowly nods. Vincent turns to me again, his face beaming as though he's won a great debate.

"I know your husband. I've been in his very same position, and I've had to make hard decisions." He pauses. "That's what Andrew is doing now. He's trying to protect you."

"If you want to protect us, let us go," I plead with Andrew.

He stares at that same spot on the ground, as though there's a sensible response written there, and he can't yet decipher it. Finally, he whispers, "How am I supposed to go through life with someone I can't depend on?"

"What?" I ask in confusion.

"That's what you said to me after Noah fell off the boat."

A wave of guilt passes through me at the thought that my expectations might have moved Andrew in this direction. I blink hard, shaking my head. "We have issues, Andrew, but this isn't the way to sort through them!"

"I'm never going to be the husband and the father you need me to be."

"You can. Prove it right now. Let us go."

"I can't." A whisper. He looks away, as though the sight of us pains him. "It wasn't supposed to be like this, you know. No one was supposed to be scared. We were supposed to make the most of these days together. Be happy. You weren't supposed to find out about any of this until…"

Until it was too late. My mind finishes the sentence for him. That's why he wanted me to join them on the boat. He wanted to kill us out there, not here in front of an angry Vincent and a dead man on the floor.

"This will all be over soon," Vincent says. He walks past me, standing beside Andrew.

"What's he talking about, Dad?" Noah asks. There's a catch in his voice that makes my heart ache.

Andrew doesn't answer him. He turns to Vincent instead. "You didn't have to do that in front of them." He motions to Dan on the floor. "This guy didn't have any part of this."

Vincent steps forward, places both hands on Andrew's shoulders, like a well-versed teacher might react to their great apprentice. "Don't lose focus now. We're so close." Vincent turns slowly. "Let's take out the boat. Follow through with that ride with the family."

"Are you crazy?" Willow asks.

"What about the storm?" Noah adds.

"There's no storm that a strong family can't weather together," Vincent says.

"We're not going anywhere with you," I say defiantly, squeezing my children closer.

Vincent doesn't say anything. He takes a long, deliberate look at Dan on the floor, his blood now pooling around the seal of the front door. He walks into the kitchen and puts his hand on the knife. He looks at me.

We don't have a choice.

CHAPTER 46

Now

The wind has picked up substantially. The curtains follow us outside when Vincent orders us onto the back deck. The descending storm makes it feel like night. The pool lights have flicked on, the waves moving rapidly in aqua and white ripples. Rain splatters against my skin, producing chill bumps immediately.

"Where are we going?" Willow shouts above the wind.

"Follow me." Andrew leads the way, guiding us down the dock to where the boat sits. Vincent follows behind us, the knife in his hands.

"I'm not going," Willow says, planting her feet and refusing to move.

"Just keep walking, honey," I say, refusing to make eye contact. I'm ashamed that I can't think of anything better to tell her. I can't think of a solid way out of this situation, not when we've all just seen what Vincent is capable of doing.

Noah puts his hand on the small of his sister's back and pushes her forward.

"Is he going to hurt us?" Noah whispers.

"I don't know." It's a heartbreaking answer to deliver. I don't want it to be true, and yet I can't deny the severity of this situation. The danger of this man Andrew has willingly brought into our lives. More tragically, I don't know if the *he* Noah is referring to is Vincent or his father.

The water below the dock thrashes violently. Andrew looks back to Vincent, a silent question about whether to proceed.

"Go on," Vincent says. Andrew steps on the boat, holding out his hands for Willow, then Noah, to follow.

"Please just stop this." I turn to Vincent, offering a final plea.

"It wasn't supposed to be like this, you know, and you have more fault than you're willing to admit. The plan was to make this as painless as possible. No one was supposed to have any fear." Vincent looks back towards the house. "And as for that man lying dead in the kitchen, the blood is on your hands. So please, let's not drag this out any longer."

I look at him, then back at the house we've called home for the past two weeks. This was supposed to be our getaway, our chance to reconnect. Now, it's very possible this is the scene of our last days together as a family.

"Go." Vincent raises the knife in his hand as a reminder.

I reluctantly step onto the boat.

Vincent unties the ropes keeping us tethered to the dock. There's a sinking sense of hopelessness; whatever they have planned, I know it will be impossible to overcome them once at sea. Adrenaline spikes, and without thinking, I lunge toward Vincent, trying to knock the knife from his hands. With his back to me, I'm able to knock him off balance. The knife falls from his hands, tumbling into the gray waters below. He turns, slapping me hard across the face. I stumble backwards, until I feel my body hit Andrew's.

"Vincent, that wasn't necessary," he says.

"Then keep her back." He starts the boat's engine, backing into the bay, away from the house and the safety of shore.

I look into Andrew's eyes, a quiet moment between the two of us when I'm silently asking him, why? How could our missteps have led to this? He appears concerned, and yet, there's a barrier between us. Between him and his real self. I believe he recognizes this, that he's not acting in his right mind, but it's already too late to stop what he has put in motion.

In the middle of the storm, we're surrounded by noises. The engine. The waves. The rain pattering against the deck. Softly, the children's cries. Andrew is huddled close to us.

"You don't want to go through with this," I say to him, trusting the cacophony of sounds around us will drown out our voices.

"I have to," he replies.

I move closer to him. "You would have done this while we were at sea the first time if that were the case. You wouldn't need Vincent to intervene if this is what you really wanted."

"It wasn't supposed to be like this. It was supposed to be peaceful, happy."

"Is that what you think happened to the others? Do you think they were happy?"

"I don't know. I—"

"I read what happened to them. The Rogers. They were shot, executed one by one. At some point, the others had to know what was happening, had to realize there was nothing they could do to save themselves. That's not peaceful, Andrew. That's torture."

"Cal loved his family. That's why he—"

"That's why he murdered them?" I scoff. "Andrew, you have to see through this. Whatever fantasies Vincent is putting in your head are just that: fantasies. Nothing about this stems from love."

"I just wanted to find a way to keep us together. I didn't want to run the risk of losing you, or watching the kids struggle."

"Look at them," I say, pointing in their direction. Willow has her arms wrapped around Noah. Both their heads are down, afraid to look. "They're terrified. It's like they're experiencing the horror of the invasion all over again."

"Don't say that. You can't compare what I'm doing to Paul. He tried to tear our family apart."

"Vincent is trying to tear our family apart. He's trying to justify his own actions, like he did something heroic." I wait, letting my words sink in. "It's not too late for you to protect us. We can still stop this."

"We can't." He laughs, a pitiful, losing sound.

"We can try." I look over at the kids again. "We owe them that. They need us now more than ever."

Andrew's gaze lands on the children, seems to stay there for an eternity.

CHAPTER 47

Now

We're going faster, moving farther and farther away from land. After a few minutes, Vincent kills the engine. I'm surprised he's stopped here, but in this storm, it doesn't really matter. Even a few feet away from the shore would be dangerous.

"Ah, ha! Nothing like that sea air."

"Why are you doing this?" Noah shouts.

"It's important that all of you are together. As a family. It's hard for you to understand just how much your father loves you. He's willing to do whatever it takes to protect you. Aren't you, Andrew?"

"Yes." The response is loud yet unconvincing.

"The world wants to pull you away from each other. This is your father's way of bringing you back," he continues to ramble, and yet I'm not convinced he's speaking to any of us directly. I believe he's talking to himself, appeasing his own guilt over the things he's done.

"What do we do now?" Andrew asks.

"What needs to be done. You've made it to this point. I understand how frightening it can be." He rests both of his hands on Andrew's shoulders. "This is the bravest choice you can make for your family. They need you now more than ever."

Andrew nods, his acquiescence making me wince. I look to the children, still clinging to each other in the cold rain, then back at Vincent.

"And what about you?" I shout against the wind.

He looks over me to Andrew, addressing his answer to him. "You'll have to do this part on your own."

There's a cabinet to his left. Inside, are the emergency life jackets and a floatation device. We're maybe a mile away from shore, the dock still visible. He's going to leave us here, return to whatever life he felt he deserved once he got his family out of the way.

"Maybe we could all go back," Andrew says, his voice catching. "Maybe this isn't what we need after all."

Vincent's posture straightens. "After the sacrifices of all the others? After Cal. After my own family. And Trent is relying on us, too. You can't back out now without throwing all that away."

"I love them."

Vincent kneels down in front of Andrew. "Then follow through. You owe it to us. You owe it to yourself."

He stands, taking a confident turn back to the floatation devices.

"Dad," Willow calls outs, her first words since entering the boat. "Please, don't do this."

She understands what is happening now, that her own father intends to hurt her, and it's heartbreaking. Not only for me, but for Andrew, too. He winces, as though physically pained. It's her words, her palpable terror, that inspire him to act.

He stands, lunging toward Vincent. Andrew's strength is no match for his adversary. Vincent shuffles to the left, knocking Andrew to the ground with one steady swing.

"Don't lose faith now," he says. "My God, Andrew. Be a man."

But Andrew doesn't give up. He stands again, this time wrapping his arms around Vincent's middle in an attempt to tackle him. Vincent begins pounding onto Andrew's back, but he holds tight, refusing to let go.

Seeing that Vincent is distracted, I scan the deck for the heaviest object I can find. There's a miniature fire extinguisher—it's not the size of something you might find in a school or office building, but it's made of the same steel. Using both hands, I whack Vincent in the back of the neck.

His right hand reaches to his neck, while his left arm springs out to grab me. I step back, then suddenly Andrew is between us, blocking Vincent's grasp. The two men struggle, Vincent's strength overwhelming, but Andrew manages to get a few hits in. When they turn, I lift the weapon over my head again, slamming it hard onto the top of his head. This time, the hit breaks the skin, and there's a gash of blood across his skull.

When Vincent pulls his fingers away from the second wound, he sees the blood. His eyes bulge, as though he can't quite believe it. I take this moment of uncertainty to push him closer to the edge. He's off balance, the loss of blood surely dulling his senses.

Andrew follows suit, the two of us pushing the massive man towards the side. The deck is slippery, causing all three of us to slip and slide. Finally, Andrew picks up the fire extinguisher. He delivers one final hit to Vincent. It's enough to make him go limp. My body almost collapses in relief, but I can't fully relax until he's off the boat. Together, Andrew and I hoist his body to the boat's edge. It's a difficult task, considering his size, coupled with the fear that at any moment he might reanimate and start fighting back.

After what feels like several minutes, most of Vincent's body hangs over the boat's ledge. Together, Andrew and I give him a final push. We watch as his body disappears into the deep.

CHAPTER 48

Now

For a few seconds, I stare at the water, waiting for Vincent to break through the surface. Like I'm in some horrible movie where the villain refuses to die. That doesn't happen. My fears aren't immediately settled, though. We're still at sea in the middle of this horrendous storm. The skies above are an eerie shade of gray bordering on green, and the waves seem to grow in intensity with each passing minute.

"Is he gone?"

It's Noah's voice I hear. Immediately, I scramble to the other side of the boat. For a brief moment, I feel peace, holding both my children in my arms. Then I lock eyes with Andrew. He helped me overpower Vincent, but it's difficult to know what he's thinking. Whether or not we should still be afraid. I don't have time to retaliate against him. All that matters is keeping the children safe. We've made it through one danger, now we're onto the next.

"The keys," Andrew says, his voice soaked with defeat. "They're gone."

"What do you mean they're gone?"

"Vincent put them in his pocket when he killed the engine, and he's…"

His voice trails off. We can all figure how he would have finished the sentence. Vincent is gone, taking with him our only chance of getting the boat back to shore.

"What can we do?"

"The storm is getting bad. Without the engine, the boat will continue to drift out to sea."

"Can we wait it out?"

"This boat isn't designed for a storm like this. It's too dangerous. Our best bet is to get back to shore." I'm relieved to know he's continuing to help us, that he's no longer willing to complete whatever plan he had, but I'm still cautious.

"What about the radio?" Willow asks.

"It's disconnected," he says. I don't bother to ask how, whether the connection was cut intentionally. I shudder to think he never intended for any of us to leave this boat. "We're only about a mile off. The best bet would be getting in the life raft. You can paddle your way back to shore before the tide gets stronger."

"Put these on," I say to the children, handing them life jackets. I put on my own just as Andrew pulls the string of the lifeboat. The orange material inflates, appearing like no more than an inner tube against the angry sea.

"No way," I say, stepping away from the edge. "We can't get in that thing in the middle of the storm."

"It's made for situations like this," Andrew says. "It's sturdier than it appears."

He lowers it into the water, and I watch as the flimsy material rocks and shakes with the currents underneath. My breathing stalls. My mind wrestles with the dangers of the water. Before, I'd jumped into the ocean without hesitation. It was either that or watch my son drown. Now… I can't willingly step onto the raft.

"I can't do it."

"You don't have a choice, Kate. It's only a matter of time before this boat is overturned. You can't steer it in any direction." He's more than concerned, he's frightened. For our safety. "On the raft, you might have a chance of making it back to shore."

Might. A terrifying word. Willow and Noah stare up at me, bundled into their life jackets. They're following my lead. I don't think either one of them feels they can trust what their father says, and it saddens me.

Andrew lowers the boat's ladder into the water so it's only a small step to the raft.

"You have to go. Now."

"We can do this, Mom," Willow says. "We're together."

I take a deep breath, lowering myself into the raft. The bottom is sturdier than I'd imagined, but it's still too flimsy to stand. I balance on my knees, holding out my hands to help the children onboard. First Noah, then Willow.

"Hurry," I shout back to Andrew.

He takes a step away from the edge. Only then do I realize he's not wearing his life jacket.

"I love you all very much," he says. "I'm sorry for everything."

He tugs at the ladder.

"Andrew, what are you doing? Get in the raft with us. You can't stay out here."

"You have a better chance of making it to shore without the extra weight."

Even though he brought us here, even though I know what he intended to do to us, my insides ache at the idea of leaving him behind. I reach back toward the boat, but it's pointless. Already the currents are pulling us away. A large wave crashes against the side, splashing my face. I wipe away the water, ignoring the sting in my eyes, and look back.

"Come with us!" I shout. He's still my husband. He's still their father. His actions in the last few minutes prove that man still exists.

"Dad, please!" Noah yells. Willow remains silent, as though she's already accepted the inevitable. However this day ends, we'll never be the family we once were.

"I love you all. I'm so, so sorry," Andrew says. I'm not sure if he sits or takes another step back, all I know is he's no longer in my line of vision.

"Andrew!" I scream with all the strength I have left.

There's no response. All I can see is the side of the boat as it drifts out to sea.

CHAPTER 49

Now

All three of us are turned, peering out at the brown shore in the distance, the rental boat fading like a ghost behind us. The sand seems forever away, and yet it's already closer than it was when we were on the boat.

"Mom, we have to start rowing," Willow says, her tone tactical.

I place my oar into the water, trying to maneuver straight, but it seems pointless. With each motion, the water is heavy, and we don't seem to move anywhere other than where the waves want us to go. I'm disoriented by the sensations around me. The chilly gale rocking us, the falling rain. I think of what monstrous beasts might be beneath us at this very moment, Vincent included.

I think of my father. His last moments were in tumultuous waters, a storm he didn't see coming. It was only a matter of time until he was overcome, his lungs filling with the water I'm sure he fought like hell to withstand. Was it peaceful or painful? I don't know. In this moment, I can't imagine his death being anything other than terrifying.

"We're not getting any closer," Noah shouts. He's sitting between us in the middle of the raft.

"We have to take turns rowing," Willow shouts, sounding much more mature than I've ever given her credit for. "When I yell pull on the left, you row on the right, okay? If we do that long enough, the tide should carry us the rest of the way in, but we have to hurry."

"Okay," I say, nodding. I'm not sure where she got this sense of urgency; none of us have ever been in this type of situation before, and Andrew is the one with the most experience on the water.

Andrew. He's still back there. Even though he's the one that got us into this mess, a part of me mourns him. He's my first love. The father of my children. My husband. And even if the trauma he's been through in the past year made him forget those roles, I can't. I still want him here, but he's gone.

"Mom." Her voice commands my attention, a literal calm in the middle of this storm. "We can do this."

"Okay," I repeat, and this time I'm focused. I can see the shore on the horizon, the marker at the end of the lane, the target in front of me.

"Pull," Willow shouts. I do. When I stop, she moves. Then again, "Pull!"

I'm no longer at sea, I'm no longer in danger. Instead, my mind is treading back to happier memories. Lazy Sunday mornings with Andrew back in college. The tears in his eyes when I handed him Willow for the first time. His excitement when Noah caught his first fish some years back at the lake house. It wasn't all bad, was it? Even if this is where we ended up, there were happy times before this. Before Paul. Before Vincent. Before we lost sight of each other.

"We're getting closer," Willow shouts, and I'm back to focusing on the waterline. Noah is hunched down, afraid to look.

The waves are vicious, splashing against the raft, spraying into my mouth and stinging my eyes. The clouds above grow darker as the storm blends into the early hours of evening, blurring one from the other. I continue the cyclical motion, ignoring the pain in my shoulder, focusing instead on the sound of Willow's voice, rhythmically leading the way.

The children are safe with me—that's what mattered the most on the night of the invasion, and that's what matters most now.

We edge closer, and I can feel the push of the waves moving us forward until the shoreline grows in width and clarity. We're so very close.

CHAPTER 50

4 Months Later

I snag a corner booth toward the back of the café and watch as students migrate across campus, clusters of snow clinging to their coats and hair. Some I know from class, but mostly I recognize them in a different sense. I remember a time when I used to be like them—carefree, curious, naïve. It seems like a lifetime ago.

I hear footsteps approach my table. I turn and see Detective Marsh. She's wearing a light blue puffer coat and khaki pants. I stand and don't shy away when she initiates a hug.

"Kate, it's so good to see you."

"How long are you in town?"

"I leave right after the holidays. It's good to come back and see people." She pauses. "How are the kids?"

"Adjusting. Willow thinks she's an adult now that our apartment is so close to campus. And Noah is due to get his green belt next month."

"Green belt already?" She beams with pride. "Impressive."

After we returned home, we couldn't bear to stay in the house. Living there used to bother me because of what happened the night Paul Gunter broke in, but now the house haunts us for different reasons. There are too many memories there, and the happy ones are worse.

"And you?" she asks. "How are you holding up?"

I'm still in counseling, with a different therapist. It didn't seem productive to go back to Dr. Sutton, the same person who listened to conversations with Andrew by my side. I don't blame her. After all, Andrew was my husband and I still didn't recognize the warning signs, but I still needed a new set of ears.

I only sleep a few hours a night. The apartment we've rented has two bedrooms. I sleep on the couch; it makes my frequent patrols of the apartment less disruptive, but the kids are aware of how little I sleep. They know I'm in a constant state of defense.

I haven't had the choice to stop working, although I'm the first to admit I'm not in the best place to fulfill my responsibilities as I once did. Our financial obligations outweigh my mental health at the moment. Andrew wasted a big portion of our savings in the months he lied about quitting his job, purchasing our time at that godforsaken vacation home. Until the sale of the house goes through, my salary is our only income. I'm hoping we can make it through the end of the school year, keep the kids in a familiar town, then we can see about starting over somewhere new. Maybe move closer to Mom.

Aster has been a surprising support in recent months. She's used her background studying psychology to help me make sense of what Andrew cooked up with his friends. She's mentioned, more than once, that maybe we could join forces. I could use my writing skills and experience combined with her criminal expertise. We might be able to put out a book that's even more successful than the one she'd originally pitched. I could finally carry out my dream of writing, although this wasn't what I had in mind. Besides, it wouldn't just be my story I'm telling. Noah and Willow are part of this. It's our story.

All of this runs through my mind in a matter of seconds, but I don't share all this with Marsh. She's smart enough to know the complexities of our predicament without me having to break it down for her.

I smile. "I'm getting there."

She nods. "You are all so very lucky. Usually, the type of men who commit these crimes give off very few warning signs. It's not until afterward that people start remembering red flags."

"That's exactly how I feel. Looking back, I can see Andrew wasn't right. He was clearly up to something. The way he started hiding things from me. The way he tried to cut us off from those around us. His quitting his job. But in the moment, none of it felt dangerous. It just felt like we were going through life." I look down, playing with the edge of my napkin. "He wasn't in a healthy mindset, but it was that damn group that put him over the edge."

It's interesting how certain crimes gain media attention, while others remain little more than whispers. I rarely hear people talk about Dan's murder, the well-meaning husband and father who stumbled into a dangerous situation and paid with his life, but people are all about the Second Chances Sect.

That's their name now, and I actually feel sorry for the Second Chances organization. They've tried their best to distance themselves from the media spectacle, but it's impossible with an alliterative name like that tacked onto every headline. After intense investigation, it's clear Second Chances had no involvement with what Vincent and some of the other participants were doing. Like so many other groups before, Second Chances started off with good intentions, to be a sounding board for men with mental health issues—it was only a few radical members who took those same teachings and manipulated them into something darker.

Clearly, Vincent was the leader. He was a man overwhelmed by his wife's diagnosis and his daughters' increasing volatility. He found solace in another woman and began envisioning a life where he could simply walk away. Of course, that's only a vision. In reality, there's divorce and alimony and resentment—an increasing laundry list of complications he preferred not to deal with. Instead, he convinced himself that murdering his family was for their benefit, ignoring that it was only him who went striding away into the sunset.

I like to think he got what he deserved. After we maneuvered the raft onto shore, we ran for help, pounding on the doors of nearby neighbors. The police were called. Once the storm settled, they sent out crews looking for Vincent, Andrew and the remnants of the rental boat. Vincent's body was found the following day. His cause of death was drowning, although trauma to the body suggested sharks had toyed with him a bit. I didn't want to know whether it was before or after his death.

In the early weeks, the media seemed fascinated with Vincent's mistress, Trixie. It's hard to say how much or little she knew about Vincent's actions. Did she know he had murdered his family for her? Or, like so many others, did she make the mistake of believing everything he told her? She's gone into hiding now, and in some ways, I envy her. I wish I could run away and pretend none of this ever happened.

Police were able to access the chat logs between Vincent and the other Second Chances members. They determined Cal Rogers was definitely influenced by Vincent, that even when he had second thoughts about murdering his family, Vincent urged him to go through with it, but there's no evidence whether Vincent helped him carry out his actions physically. He spent weeks preaching to Cal Rogers that this was the only way for him to take back control of his family. He spent the same amount of time communicating with Andrew.

The messages also helped investigators find Trent, the person who impersonated Detective Barnes. He apparently had plans to kill his own family, although he was likely to take Vincent's route and remain alive. It's believed his actions were meant as a form of revenge against his estranged wife. If we hadn't survived that night at sea, another family could have been lost. Trent was arrested and found hanging from a bed sheet in his jail cell a week later.

Even with all this information available to me, I still can't figure out why Andrew spiraled the way he did. Why he believed there was no other way to take back the control he felt he'd lost. I wonder if, like Vincent and Trent, his plan was to start over after getting us out of the way. Deep down, I don't believe that. I think, like Cal Rogers, he always intended to leave this world by our sides. In his own twisted way, he thought he was protecting us.

I picture his face during the final moments on the boat, the storm raging around us, our children clinging to one another. I believe Andrew knew there was no way to repair the damage he'd caused, which is why he stayed behind. He's right. Even if he'd made it to shore, our marriage would be over.

I only wish I could have seen how he was struggling sooner. I wish I could have had the chance to save him before it was too late.

"I have another reason I wanted to meet with you," Detective Marsh says, bringing my thoughts back to the present. "Paul Gunter."

A familiar shiver climbs my spine. "What about him?"

"As you know, they've pushed back his trial. Looks like it's given him time to think. He's going to plead."

"Plead?"

"He's accepting responsibility for all charges."

"What's the catch?"

"He'll still be serving time, but he'll be in a mental health facility instead of prison. It seems he's been taking advantage of counseling sessions and taking medication."

"So, he won't be going to prison?"

"He'll be getting help. As long as you sign off on it."

"Me?"

"Part of the deal means you have to agree to the terms. If you'd rather he serve time, he will. Either place, he won't be released for a long time."

She reaches into her jacket and pulls out a piece of paper.

"His lawyer gave me this and asked me to pass it along. He's still forbidden to contact you directly, but this has gone through all the proper protocols. I thought you might want to give it a read before you make your decision."

I leave the letter on the table, not yet wanting to touch it.

"What would you do?"

"After what your family has been through? I wouldn't let me, Paul Gunter, lawyers or anyone else sway your decision. You've got a clear head on your shoulders. I trust whatever call you make will be the right one."

"Should I even read it?"

"Read it, trash it." She stands, tucking her hands into her pockets. "Good seeing you again, Kate. Take care of yourself."

I finish the rest of my coffee, swirling the tepid liquid around my mouth. I keep my gaze on the crowded students walking across the quad, but every so often, my eyes land back on the letter. I pick it up and begin to read.

Dear Kate,

I appreciate you taking the time to read this. I know you must have conflicted feelings about me and everything I put your family through. I promise this will be my only correspondence with you, but I felt it was necessary to give you an explanation, regardless of whether or not you choose to accept it.

I don't have any excuse for why I treated you the way I did. I realize now it was my own insecurities rising up. You weren't the only person I hurt, but I fear what I put your family through that night was the worst of my actions.

I want you to know how very sorry I am for treating you the way I have; nothing you've ever done to me deserved such behavior. You have no reason to believe me when I say I'm improving, but I finally have found the right resources to help me cope. I'm confident that moving forward I won't put you or any other person at risk. I hope you find comfort in that. I know I have.

Sincerely,
Paul

I fold the letter and place it back on the table. After another minute of thought, I stick it into my purse. It doesn't hurt to have a written reminder that Paul has admitted to what he's done. I know now he never tried to contact me after his arrest—that was all the work of Andrew and his friends. They wanted to fill me with fear, force me to rely on Andrew, so he could carry out the plan.

I can't say this letter has completely wiped my fears concerning Paul or dampened the terrifying memories of that night, but I do feel a sense of peace knowing he has at least acknowledged his mistakes and is committed to getting better. I may never forgive Paul for what he's done, but I'm not above giving him a second chance.

Then again, maybe that's not the best phrase to use.

I stand, pushing my chair under the table. As I'm walking out of the coffee shop, I catch sight of a man standing by the counter. It's a familiar profile. The corner of a jaw, the glimpse of a hairline. I move toward the register, my heart beginning to race.

When I approach, the man turns. He's a stranger. A person I've never seen before. My pulse settles.

The wreckage from the rental boat was found in the days following the storm. As Vincent had intended, the craft eventually capsized, losing its battle with the tempestuous sea. Andrew's body, however, was never found. I understand the chances of him surviving the storm are improbable, if not impossible. Besides, when he left us alone on the raft, it appeared he too was at peace with his fate.

There is no evidence that the sea got him like it did the rental boat, or the sharks got him like they did Vincent. There's no confirmation that the man I once loved, the father to our two children, is gone forever, although I believe he withered away long before last August.

Still, without proof, I sometimes wonder.

I may always be looking over my shoulder, trying to prepare for the next threat, but there will be no more running.

There will be no more hiding.

There will be no more fear.

A LETTER FROM MIRANDA

Dear Reader,

Thank you for taking the time to read *His Loving Wife*. If you liked it and want information about my upcoming releases, sign up with the following link. Your email address will never be shared and you can unsubscribe at any time.

www.bookouture.com/miranda-smith

In many ways, this has been the darkest subject matter for me to tackle, but I tried my best to deliver a story that was full of heart, especially when it came to Kate and her children. Be aware, there are spoilers for *His Loving Wife* below.

Familicide (the culprits are often called family annihilators) has always struck me as one of the most horrendous crimes. Don't get me wrong, all violent crime is awful, but there seems to be something particularly warped about hurting those closest to you, the very people you are responsible for protecting. These crimes are unique in that they often result in the demise of an entire family.

Even more disturbing is that those closest to the families rarely predict what is about to happen. However, in hindsight, I believe there are often red flags that go unnoticed. I wanted the reader, along with Kate, to experience these warning signs and how they can be misinterpreted. There are a handful of reasons for why a person might resort to this level of violence, and I tried to portray them in the various characters from Second Chances.

Kate has been one of my favorite characters to write. Despite her fears and anxieties, she's a fighter, a protector. She's all the things her husband aspires to be. I was happy to tell a story where the bad guy—in this case, multiple bad guys—didn't win, and a badass woman came out on top.

If you'd like to discuss any of my books, I'd love to connect! You can find me on Facebook, Twitter and Instagram, or my website. If you enjoyed *His Loving Wife*, I'd appreciate it if you left a review on Amazon. It only takes a few minutes and does wonders in helping readers discover my books for the first time.

Thank you again for your support!

Sincerely,
Miranda Smith

MirandaSmithAuthor

@MSmithBooks

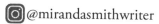@mirandasmithwriter

mirandasmithwriter.com

ACKNOWLEDGMENTS

I'd like to thank my editor, Ruth Tross, for all her support and encouragement. This is the fifth book we've worked on together, and I wouldn't have made the progress I have today without her guidance. She's a brilliant collaborator who always pushes me to take my work to the next level. Thank you for continuing to believe in my writing.

There are several other people at Bookouture I'd like to thank, including Jenny Geras, Kim Nash, Noelle Holten, Sarah Hardy, Alex Holmes, Jane Eastgate and Liz Hurst. Thank you for your help during the various stages of the publishing process.

I found *The Anatomy of Motive* by John Douglas and Mark Olshaker to be a great resource when writing this book. Any mistakes I made are my own, and likely done to enhance the story.

Thank you to each person who has read, bought or reviewed my books. I'm forever thankful for your support. Special thanks to the book promoters and bloggers who help spread the word about my old and new releases.

To my friends, community and extended family, thank you for your encouragement and support. It means more than you could ever know.

I'd like to thank my parents and sisters for their continued love and support. Lastly, thank you to Chris, Harrison, Lucy and Christopher. I love you all very much.